OLIVIA ELLIOTT

A Baron's Son is Undone

Book Three in The Pemberton Series

Copyright © 2025 by Olivia Elliott

All rights reserved. No part of this publication may be reproduced, stored or transmitted in any form or by any means, electronic, mechanical, photocopying, recording, scanning, or otherwise without written permission from the publisher. It is illegal to copy this book, post it to a website, or distribute it by any other means without permission.

This novel is entirely a work of fiction. The names, characters and incidents portrayed in it are the work of the author's imagination. Any resemblance to actual persons, living or dead, events or localities is entirely coincidental.

Olivia Elliott asserts the moral right to be identified as the author of this work.

First edition

This book was professionally typeset on Reedsy. Find out more at reedsy.com

Contents

1	The Pirate's Daughter	1
2	The Ocean is a Dangerous Place	18
3	David and Goliath	36
4	A Room Made of Sky	51
5	Costumes	67
6	A Game that Matters	82
7	Brilliant and Unique	98
8	Souls and their Salvation	113
9	A Rare Breed	125
10	Pixies and Politics	139
11	Intimate Thoughts	152
12	All of You	166
13	A Man Like Me	180
14	What Have We Here?	201
15	Family Matters	215
16	Accounts to Review	229
17	Target Practice	243
18	The Sensible One	256
19	A Disobedient Wife	271
20	A Vision of Sunshine	290
	Epilogue	311
	Thank You	317
	Also by Olivia Elliott	318

Content Warning: This book includes vague references to an off-page sexual assault as well as on-page psychological fallout from this assault. Please read with care.

One

The Pirate's Daughter

No day was safe.

This knowledge was a dark gem George Pemberton kept in a small box in his inner breast pocket—easy to reach. As he gazed out of the carriage window at the summer fields passing him by, he reached into his pocket and pulled forth the tiny box—the box of his mind, his memory. It always told him the same thing . . .

Even if the sun was shining in a clear blue sky. Even if your sister was teasing you as she always did. Even if you were only ten years old and out of breath and pretending to be invisible. Even if it was a day like that, it could also be a day that turned cold and bitter before you were forced to swallow it whole.

The memory of that day descended on him then, crisp and bright.

"What should we play?" Serafina looked to George as if he were in charge because he was. He appreciated this about his

A Baron's Son is Undone

sister's friend. She was sensible.

Serafina's dark hair was decorated with several white daisies making her look like a fairy in the green garden.

"Why does Serafina get daisies when I don't?" complained Patience.

"Because Serafina deserves them," said George without looking at his sister. She was always interrupting when he was thinking.

"Pirates?" offered Serafina softly. She was asking George. Again, he appreciated this.

Patience turned on her friend, blonde ringlets flying.

"I'll not spend all afternoon waiting to be rescued again. There's nothing more boring," she said.

"The Invisible Game," announced George.

"The Castle," corrected Patience.

"You can call it what you like," said George.

"Yes, all right. I don't mind playing that one," said Patience.

"No one asked if you minded," said George, but the girls had already taken off towards the house which was now the castle.

When George revisited this memory, he always paused here. Fifteen more minutes of childhood, maybe twenty. He lingered over them. Taking his time. Delaying the inevitable. He could see the starched white apron of the scullery maid stepping out into the herb garden at the back of the house. He could see Patience deftly kicking off her blue shoes as she ran so as to better win the race to the castle—the race only she was running. She would win of course since no one else knew they were competing for speed. This would soon cause another argument between them.

It was hot that day, and he had suggested playing The

The Pirate's Daughter

Invisible Game because he fancied returning to the cool of the house. If there had been a few more clouds in the sky, they may have remained outdoors. Everything would have been different. The boy he had been would not have died inside himself that afternoon. He would be someone else. A few more clouds could change a life.

Normally, The Invisible Game involved a story-line that had the three of them fleeing their terrible step-mother (one of the horses), running away from home (the stables), then wandering through the woods (an expanse of lawn) until they encountered a strange castle (the Pembertons' actual house).

"We don't need to make a whole to-do about running away from home first," said Patience. "I'll not walk all the way out to the stables. Let's just start at the castle."

George did not want to agree with his sister, but perspiration was prickling at his brow, and his jacket was becoming uncomfortable in the heat.

"Fine," said George.

They crept into the house by the back door and pressed themselves flat against the cool wall by the kitchen entrance. George peered into the kitchen to see the sweaty cook and two maids chopping and kneading and laughing.

"They're distracted," he whispered. "Now!"

He led the way as Patience and Serafina followed past the open kitchen door as quiet as two little girls can be if those little girls are also giggling under their breath.

George turned on them.

"Shhhh! Do you want to be caught? It'll be the dungeon for both of you!" He gave Patience a hard look. "They'll probably string *you* up by your thumbs."

"Why me?"

A Baron's Son is Undone

"I'm sure you'll annoy them in some way. Then. Thumbs. It won't be pretty."

The sound of footsteps coming from around the corner quickly sobered them. They all scrambled into the nearest stairwell with their hearts thumping against the possibility of capture. Serafina brought her hand to her mouth to hide a terrified laugh.

"Don't get her started," whispered George.

Patience's eyes were wide with mirth.

"Not a sound, Patience!"

His barefoot sister led the way up the staircase clambering on hands and feet like a dog. It looked like a satisfying way to climb the stairs, so George followed suit and Serafina after him. By the time they arrived at the drawing-room door, they were out of breath. Peering in, they could see Miss Tindale, their thin-lipped housekeeper, fussing with a yellow embroidered runner that was draped unevenly over a sideboard. Crouched to the side of the doorway, George watched as Patience and Serafina crawled into the drawing room. That was the game. Sneak into the castle and then remain invisible to its inhabitants for as long as possible.

Miss Tindale must have heard them because she looked up from her runner and started to turn. George held back a bark of laughter as Patience and Serafina threw themselves face-down behind a settee. George slid himself back against the wall by the doorway grinning. When he peered into the room again, Patience and Serafina were slithering their way under the settee and completely out of sight. The high click-clack of Miss Tindale's shoes heading for the door had George fleeing down the hall. He would certainly not be caught before Patience was found out. Invisible was what he did best.

The Pirate's Daughter

He nearly passed by the library altogether assuming it was unoccupied. (There was no point trying to be invisible if there was no one about. The Invisible Game was all about the excitement of getting caught.) As he passed the door to the library, he heard someone drop a book. George stepped back two paces and peered in. His mother was turned away from the door as she bent down to retrieve her book from the floor. George slipped into the room like a sweaty shadow, crouching behind a silver-blue wingback chair as his mother stood. She turned back to the shelf to replace the book, and George took the opportunity to step gingerly across the soft carpeting to the enormous window at the far end of the room. Teal blue velvet curtains had been drawn back to let in the light, but they had not been fastened, and part of the wide window-sill was obscured from the room. George slid up onto the sill and pulled his knees up to conceal himself behind the drape of velvet.

The sun beat down on him, somehow hotter for passing through the window pane. A large black fly with green eyes buzzed against the glass. George hugged his knees. Annoying as Patience was, he found himself having considerably less fun without her there in the library. It didn't feel at all as if he were playing a game anymore. He only felt hot and cramped and alone.

George froze this memory in place. Only two more minutes remained of his childhood.

No further. Not yet.

Twilight had descended, and his carriage pulled to a halt outside a thatch-roofed building. From the window of the carriage, George could read the sign as it lifted on a gust of wind. The Old Inn. Descriptive if not imaginative. The driver

A Baron's Son is Undone

opened the door, and George made his way to the rough-hewn door of the inn. It opened inwards onto a scene of golden lantern light and warm revelry. Tankards landed on tables, sloshing their contents. The low laughter of men. Apart from one serving woman, there were only two other women in the place, seated together at a table near the bar. What was an inn if not a tavern with a few rooms to let? George allowed himself to relax. No one knew him here. His stay would give him some time to think, a brief reprieve before he threw himself back into the sham that was his life.

The inn-keeper—a Mr. Harris—was also the bartender. He eyed George up and down.

Damn.

George had gone to some effort not to look too well-off. He had even dispensed with his valet and footman, carrying his own case in himself. Nevertheless, the innkeeper was clearly rejigging the room prices in his head to match the man of means standing in front of him.

"I've just the room!" boomed Mr. Harris altogether too exuberantly. He wiped his hands on a towel and made his way out from behind the bar to show George upstairs.

After settling his things in his room, George proceeded back downstairs to the tavern and found himself a small table in an inconspicuous corner.

"You'll be wanting a drink then," said the elderly waitress. She looked old enough to be the inn-keeper's mother. Perhaps she was.

"Whisky," said George.

"You talk nice. You sure you're in the right place?"

Another man might have smiled, but George rarely smiled. He didn't answer the question.

The Pirate's Daughter

"Whisky it is," she said.

As he sat in the corner with his drink, George surveyed the room. The dozen or so men spread out over several tables were growing louder by the minute. In contrast, the two young women seated together were chatting quietly. Unescorted women at this time of the evening could only be women of pleasure, and one of the two—the blonde—was dressed to match that assessment. But the second young woman was dressed like a spinster setting off for church—a dark green dress made of some heavy material, long sleeves buttoned at the wrists, and a collar that was so high it grazed her delicate chin. Her black hair was done up in a kind of plaited crown that swept her hair into a woven circlet across the top of her forehead down to the nape of her neck and back up again. There seemed to be no beginning and no end to it.

George leaned back in his chair, his reverie from earlier in the evening returning to him in full force. The heat of the sun streaming in through the window. The doomed fly battering itself against the glass.

"There you are!" It was the voice of his mother's sister—Aunt Sara. She had arrived several days earlier unannounced.

His mother did not respond.

"It's quite a fairytale life you live here, Agnes," said Aunt Sara.

Again, silence.

"And to think it could have gone so terribly wrong."

"What do you want, Sara?"

George hugged his knees tighter. He had never heard his mother speak in that tone of voice before. There was an edge to it that unnerved him.

"Has Edward never noticed? Your boy looks nothing like

A Baron's Son is Undone

him." George could hear the insincere smile in his aunt's voice.

At first, he thought nothing of it. She was simply commenting on his appearance.

But he was ten years old, and he was (as people kept telling him) a clever boy. It took the length of eleven heartbeats and his mother's silence to put it all together. The sudden realisation of what those words meant caused a burning sensation in the hollow of his chest. He struggled to take a breath as the searing pain shot up from his chest to his throat and then collected behind his eyes. His hands curled into fists. He did not cry. Boys didn't cry. Not even if they were strung up by their thumbs in a dungeon.

In the tavern, George's hands had also closed into tight fists on the table in front of him. He could feel the tension of the past several months waiting to be released. It had been quite some time. The last time he had planted a fist into anyone, it had been his brother-in-law Winter, and that had been no release at all. The man had gone limp, refusing to fight back as George landed blow after blow on behalf of his sister.

George unfurled one hand to grasp his glass. He took a gulp of his whisky and swivelled his gaze to the most dangerous-looking man in the room who was standing in the far corner as if simply waiting. The man was bald and middle-aged, perhaps forty years or more. He looked dry and hard like a clay pot left to bake in the sun, and his skin cracked along lines that life had carved out for him. He had a crooked nose and a scar running from the top of his shining forehead down through one eyebrow and his cheek until it hit his mouth. The scar seemed to pull one side of his mouth down towards his chin.

"Get off, Tom—I'm not working yet!" It was one of the

women. The blonde one.

A burly man—clearly drunk, clearly someone called Tom—was stroking the woman's pale cheek with one hand while attempting to pull her up by her arm with the other.

"But you're here. And I'm here. And we had such a good time last week. I just been paid," he said, taking his hand from her cheek to pat the pocket of his jacket.

The young woman made to shrug him off, but he tightened his grip. The other woman at the table appeared frozen in place. George knew an opportunity when he saw it. He placed the flats of his hands down on the table and slid back his chair.

Sophie watched as the handsome gentleman (for he was obviously a gentleman) with the tousled sandy hair stood from his table. His movements were casual, cool as you like. He even slid his chair back into place beneath the table before walking slowly over to hers. As he drew closer, she noticed that the smoky grey of his travelling jacket matched the grey of his eyes. He didn't even bother to look at Tom but reached down and moved the three empty glasses on her table into a neat row. His actions had the effect of stopping everyone in their tracks.

Finally, he did look at Tom.

"The lady says she's not working right now," he said. His voice was hard and sharp, like the edge of a blade.

"Lady?" said Winnie. Sophie noted that Winnie was not so upset about the goings-on with Tom that she did not notice being called a lady.

"Is none of your business!" said Tom. "I have the money."

A Baron's Son is Undone

"That's not the point though, is it?" said the grey-eyed gentleman. "She's saying no."

"Don't you have a ball to attend?" asked Tom in a blazing moment of wit that had Sophie smiling behind her hand. She looked to the grey-eyed gentleman. He *did* look like he might have a ball to attend.

"We can take this outside if you like," said the gentleman evenly.

Tom looked behind him to his table of mates as if for backup. No one came forward. They were all watching the show and grinning.

"The toff wants a fight, Tom!" yelled one of the men. "Give it to 'im."

"I'll wager Tom takes him in less than fifteen minutes," laughed another.

"*I'll* wager," said the gentleman slowly without taking his eyes from Tom, "that Tom won't last five minutes, let alone fifteen."

The men let loose a cheerful roar. Someone pounded one of the tables with a fist.

"Go on, Tom. It'll be easy money!"

Excitement began to tingle within her like tiny birds fluttering against her chest. Sophie decided that if it came to it, she would certainly go outside to watch the fight. She may even place her own wager. Duncan wouldn't like it, but Duncan wasn't paid to like it. Unfortunately, as she watched Tom's drunken face deliberate upon the situation, she realised before he did that he was about to back down. She could see why. She looked from Tom's face to the gentleman's. There was a fire behind all that grey smoke in his eyes, and he was considerably more sober. Tom might be a large man, but what

The Pirate's Daughter

this gentleman lacked in bulk, he would surely make up for in coordination.

It took Tom a moment, but he did release Winnie's arm.

"She's not worth it," he said, turning back to his friends. "She's just a whore."

Sophie saw Tom's words land like a slap across Winnie's face. The gentleman himself looked strangely disappointed that Tom had backed down. In fact, he looked almost as disappointed as Sophie herself felt. He watched Tom rejoin his friends.

"You're lucky," she said. "Tom would have punched the plums clean out of your mouth."

Her words drew his gaze to her (which she supposed was what she had wanted). They locked eyes, and Sophie could feel a coiled aggression directed her way.

"And what time," he asked her slowly, "do *you* start work?"

Sophie's eyes went wide. *The sheer nerve! Who was this man? He had the bearing of a gentleman, but he was behaving like . . . well . . . like an ass.*

"You couldn't afford me," she said. "My services come much too dear for the likes of you." She reached out and shoved one of the empty glasses he had lined up earlier out of its neat little row. For some reason, she knew this would upset him.

He looked at the glass, then at her.

"Try me," he said.

Sophie could sense Duncan's approach from behind her with some irritation. She lifted a hand to stay him.

Winnie laughed. "You'll not want to be caught fiddling with a pirate's daughter," she said. "When he returns, he'll gut you like a pig at the market. If Duncan over there doesn't do it first," she added.

A Baron's Son is Undone

The man spared a glance for Duncan but didn't seem particularly put off by his battle-worn appearance.

"Pirate's daughter?" said the gentleman, eyebrows lifting.

Sophie turned on Winnie. "I never told you that."

"Everyone knows," said Winnie. "You can't keep that kind of secret in a town like this." She turned to the gentleman with exaggerated grace. "If I may make the introductions," she said in her best impression of an upperclass accent, "Miss Lovell, this is Mr. —"

"—Pemberley," said George. "George Pemberley."

He reached out his hand, and for some reason she could not explain (for he had been quite insulting to her not three seconds ago, and he was, she had decided, a world-class ass), she placed her hand in his. Neither of them were wearing gloves, and she could hear Duncan behind her taking in a rattled and angry breath. Sophie found herself staring at her own hand clasped in his. She usually avoided being touched, so she was surprised beyond measure that she had initiated this rather intimate contact with a stranger. Her heart began to beat a little faster, and she withdrew her hand swiftly as if perhaps she had touched a flame rather than a man.

"I've never met a pirate's daughter before," said Mr. Pemberley.

"It's mere hearsay," said Sophie. Because it was. Convenient hearsay, but hearsay nonetheless.

"Mmm," was the sound Mr. Pemberley made. It was a nice sound, a low vibration that set her every nerve aquiver. It was the kind of sound Sophie would pay good money to hear again. She wondered what Mr. Pemberley would charge for the service, and wondering this, she laughed out loud.

"Do I amuse you?" asked Mr. Pemberley releasing her hand.

The Pirate's Daughter

"Not at all," said Sophie with a condescending smile. "I amuse myself. Always have."

Back at Seymour Cottage, Sophie and Duncan were greeted by one of the footmen who had stayed up late do do just that. She handed her coat to the footman and turned on Duncan who stood behind her waiting with his hands clasped behind his back. His scar gleamed white in the light of a lantern resting on a side table in the hallway.

"Why didn't you do something to help Winnie?"

"Not paid to guard whores," said Duncan.

"Don't use that word," said Sophie.

Duncan grimaced, but Sophie knew he would not be using that word again. In most ways that mattered, Duncan was in charge, but he allowed her these little wins now and then. She wasn't sure if he did it out of pity or simply to keep her compliant and easy to manage.

"What do you think of Mr. Pemberley?" she asked.

"From London," said Duncan. "A gentleman of the ton."

"Anyone can see that," said Sophie picking up the lantern and stepping along the hallway. Duncan followed like a dutiful shadow. "I'm asking what you think of him."

"Not paid to think," said Duncan.

Sophie spun around.

"That is a lot of nonsense, and you know it!" she said. "You're paid to assess and secure my safety. If that's not thinking, what is?"

"He's got problems," said Duncan without flinching. "Up here." He tapped his temple with a finger.

A Baron's Son is Undone

"Don't we all?" said Sophie.

Duncan stretched his lips into what passed for a smile on his face.

"He's also a bit of a shitter," said Duncan, reaching his ugly smile even further.

Sophie laughed as she began ascending a flight of stairs with Duncan at her heel.

"Accurate, as always," she said. "You're a good dog, Duncan. I only wish I had a treat for you."

"I live to serve," said Duncan without any hint of irony.

"It's a shame you're my father's dog," said Sophie turning to him outside her bedchamber door. "I should like to keep you for always."

Duncan gave her a short bow before leaving, but she could see from his face that her words had touched him.

At breakfast the next morning, Sophie painted a pained smile across her face as her aunt—great aunt to be precise—held court. Sophie was the court. A court of one, but that didn't matter. Her aunt took great pleasure in presiding over someone, and that someone just so happened to be Sophie at this point in time.

"And where were you last night?" asked Aunt Margaret.

Sophie looked up from her toast.

"Out for a walk," she said.

"All night?"

"Not all night. Only until eleven-thirty."

"I have a good mind to write to your father," said Aunt Margaret. It was a threat she repeated about three times a day.

The Pirate's Daughter

"Young ladies have no business *going for walks* at all hours of the night."

"Duncan would never let me do anything unsafe," responded Sophie. "That is why Father sent him."

Her aunt pulled at her black collar. She was not in mourning, but she only ever wore black or grey on account of her being averse to any gaiety whatsoever. The colours of the rainbow offended her.

"I have an itchy throat," she said. "Not inside, mind you. On the outside."

"Neck," said Sophie.

"Pardon?"

"If it's on the outside, it's your neck. If it's on the inside, it's your throat."

Aunt Margaret twisted her face with disagreement.

"What did that governess of yours teach you? The front of your neck is your throat—and mine's itchy!"

"Perhaps it's all the starch in your collar," suggested Sophie taking a bite of her toast. She knew how this conversation was going to go because they all went the same way.

"I'll not be condescended to by the likes of you!" said Aunt Margaret. "Gallivanting all night with who knows whom. You have utterly destroyed your father's reputation already."

And now she'll say something about Mother, thought Sophie.

"That mother of yours was a hussy as well. Don't think I didn't make myself heard when that insensible arrangement was cooked up. A Portuguese trollop is what she was. You're no better."

"So I've heard," said Sophie before taking a sip of her tea.

When she had first arrived at Seymour Cottage, her aunt had looked her up and down with a sour expression puckering

A Baron's Son is Undone

up her judgmental face. She had actually never met her aunt until that very moment. There was no hello or how-do-you-do? No welcome-to-my-home or so-sorry-about-that-awful-business-in-London. No. The first words from her aunt's lips were, "Heaven help me, you look like you've been sitting in the sun! You'll not find a husband looking like a field hand."

Sophie was well aware that her complexion was not the standard of English beauty. As a child, she had not understood that the remarks of her family's various acquaintances had been uncomplimentary, even snide. It was only after her mother passed away and she was forced to navigate the waters of new adulthood alone that she realised the negative undercurrent of the commentary directed her way.

At the breakfast table, her aunt tugged desperately at her collar.

"It's so very itchy!"

"Aunt Marg—"

"—I told you not to call me that!" interrupted her aunt.

"Miss Byrd," corrected Sophie. "I do think it's the starch."

Her aunt had insisted (after her initial inspection of Sophie upon her arrival) that she would not countenance the local population finding out they were related. She insisted Sophie go by the name of Lovell.

"I'll not be having you throwing the name 'Byrd' around town," she had said. "You can be Miss Lovell. I am hosting you for the summer. Under duress."

Sophie smiled as she thought back to this decision of her aunt's. It had been quite fortuitous as Lovell just so happened to be the name of a local pirate who had not been seen in several years. Had her aunt known this all along, or had the name simply been imprinted on her scattered mind at some

The Pirate's Daughter

point?

When Sophie started introducing herself around town, people began to whisper, and rumours that she was Captain Lovell's daughter began to swirl like mist in her wake. Which was quite fine, she thought. As a London lady, she would have been treated rather differently, kept at a distance by the locals. As Captain Lovell's daughter, she was welcomed into the fold. This touched her in an inexplicable way. It warmed her heart in places that she hadn't realised were frozen.

Sophie recognised that people love a good story, and right now she was that story. It mattered not that she had the bearing and manners, the accent even, of a member of the beau monde. These remarkable achievements (for a pirate's daughter) were attributed to the fine finishing schools she had attended—Captain Lovell was rich and would have spared no expense for his treasured daughter.

At the breakfast table, Sophie chuckled quietly to herself.

"I'll not be laughed at!" said Aunt Margaret. "You can spend the rest of your day in your room."

She pointed to the door of the morning room with a bony finger that trembled with agitation.

"Very well," said Sophie, placing her napkin on the table and standing. "I shall remain in my room for the day."

"And don't think about luncheon," said Aunt Margaret. "You don't deserve a mid-day meal."

"Quite," said Sophie.

She didn't care. Duncan had mysteriously disappeared on what he had gruffly referred to as "an errand" earlier that morning, and Sophie had plans to make the most of her day of freedom. She would certainly not be spending it in her room.

Two

The Ocean is a Dangerous Place

George woke early the next morning with the beginnings of a headache pulsing behind his eyes. The sun had slipped a finger of golden light through the crack in his curtains, and he could hear a bird chirruping madly in the tree outside his window. He rolled away from the window, pulling a pillow over his head. He had a brief vision of himself walking outside with a pistol and shooting that bird from the tree. It would land like a heavy drop of rain on the ground below, and then he might return to his room to sleep the rest of the day away.

Bird murderer, he thought. *Ruffian.* Of the two, he found bird murderer to be the more damning. He hadn't done it yet. Murdered any birds. But he knew he could. And he knew he would enjoy doing it, so as far as he was concerned, *as far as his soul was concerned*, it really didn't matter that he hadn't done it. This was just the kind of person he was.

The Ocean is a Dangerous Place

He rose and washed and dressed, then sat down at the small table in his room and opened his diary. This was no literary diary of his thoughts, no record of past events, but rather a book he used to schedule the minutes of each day. If one planned the day and then executed the day as planned, time seemed tidier. The world seemed safer. Minutes and hours and years could be swept up with a pen and arranged into nice orderly rows the same way he had done with his toy soldiers when he was a boy.

A schedule was what he needed here at the inn, here in this town. He was up early, but he was hungry so breakfast first. Then a walk along the cliffs. Then . . . what? George realised as a sharp pain stabbed him behind the eyes that he did not know how to spend a holiday by himself. He normally had a sister or two to corral and entertain—a focus for his efforts. He was hopeless if left alone with himself. *What had he been thinking? Why was he even here?*

Downstairs, the elderly waitress greeted him with a gap-toothed smile, bright as the damnable sun outside.

"A gentleman will be wanting his tea in the morning," she said.

"Coffee," said George. "Bring the pot."

She lifted her eyebrows.

"Oh, aye, and will ye be wanting a hair o' the dog as well?"

George didn't like the fact that she was so observant. He had drunk too much the night before. Alone in his corner of the tavern. After that woman had left with her scar-faced goon. Pirate's daughter—what a load! But she did have a look about her. As if her mother had hailed from stranger parts, a place where a pirate might have harboured his ship, might have harboured his heart.

A Baron's Son is Undone

What nonsense. George shook his head to clear it.

"So that's a no to more whisky this morning?" asked the waitress quite seriously.

"Yes," said George. "I mean yes, it's a no." It was a silly thing to say, and the woman smiled at him.

"I'll bring you some bacon. There's fresh bread in the oven."

George nodded his thanks.

Apart from himself, there was only one other man in the tavern this morning taking breakfast. Mr Harris the innkeeper was up and out early to greet his guests.

"Mr Pemberley!" The man spoke much too jovially, as if every sentence ended with an exclamation point.

It took George a second to register that the name was his. He hadn't wanted to be recognised as a Pemberton. He had relatives living two towns over, and he did not want to spend his short sabbatical answering Uncle St. John's questions about Parliament and being sequestered by his Aunt Evelyn for every dinner from now until September.

"Mr. Pemberley!" said Mr. Harris once more with feeling. "I hope your bed was comfortable. Please let me know if there is anything more we can do for you!"

"Have you a map?" asked George. "Of the area," he added when Mr. Harris did not respond immediately.

"Oh yes! A map! I could rustle up a map! No problem!"

The man's grin was broad, and if he hadn't seemed so sincere about it, George might have been annoyed with his exuberance.

"Has Maddy told you about second Wednesdays?" asked Mr. Harris, beaming down at him.

"Maddy?" asked George.

"Wednesdays at Almack's!" said the innkeeper.

The Ocean is a Dangerous Place

George stared at him, completely at a loss.

"We set it up here in the tavern!" Mr. Harris swept his arm across the room. "On alternate Wednesdays! Hazard, baccarat, whist, what-have-you. And it's an opportunity to mingle with the good people of the ton!" Here he laughed, a deep belly laugh that ended in a fit of coughing.

Mr. Harris placed his hand on George's shoulder and leaned in conspiratorially. George looked to the red hand that was touching him, then to the man's equally flushed face.

"She'll be here on game nights." He said it quietly. "Miss Lovell. She likes a game." He gave George a scolding look, and he shook his head once, as if in disbelief. "I heard you proposition her last night. Not clever. Though I imagine a gentleman like yourself is used to getting what he wants."

Mr. Harris lifted his hand from George's shoulder and stood to his full height.

"Stick with Winnie," he said. "She's clean, and she's sweet for a whore. And no one will slice you up afterwards. I'll not have a murder on the premises." His face went solemn, as if he truly believed that George might be killed in front of him, that he would have to ask the elderly Maddy to mop up the blood.

"I hardly think—" began George.

"—I'll get that map!" said Mr. Harris spinning away on his heel. "You'll want to explore the beauty of Cornwall on foot I imagine. The good people of the ton do like to perambulate!"

When he was away from Cornwall, George imagined her at her best—a blue sky and turquoise waters breaking into white

A Baron's Son is Undone

foamy runners that crawl up the golden sand. He would turn inland in his mind in order to drown himself in a hothouse of lush greens. Fields of yellow-flowering gorse packed so tight and so high that they were impossible to traverse.

George noticed that his fond memories of the place were not materialising today as he strode out against the wind. Pale grey clouds skittered nervously across the sun that had been so bold and so bright just half an hour before, and the sky sprinkled a hesitant drizzle down upon his head. He felt like a hothouse flower being given a good spritzing. When he arrived at the cliffs overlooking the sea, however, nothing mattered. He stood, and he took it in. Water stretched out to meet the bowl of the sky, the expanse of it all making him feel as if he were being lifted up and carried off like an insignificant piece of flotsam.

I wish I were a piece of flotsam. That would be a fine thing.

He could feel his entire being coiled tightly around the role that he played in his life, the life of his family. The role was so much more solid, more real than he himself could ever be. *The baron's son.* What a joke! And not a funny one. It was the kind of joke that pokes you full of holes and leaves you to bleed out onto the expensive carpet.

As a child with his knees pulled tight to his chest up on the window sill that day, his first thoughts had not been, *Father is not my real father*, or *Patience is only my half-sister*. Instead, his first thoughts had been, *I am not Father's real son*, and then, with a pang he felt might shatter his chest, *I am only half a brother.* The child that he had been set his mouth in a grim line and squeezed his eyes shut against the onslaught of tears. He would make it up to them. He could be a whole person for his father, for Patience, and much later, for his little sister

The Ocean is a Dangerous Place

Grace.

Maintaining a view of the sea from the cliff edge, George turned and began his morning trek. He would hike along the cliffs, then return to the inn by lunchtime. After that, he would check his diary to see what was next on the agenda even though he knew what was next, for he had only just written it down that morning.

George strode swiftly along the cliffs as if someone were in pursuit of him and closing in fast. The drizzle turned to drops of rain, but it was the kind of rain that lacks commitment, and it soon gave up, leaving George damp but relieved to see that the clouds were making way for the sun. He had passed two coves now. From his height, they looked like landscape paintings, idyllic little worlds of rock and sand and sea. He fancied he should like to climb down and stand in the middle of one of them. The sea was different at eye level, much more foreboding. The strength of it, the sheer weight of water. George decided that when he reached the next cove, he would climb down.

After another twenty minutes or so of brisk walking, he found it—the perfect beach rested beneath him at the base of the cliff. The clouds had been blown out to the edges of the horizon. There was still a wind, but the water was as turquoise as he remembered it. George began a precarious descent along a staircase cut into the side of the cliff. He had to pay attention to his feet lest he slip and slide the entire way down, so when he finally alighted at the bottom and looked up, the surprise of seeing her there took his literal breath away.

"Miss Lovell," he said after gathering up a lungful of air. "I did not see you from the cliff."

He looked around, imagining her man Duncan was hiding

A Baron's Son is Undone

somewhere nearby with a knife and a satisfied gleam in his eye. But there was no Duncan. This disturbed George perhaps even more than if Duncan had actually been there.

"Mr. Pemberley," she said.

Her hair was done up as it had been the night before. That plaited crown, but today it was frizzing and straining against its woven bonds. Her eyes shone a luminous amber brown, the colour of a glass of sherry held up to the light.

"Your bathing costume," said George awkwardly, for she was wearing a white garment that stretched (he noted) not quite down to her shapely ankles. And it was wet! *Dear God.* These bathing costumes pretended to be modest affairs, but a woman in a wet dress was still a woman in a wet dress—every curve and crevice on display.

"Observant," she said.

He knew she was mocking him, but it was difficult to take offence while he was staring at her breasts. He had to tear his gaze up from her tight little nipples which were straining against the wet fabric.

George was having trouble thinking. His brain was screaming, "Retreat!" but his legs would not obey the order.

"This is no place for a lady alone."

"I'm always alone," she said, and she turned away from him and walked out into the sea!

Sophie knew she was in a precarious position as she waded past the breakers and swam out from the shore. Mr. Pemberley intrigued her, yes, but that did not mean that Mr. Pemberley was a nice man. She and Duncan had established

The Ocean is a Dangerous Place

the night before that he was in fact (what had Duncan called him?) "a bit of a shitter". And here she was. Alone with him on a deserted beach. No one would hear her cries for help. She should have made straight for her blanket on the beach and retrieved the pistol, but she hadn't been thinking clearly. That smoky grey gaze was enough to addle an otherwise logical mind.

Don't be a fool, Sophie. He's just a man—a man you don't know in the slightest. See him off.

Despite the cold water, Sophie flushed with the realisation of how foolish she had been to sneak out alone. Duncan would bite off her head if he found out. No, he would bite off Mr. Pemberley's head. Sophie imagined Mr. Pemberley without his handsome head, and it made her momentarily sad. She turned herself to the beach and saw him standing there, hands in his pockets, watching her. She waved, not a wave of hello, but rather a dismissive wave that said "go away, be gone". He lifted a hesitant hand to wave back so clearly did not *or would not* comprehend the message. He came closer, right to the edge of the water, and called out to her, but she couldn't hear him over the sound of the ocean. Perhaps she could swim along the coast to find another inlet and make her way home from there. It was a fleeting thought because it was clearly an impossibility. The rocky promontories at both ends of the cove would force her out into deeper and more dangerous waters. She was not so strong a swimmer and not so brave a woman as to entertain death to avoid . . . avoid *what* with Mr. Pemberley? She was not entirely convinced that he would assault her.

But he might.

Time passed. She swam, and Mr. Pemberley kept his vigil.

A Baron's Son is Undone

Eventually, she grew tired and had to return.

"Why have you not left yet?" she asked as she approached him from the water. "It would be the gentlemanly thing to do." The wet tongue of the sea licked up to her ankles and withdrew.

Mr. Pemberley looked down at his shoes.

"These are ruined," he said with agitation.

"Then don't stand in the water," replied Sophie irritatedly.

"What would you have me do?! I can't very well leave. You should not be swimming alone! The ocean is a dangerous place—"

"—for a woman," added Sophie, finishing his sentence for him.

"For anyone!" Mr. Pemberley drew both hands through his thick sandy hair, standing it on end in the most appealing way. "You should not be here alone, full stop."

Sophie was as torn with this man today as she had been the night before. His concern for his shoes grated on her, but his concern for her was mildly . . . pleasing? Would she still be pleased if he touched her? She thought not. Would he force himself upon her here in the sandy cove? Looking at him now, again she very much doubted it. But she had been wrong before. A mild panic began to rise up into her throat. Regardless, all she had to do was make for her blankets under the rocky overhang. She would dry off and casually retrieve the pistol hiding there. Then she would wave it at him, and he would be on his way. Duncan would be so proud if she were to tell him later. Which she would not.

"Have you come to your senses? Are you leaving now?" asked Mr. Pemberley following her over to the red blanket she had laid out under the cliff.

The Ocean is a Dangerous Place

"No. I'm drying off," said Sophie. "Then I shall have a bite to eat. And *then* I shall go home." She hoped that her cavalier tone of voice did not betray her fear.

She turned to see him checking his pocket watch. Not the behaviour of a man who was about to assault a woman, unless of course he intended to do it in a timely fashion. Still. Best be completely safe. She would fetch the pistol.

"Do you have somewhere you need to be?" she asked.

"I have a schedule to keep," said Mr. Pemberley. *Was he getting impatient with her? Why didn't he just leave?*

"So keep it," said Sophie, reaching down as if for a blanket but slipping her hand beneath to grasp the rounded handle of her pistol (actually, Duncan's pistol).

She turned on him as she said it, pointing the weapon at his face.

"Bloody hell!"

"Leave!" she said.

Mr. Pemberley raised his hands into the air, and after a startled moment, his face broke into a smile that sent a shock of liquid pleasure right through her.

He was pleased!

"Well done," he said, chuckling now. "That was . . . well played. Full points as far as I'm concerned. You clearly know how to deal with pirates. I'm sorry if you thought I was one. I didn't mean to scare you. Only, I couldn't leave you here. If I later found out your body had washed up somewhere drowned, I could never have forgiven myself."

"Pirates? What are you talking about?"

"How about this?" suggested Mr. Pemberley. "I shall retreat up the cliffside. You can have your picnic, and then I will keep my distance as I see you safely home. Your man Duncan will

A Baron's Son is Undone

be worried."

"My man Duncan?" asked Sophie incredulously.

Mr. Pemberley started to back towards the cliff, hands still raised, his beautiful mouth still smiling. When he reached the staircase, he turned and started his ascent.

Sophie lowered her weapon. She felt strangely empty now that he was leaving. She had felt this way before. Everyone always leaving. And her alone, playing spillikins all by herself until, inevitably, she pulled the wrong stick and everything came crashing down.

"Wait!" she called out.

Mr. Pemberley turned towards her.

"Come back." Sophie heard herself speak the words, but she couldn't quite believe what she was hearing.

Mr. Pemberley stepped back down the staircase and crossed the sand to her, a quizzical look upon his face. It was almost as endearing a look as the smile he had graced her with earlier.

"You can stay if you keep your distance."

"But I don't want to stay, Miss Lovell. I told you, I have a schedule to keep. So eat your sandwich or apple or whatever it is you have brought with you, and let's be on our way." He checked his pocket watch once more.

Sophie sat down at one end of the red blanket and wrapped a blue shawl about her shoulders. She placed the pistol down beside her within easy reach.

"I brought pasties," she said, ignoring the fact that he did not want to be there. "Do you want one?"

Mr. Pemberley looked up from his watch.

"Pasties? Is there dessert at the bottom?"

Sophie nodded. "Cooked apples and cinnamon."

She tossed a pasty to the far side of the red blanket, and it

The Ocean is a Dangerous Place

landed near Mr. Pemberley's feet.

He crouched down to pick up the pasty, and the movement drew his buff-coloured trousers taut across his thighs.

"It's such a tidy and efficient meal," he said. "I shouldn't mind climbing down a mineshaft each day if I had one of these waiting for me at the bottom."

"Oh, I think you would mind," said Sophie with a small laugh. "Mining is difficult work. Not to mention dirty and dangerous."

Mr. Pemberley pierced her with a look. "You think me incapable of hard work?" he asked.

"Oh yes. A gentleman of the ton?"

"And what would pirates' daughters know of the ton?" asked Mr. Pemberley biting into his pasty.

"We circulate secretly among you," she said cryptically. "Life is one big masquerade."

Mr. Pemberley looked up from his pasty. His face had set along solemn lines.

"It is," he said seriously. "No one can truly know another."

Sophie was touched to her core by the candid sentiment. Most people, she had noticed, liked to 'make conversation', but they didn't really *talk*. Mr. Pemberley was actually talking to her. It felt the most wondrous thing, like a moth caught in the cage of her hands, and she didn't for the life of her want to let it go.

"What do you mean by that?" she asked.

"Nothing," he said, but he took a shuddering breath. "I'm just tired."

"Of pretending?" she asked.

"This is quite good," he said lifting his pasty. "Did your cook make it?"

A Baron's Son is Undone

"You haven't answered my question."

"I don't plan to," he said locking eyes with her.

"But you forget, Mr. Pemberley, I'm the one with the gun." She picked it up and waved it in his direction. "Answer the question."

"For Heaven's sake! I hope that thing isn't loaded!"

"Oh, it's loaded."

"It's clear you don't know how to use it, Miss Lovell, so put it down before one of us gets hurt."

"Answer the question," she said, holding the gun in place.

Mr. Pemberley lifted his gaze suddenly up the cliff side in a way that suggested something had caught his eye, and Sophie's eyes involuntarily followed his. It was only a moment, but in that instant of distraction, Mr. Pemberley threw himself across the blanket and tackled her to her back. *Good Lord, the man's body was hard!*

For a brief moment, the sensation of so much raw contact with another human being threatened to overwhelm Sophie's faculties, but she managed to rally herself in order to attempt a hard kick. It didn't matter—he had her pinned with one hand to each of her wrists and his body flat against hers to keep her from moving. He gave her right wrist (the one with the gun) a mild squeeze.

"Release the pistol, Miss Lovell."

His voice was stern, but despite the fact that he had her pinned, he was being as gentle as possible. The side of his face skimmed her cheek, and his breath was hot on her ear. He smelled like freshly cut wood and, unbelievably, sunshine. Sophie squirmed and struggled against him which had the unwelcome effect of making her quite damp between the thighs. A sudden wash of shame spread through her like a

The Ocean is a Dangerous Place

watercolour stain through paper.

Had this happened to her ten months ago, she probably would have gone into a fit of hysterics and eventually blacked out. But time, it seemed, had worn away the sharp edges of her terror leaving her with a softer, more manageable ball of fear.

"Get off!" yelled Sophie.

"Apologies, Miss Lovell," said Mr. Pemberley in a voice gone gravelly with the effort of holding her down. "I don't normally throw myself on top of young ladies, but you left me no choice. This is for your own safety as much as mine. Give me the pistol."

Sophie manoeuvred her head to look him in the eyes. Was his breathing laboured? His face was flushed.

"I promise I won't hurt you," he said.

"I've been promised that before," said Sophie.

She could feel his chest moving with his breath, and it actually hitched as he registered the meaning of her words.

"I always keep my promises," said Mr. Pemberley seriously, his eyes on hers.

There was something about the way that he said it—a gravity to the statement that settled down heavily into Sophie's bones. She released her grip on the pistol. He took it from her and immediately knelt up on the blanket. In a few deft motions, he had it unloaded.

"Game's over," he said, giving her a scolding look that made her feel all of eight years old. "I don't think I need to say it, but I'll say it anyway: I won." (This last statement made *him* seem all of eight years old).

Mr. Pemberley looked down at his pasty which he had dropped in the sand.

A Baron's Son is Undone

"Look what you made me do," he said with some petulance.

His concern for his pasty not a few seconds after their physical altercation had a relaxing effect upon Sophie's nerves. She appeared to have been right in her initial assessment—Mr. Pemberley was not to be feared. She allowed herself (for the time being anyway) to want his company.

"You can have mine," offered Sophie sitting up shakily. The words arrived involuntarily on her tongue. They took flight without her say-so.

He turned to her with a look of surprise on his face.

"I won't touch you again. I promise," he said as he slipped the lead ball into a pocket. He followed her gaze to his pocket. "Duncan will want it back. No point wasting good ammunition."

"Duncan again?!"

"What?"

"You seem to have a lot of concern for a man who is more likely to batter that pretty face of yours than to actually thank you."

"You think my face is pretty?" asked Mr. Pemberley. He didn't smile, but the corners of his mouth twitched in a way that suggested they wanted to do so.

Sophie rolled her eyes and thrust out her hand to offer him her pasty.

"I couldn't take yours," he said. "Finish up, and lets get going."

Sophie ate her pasty slowly, watching as Mr. Pemberley became more fidgety with every passing second.

"What's next on your agenda?" she asked. "Is it important?"

Mr. Pemberley stopped fidgeting.

"It's always important," he said.

The Ocean is a Dangerous Place

"So what is it?"

"Nothing."

"It can't be nothing. You said it was important."

"Glass," said Mr. Pemberley giving in. "I was going to visit a glass shop one town over. There's a wizened old man there who creates wonders in glass. Tiny filigree pendants, miniature flowers to stand in a vase made entirely of netted glass, a herd of small transparent horses. He makes everything to the scale of a flower fairy."

Sophie found herself laughing.

"I'm amusing you again," said Mr. Pemberley.

"Again?" asked Sophie.

"You laughed at me last night," replied Mr. Pemberley.

"It's just . . . the scale of a flower fairy? Really? You sound like a little girl."

"That's because I'm thinking of a little girl," said Mr. Pemberley as he stood. He motioned for her to do so as well, then lifted up her red blanket and gave it a shake. "My sister Grace is only ten. She will love me forever if I bring her a little trinket from the magical old man in Porth La."

"You have a sister?"

"I have two," said Mr. Pemberley. "But one has left me. Patience. She was married only a few months ago."

"You miss her."

Mr. Pemberley folded up the blanket while avoiding Sophie's eyes.

"She was a thorn in my side," he said. "Of course I miss her."

"She's quite lucky then," said Sophie wistfully.

"Do you have siblings?" asked Mr. Pemberley.

"No."

Sophie didn't want to elaborate. It was a subject that left her

A Baron's Son is Undone

feeling exposed and raw. She had no siblings who had lived. She had been an only child in an enormous house playing games with herself because all of the servants were too busy to engage with her. A dead mother and a father who considered her existence to be a blight on his otherwise perfect life. If she had been a boy, she might have been loved.

"No," she said again. "No siblings." She tried to make the statement sound like a simple unemotional fact, but it was impossible to do so.

Mr. Pemberley gave her a long look. It was a gaze that wrapped her up in the warm embrace of his eyes.

"Perhaps I will not go to the glass shop today," he said. "Perhaps I will go on Saturday, around two of the clock in the afternoon. If I were to happen upon you there, you could help me pick out a gift for my sister. That is, if Duncan can be convinced."

Sophie felt his invitation land like a cloud of butterflies. She kept her features carefully composed. A lady, she knew, must not be too eager.

"Perhaps," she said.

In the end, she agreed that Mr. Pemberley would escort her home. Maddeningly, he was of a mind that Duncan should be informed of her truancy, and she had to plead with him for some time before he reluctantly assured her that he would not speak with the man.

Sophie could not help noticing that Mr. Pemberley seemed to enjoy the pleading as much as he had enjoyed the pasty earlier. He held out for so long that she thought she might be forced to drop to her knees like a supplicant. And she probably would have. Duncan couldn't know. This was as much for Mr. Pemberley's safety as it was to guard the secret

The Ocean is a Dangerous Place

of her independent outing.

In the end, Mr. Pemberley gave in with a stern warning: "All right. But let this be a lesson to you. Had it been someone else who found you here, pistol or no, God only knows what might have happened. Duncan is only trying to keep you safe."

Sophie nodded, trying to look contrite. He reached into his pocket for Duncan's lead ball, and when she opened her hand to receive it, he dropped it into her palm from a small height in an exaggerated effort to avoid contact between them.

"A promise is a promise," he said. "I shall not touch you again."

Three

David and Goliath

Everything is out of order, thought George, as he marched himself back to the inn. *That was . . . unanticipated.*

Miss Lovell and her transparent bathing costume had derailed his carefully planned day. His schedule was now quite destroyed, and time was scattering about him in untidy clumps which was sending his heart into a mild panic. His shoes were ruined. He had dropped his delicious pasty in the sand.

So why was he grinning to himself?

It was such an unfamiliar feeling to have the corners of his mouth lifted, his cheeks pressing up to crinkle the corners of his eyes. When was the last time he had smiled? God only knew. This was not to say that Miss Lovell was the perfect woman—she was not. Words to describe her would be imprudent, brash, irresponsible . . . amusing, surprising,

David and Goliath

brave, unbelievably bloody lovely . . . After a moment, George added, 'lonesome' and 'melancholic' to the list. Then, 'untouchable'.

Arriving back at the inn, he climbed the stairs and opened the door to his room. The whole place seemed somehow more inviting, as if it were sprinkled with tiny little promises. George kicked off his wet shoes and lined them up neatly in a patch of sun by the window. He shrugged off his jacket and hung it on the back of a chair.

He looked down at his open agenda on the little wooden table. His outing to the glass shop would now need to be shifted to two o'clock this coming Saturday. He thought of Duncan again and couldn't help but feel as if he were baiting a rabid dog. That man was not going to like this at all.

Perhaps I'm the imprudent one, thought George. *Or the lonesome one*, he added.

Evenings at the inn, it turned out, were always merry affairs. Travellers took their supper. Working men came for a drink and a laugh. Winnie plied her trade without much subtlety, and burly Tom sat in the corner sulking as she did so. George knew that his own days here were numbered, that eventually, he would have to return. He would have to lift his chin and swallow his self-loathing and continue to act out his role as the baron's son. This knowledge pulled his muscles so tight that his stomach had become a hard rippled board. The stiffness with which he had arrived had not dissipated, and George knew there was only one way to find some relief.

Miss Lovell had not returned to the inn on any of the

following evenings, and her absence somehow wrung the pleasure from George's days so that he felt as if even here, even on holiday, he was simply going through the motions. The feeling of elation that had embraced him after their last encounter had gradually dissipated. The logical part of George's mind had stepped in to remind him that nothing could come of his time with Miss Lovell. For one thing, he was deceiving her—his name was not Pemberley. For another thing, a dalliance with a supposed pirate's daughter was not exactly the done thing for a man in his position—men who were to take positions in government should not by rights be frequenting with criminals or their daughters. And then, even if he were to ignore these last two points, there was the nuisance that was his promise: no touching.

This evening was like any other. A full house at the tavern but no Miss Lovell. George strode over to Tom who was sitting alone at the end of a long table. He planted a tankard of ale in front of the man.

"Tell me," he said sitting down, "about the pirate's daughter."

Tom tore his gaze from Winnie who was sitting on another gentleman's lap.

"What's that?"

"The pirate's daughter. What do you know about her?"

Tom smiled. "So you fancy a bite o' the forbidden fruit, do ya? Can't say I'll be disappointed when your guts are spilling out of your belly onto the floor."

George slid the tankard towards Tom who grasped it in both hands.

"Captain Lovell's well-known 'round these parts," said Tom. "Not actually a pirate. Least as far as I know. Privateer? Yes. Smuggler? Sure, but who isn't? Has a bit of a violent streak, so that's probably where the whole pirate notion came from. Haven't seen him for some time though. Years. Sophie's been livin' with Mad Margaret for the last two months."

"You call her Sophie?" asked George taken aback.

"Everyone does apart from Mr. Harris." Tom looked to the inn-keeper behind the bar. "He tries to be proper. Has a business to run."

"Who's Mad Margaret?" asked George. He had seen Miss Lovell home to her rather large cottage but had not realised that anyone else lived there.

"Margaret Byrd," said Tom lifting the end of his nose with one finger. "She imagines she's a lady, but everyone knows she's short of funds. Captain Lovell must be paying her to house his daughter. She certainly doesn't want her there. Makes that very clear to anyone who'll listen."

"I see," said George. His mind was a trap for facts, and he knew the name Byrd. That woman, mad or not, wasn't imagining that she was a lady. She was very possibly related to the Duke of Somerset! A relative of the Duke's would have to have fallen a long way down to be frequenting with the likes of pirates, or even privateers for that matter. There was something else about the Byrds that George knew might be important. He had a vague memory of Patience and his mother discussing some piece of news (or, more likely, gossip). George tended not to listen when they were chattering, but he knew the conversation must be lodged somewhere in his mind, for his ears had heard it even if his mind had dismissed it out of hand.

Tom glanced across the room, and George followed his gaze to where Winnie was being fondled in a not-so-dark corner. The man lifted her from his lap and taking her by the hand,

A Baron's Son is Undone

led her up the stairs, presumably to his room. Tom hoisted his tankard and drank it all down in one glugging motion.

"How's 'bout that fight?" he asked George before wiping his mouth with his sleeve. "I'm in the mood to punch someone."

"I thought you'd never ask," said George unbuttoning his jacket and hanging it neatly on the back of his chair.

Tom banged the table with a fist.

"Fight outside!" he yelled. "The toff's goin' down!"

A cheer rose up around him.

"You'll have to give it a minute," he said leaning in towards George. "They'll want to place bets."

"Of course," said George. He had stripped down to his shirtsleeves and was pulling his cravat loose from his neck.

This was more like it. A bone-jarring fight was exactly what he needed. The satisfying sound of his fist connecting with another man's jaw. The taste of blood in his mouth. This had been his solution since he was a boy. It was a draught of medicine that drowned out all those terrible feelings vying for his attention, at least temporarily. As a child, he hadn't known what he was doing. But he did know it was necessary in the same way that he knew it was necessary now. At school, he learned that most other boys were simple and predictable. Confront, belittle, taunt—it was easy to draw another lad into a fight. Almost too easy.

"You wanna say that again to my fist?" might be a typical response to one of his goads. (No one was ever particularly original with their replies).

He would counter with something like, "You probably fight like my little sister. You certainly look like her." He might kiss the air here for added effect.

He would plant his feet as he did so because he knew he

David and Goliath

would be tackled within the next few seconds. And when a boy did inevitably rise to the bait, God, it was gratifying. He felt like a puppeteer. In charge. Making everyone else dance to his say so.

As an adult, things were much easier. You could join a boxing club or simply make a gentlemanly agreement to fight someone at an arranged time and place. Everyone and their dog fancied himself a pugilist these days. George, however, preferred his schoolboy method. The fight seemed more real if you had wound someone up to do it. He had tried it on with Tom the other evening and been sorely disappointed with his response, so this somewhat amicable arrangement would have to do, at least for the time being.

They set up a makeshift ring outside. Lanterns and torches and much jostling and shouting.

George pulled his shirt up over his head and handed it to Maddy who eyed his torso up and down in the golden light. She sucked in a breath through the gaps in her teeth.

"Lord love you, Mr. Pemberley, but you're no match for Tom."

She looked across the ring to where Tom was standing stripped to the waist looking like an enormous boulder in human form.

George took Maddy's free hand and bowing down, raised it to his lips. Maddy let out a little shriek of embarrassment.

"David and Goliath," said George lifting his head from her hand. "Who won that one?"

"Don't talk nonsense, Mr. Pemberley. You haven't a slingshot. Nor the Grace of God."

"No. I have neither," he said, turning towards Tom. "It's a show, Maddy. Just enjoy yourself."

A Baron's Son is Undone

"What did you say?" asked Tom stepping forward to hear him over the shouting of the crowd.

George raised his voice: "I said Winnie's probably enjoying herself upstairs right now. I hear she's quite sweet for a whore."

Tom's punch landed on the word 'whore'. The crowd raised up a cheer.

George stumbled, then righted himself, finding his centre of balance once more. Fists at the ready.

"She's not worth it, Tom. You said so yourself."

George watched with some satisfaction as Tom flushed red across not just his face, but his torso as well. He lunged for George who, side-stepping him, gave him a kick to land him sprawled face-first on the ground. George appreciated the fact that bare-knuckle boxing was not known for its gentlemanly rules of conduct. Kicking, hair-pulling, throwing. It was all fair game, so long as the crowd got their show, so long as someone was eventually left down on the ground for longer than thirty seconds. The same rules had applied at school when they met behind the laundry on a Saturday. Someone would be eating dirt by the end of the afternoon, and then everyone would make their way back to the dormitories laughing, their frustrations momentarily forgotten, their griefs temporarily eased.

In the lantern-lit ring, Tom rose to his massive feet, and the fight began in earnest.

When Sophie arrived with Duncan at the tavern that evening, her heart leapt with excitement to see the crowd out front.

David and Goliath

A fight! She hoped she hadn't missed it. Duncan placed his hand on her arm to hold her back.

"They're all a bit blood mad right now," he said tipping his chin towards the unruly rabble. "Best not have a lady step into the fray."

Sophie shook off Duncan's protective hand.

"But I want to see the fight." She turned to Duncan and gave him her best, most beseeching look. "Please Duncan. Make a girl happy for once."

Duncan hesitated, but she knew she had him. A dog always wants to make his mistress happy. Even a guard dog.

"Stay close," he said.

They shouldered their way through the rowdy crowd until they came to the edge of the ring. Sophie could smell the ale-soaked clothes and breath of those around her. Many had brought their tankards outside with them, and their contents were sloshing all over the place as people yelled and gesticulated.

Sophie gazed into the ring, and it took a moment for her mind to register what her eyes were seeing.

Mercy.

Mr Pemberley was down on the ground, his beautiful face covered in blood, and *sweet heavens*, he was naked from the waist up! All lean muscle and sinew. Sweat glistened in the torchlight. Sophie saw Tom—himself a hulk of flesh and brawn—standing over his fallen opponent, waiting. There was another man she didn't recognise who was kneeling beside Mr. Pemberley and counting out the seconds. When the man struck upon the number 'thirty', most of the crowd let up a cheer. Mr. Pemberley stirred in the dirt.

"Dear God, somebody help him!" said Sophie stepping

A Baron's Son is Undone

forward, but Duncan had grabbed her by the back of the dress.

"What do you think you're doing?" he growled.

"Help him, Duncan!"

"Not paid to—" Sophie slapped him across his ugly face. And it felt good. So incredibly good. She could see the shock of what she had just done in Duncan's eyes. Shock and something else . . . *Was he actually hurt?*

"Not everything you do requires that you be paid to do it!" she yelled before wrenching her dress from his hand and fleeing into the ring.

"Mr. Pemberley!"

Maddy and Mr. Harris approached as she knelt beside his body in the dirt. He opened his eyes. He was alive!

"Did I win?" he asked without even the shadow of a smile.

Mr. Harris boomed with laughter. "He's a good sport and all! Ah, Mr. Pemberley, I had money riding on you!"

Mr. Pemberley looked to Maddy who bent down with a cloth to wipe away some of the blood on his face.

"Did you enjoy the show, Maddy?" he asked.

"Oh, aye, Mr. Pemberley. It was one they'll be talkin' 'bout for some time to come."

Sophie noticed that despite the fact that she was kneeling right beside the man, he was studiously ignoring her. Duncan stepped up behind Mr. Pemberley's head, crouched down, and hoisted him up by his armpits. As he did so, the crowd cheered once more.

They loved him! They loved him for losing!

Duncan and Mr. Harris helped him through the crowd to the tavern as Sophie and Maddy followed behind.

"You missed a right good fight," said Maddy. "He gave Tom a run for it, he did."

David and Goliath

Mr. Pemberley was propped up at a table, and a glass of brandy was placed in front of him. He sat up straight and wiped some dirt and blood from his eyes with his bare upper arm. It was a simple uncalculated movement, but Sophie felt an ache in her belly as she watched him. She had never seen so much skin on a man. Her eyes followed the lines of his muscles along his arms and shoulders, down the length of his hair-smattered and blood-smeared chest to his rippled belly. He downed his glass of brandy and called for another. She was standing by his table with Duncan and several others. Finally, after many minutes had passed, he looked her way. It was the briefest glance, as if he were simply tracking the crowd of onlookers, not looking at her in particular. As their eyes met, she felt her insides go all wobbly. She turned to sit down, and Duncan was already there pulling up a chair for her.

"Where's Tom?" asked Mr. Pemberley.

As he said it, the burly brute appeared in the doorway of the tavern. He looked somewhat worse for wear. His nose was crooked, his mouth was bloody, and there were streaks of that blood as well as dirt smeared across his chest. Tom froze in place. Sophie followed his gaze to the backstairs where Winnie was standing staring at him. They stood like that for a long time.

Eventually, Tom said, "Winnie."

The way he said it sent a fracture branching through Sophie's heart.

"I'm sorry, Winnie," he said.

Winnie didn't move. She didn't speak. A few more seconds passed, and Sophie realised Winnie was actually crying. Maddy rushed over and ushered her out back to the kitchen.

A Baron's Son is Undone

Tom came in and sat himself slowly down across from Mr. Pemberley.

"Thanks," he said. "That was all right."

Mr. Pemberley reached out a hand, and Tom shook it.

"Any time," said Mr. Pemberley seriously.

Sophie looked to Duncan. "I'm just going to . . ." She rose from her seat. "I'm just going to see about Winnie."

Duncan placed a hand on her shoulder and lowered her back to her chair.

"No," he said. "Not out of my sight."

Sophie spied Mr. Pemberley watching their interaction out of the corner of his eye. She felt so small and useless. She could argue with Duncan, but she didn't want any witnesses to that. It made her look (and feel) like a whiny child trying to get her way.

"I'll have a glass of sherry then.

"Duncan," she added when he didn't get up.

Duncan narrowed his eyes at her, but he soon left to fetch her order at the bar. She could hear Mr. Harris's enthusiastic attempts to engage him in conversation. Mr. Pemberley fumbled in the pocket of a jacket that was hung neatly over the back of his chair. He pulled out his pocket watch. It was the most incongruous thing to see. This half-naked, feral man with his split lip and swollen cheek using his bloody-knuckled hands to casually open up the silver-casing of his pocket watch and check the time!

"Do you have somewhere else you need to be?" asked Sophie over the chatter of the men around the table.

Mr. Pemberley directed his grey gaze her way, and she was glad she was already sitting down. No surreptitious glance this time. The way he was looking at her made her heart go wild inside her chest, as if it were some trapped creature looking for a way out.

"No," he said slowly, not taking his eyes from hers. "Everything is going according to schedule."

"The fight was scheduled?" asked Sophie incredulously.

"The possibility of the fight was scheduled," said Mr. Pemberley sliding his watch back into his jacket. "Here's your sherry."

Sophie looked to Duncan who was as grim-faced as ever. The tavern was warm with bodies, and the air was heavy with the smell of ale and male sweat which should have been distasteful to a lady, but Sophie found the atmosphere quite . . . stimulating.

I'm supposed to be a pirate's daughter, anyway, she thought. *Someone like me would be used to this sort of thing.*

As Sophie took a sip of her sherry, she looked up to see Mr. Pemberley engaging amicably with the other men around him. It was as if he had turned into a different person. If one eliminated the incident with the pocket watch, he seemed entirely more relaxed than usual. He seemed more himself, if that made any sense. *Heavens above, he was laughing!* She couldn't explain why, but his smile caught her by surprise like an unexpected undertow. It drew her in, and she imagined drowning quite happily in its depths. In one brief moment of what she could only consider to be madness, she imagined herself licking all the blood from Mr. Pemberley's golden chest. The image shocked her, and she stood suddenly.

"Duncan," she said. "I think we'd best be off."

"Thank Christ," replied Duncan.

They walked home under a bulbous moon half-hidden behind gathering clouds. Duncan was normally silent, but

A Baron's Son is Undone

Sophie could feel the weight of his silence tonight.

"I'm sorry I hit you," she said.

Duncan didn't reply.

"There's no excuse for it," she added.

Duncan grunted, which was progress.

"I was a trifle worked up," said Sophie even though she had just now said there was no excuse.

"Worked up over Mr. Shitter lying battered in the dirt," said Duncan. He didn't glance her way but kept his eyes to the moonlit path ahead of them. "What would your father think?"

"Father doesn't think much of me as it is," said Sophie. "I doubt I could fall any further in his estimations." They walked on, and she wondered if she should ask the next question. It was to her by far the more important question.

"Have I fallen in *your* estimations, Duncan?"

"Never," said Duncan immediately.

"I appreciate that you allow me these little forays to the inn," said Sophie. She had never properly thanked him. "It would be so lonely otherwise, cooped up in that cottage with *her*."

"We have to wait it out," said Duncan. "Your father will call you back eventually. People will forget."

"They won't forget," said Sophie.

"But they *will* get bored," said Duncan. "It's almost the same thing."

"I suppose," said Sophie.

As much as she disliked living with her aunt, the thought of returning to her father cut through her like an icy blade. As a child, she had always imagined that though her father was distant and strict, he had her best interests at heart. This was what she had been told anyway. Now that she was grown, Sophie knew that the interests her father had at heart were

David and Goliath

his own. She did not know what his plans for her might be when she returned to him. All she knew was that she would not be consulted.

Back at the inn, George was feeling in fine form. He was good on his feet which had saved him from most of Tom's harshest blows, except, of course, the one that had sent him down. He tilted his face up and stretched his neck one way, then the other. He would certainly be sore in the morning. Downing the rest of his brandy, George stood from the table, and several men clapped him jovially on the back.

As he made his way up to his room to wash, he wondered at Miss Lovell's sudden departure. He had not expected to see her tonight, nor for her to see him . . . like this. No one he actually knew well—not friends and not family—had seen him this way. As himself. He doubted very much it was an appealing look, and he wondered if Miss Lovell would change her mind about their outing to the glass shop. He would certainly understand if she did. When she had agreed, she had thought him a gentleman. Now she knew him to be, if not a beast, then at least a dirty tavern scrapper, which was probably worse somehow.

You really know how to impress the ladies, thought George to himself. *First you propositioned her as if she were a woman of the night. Then you went out of your way to look like the lowest kind of ruffian.*

George forced himself to turn his mind to the glass shop and his little sister Grace. He imagined the look on her face when he presented her with his little glass offering. Her face

A Baron's Son is Undone

would be as bright as a daisy. She might even give him a hug.

Four

A Room Made of Sky

George arrived at the coastal village of Porth La around nine in the morning. He had decided to spend the day. He wondered if Miss Lovell would come to meet him or if his antics two days earlier had put her off. He told himself he didn't care either way, but his belly was fizzing in an altogether unwelcome manner, and though he knew he must be hungry (for he hadn't taken breakfast at the inn earlier), just the thought of food made him feel quite ill.

He strolled along the grey stone harbour front. A fishing boat had come in, and a dozen or so locals had gone down to the beach to help pull in the nets. He could see the white-and-silver flash of mackerel writhing and gasping their last as both men and women heaved the twinkling haul up the beach to the measured shouts of one red-faced man in a worn yellow cap. It was an exceptionally large catch, and they were having

A Baron's Son is Undone

an awful time of it. The man in the yellow cap looked up as if to search the harbour front. His eyes landed on George, and he waved. George looked behind himself, but there was no one there, so he decided that the man was likely waving at him. George pressed his hand to his chest in a questioning gesture, and the man in the yellow cap nodded and beckoned him with a wave of his arm.

Down on the beach, George could hear the slap of the fish as they jostled up against each other. The smell of sea and salt was like cold water splashed in his face. The call of the gulls circling overhead was deafening. He approached the throng of people, and the man in the yellow cap yelled across to him: "Do us a favour. Another strong hand's all we need."

When George stepped closer, the man looked him up and down and laughed an apologetic kind of laugh.

"Didn't realise you was so finely dressed!" he said.

"It's not a problem," said George. He slung his jacket over a beached rowboat and took up a place along the net lines.

One more hand did make a difference. It was still hard going, and it took a considerable stretch of time, but they eventually had the nets hauled up the beach. The task accomplished, a chatter broke out among the crowd. People laughed and wiped the sweat from their brows. Several of the women collected a few fish for themselves in baskets they had brought with them for just such a purpose. Flasks of tea were passed around.

The man in the yellow cap came by to thank George.

"Not from these parts, are you?" he said, picking up George's jacket from the rowboat and handing it to him. "I don't suppose you'd like a few mackerel as payment?" He nearly choked himself laughing at this.

A Room Made of Sky

George found himself smiling at the man. He couldn't help it. He was enjoying himself.

"The tea was good," said George. "We'll call it even."

When he turned to go, his heart stopped in his chest as he came face-to-face with a man so silent and rigid that if he weren't familiar with him already, George might have taken him for a statue.

"Hello Mr. Pemberley."

"Duncan."

"You're a fisherman now, are you?" Duncan slid a knife from a sheath on his belt.

"I wear many hats," replied George, trying his best to keep his heart beating at a leisurely pace. *Was Duncan aware of his date with Miss Lovell? If not, why was he here?*

A movement drew George's gaze up to the harbour front. There she was in a dress of pale green, a lavender jacket, no bonnet. Leaning down over the stone wall. She had come to see him after all!

"Duncan! I'll be at the milliner's, then I'll meet you back at The Sloop Inn for lunch. Oh, hello, Mr. Pemberley!"

Dear God, she was making her way down to the beach. George looked to Duncan who had set his face into a grimace. He slid his knife back into its place on his belt.

"Mr. Pemberley, fancy meeting you here," said Miss Lovell.

"Yes, it is quite the fancy," said George eyeing Duncan. "Your man here was just showing me his knife."

"Was he now?" asked Miss Lovell. She gave Duncan a stern look. They seemed to be having an entire conversation with just their eyes. Finally, Miss Lovell tore her gaze back to George. "You must join me for lunch, Mr. Pemberley."

George thought he heard Duncan growl.

53

A Baron's Son is Undone

"That would be quite fine, thank you," said George. "After lunch, I was planning on visiting the glass shop around the corner. Have you been? I'm sure you would find the creations there most enchanting."

"Are you inviting me, Mr. Pemberley?" asked Miss Lovell with a smile.

"Yes, I am," said George taking a side-long glance at Duncan. "I'm to pick out a gift for my little sister, and it would be most helpful to have a feminine opinion to hand."

Miss Lovell clapped her hands together as if it were the most delightful surprise, and George marvelled at how easily she had slipped into this little game with him—a game that he suspected was not fooling Duncan in the slightest.

"Well," said Miss Lovell, her gaze resting on the rather garish split in his lip, "I'm sure you have a schedule to keep. I'll not deter you from your morning." She turned to Duncan. "As I said, I'll be at the milliner's. I'll meet you both at The Sloop Inn for noon."

She turned and gestured with her head to the inn overlooking the harbour.

Duncan gave her a nod, and she strode back up the sloop to the harbour front. They both watched her go. A silence settled between them as she disappeared around a corner.

"You're letting her go off on her own?" asked George. He was surprised.

"It's not downtown London," said Duncan. "Nor is it past nightfall in a crowded tavern. She needs to feel as if she can take a few steps by herself."

"Are these her father's orders?" asked George curiously.

"No," said Duncan quietly. "I decide."

"And you think it's a good idea to take her to taverns after nightfall?" George could not keep the accusatory tone from his voice.

Duncan surprised George with his answer.

"Loneliness is like an illness," he said as he stared off towards the sea. "It would have consumed her spirit, and once that was done, it would have begun to feast on her body. She would have wasted away." He turned his gaze abruptly to look George in the eye. "I don't know of any sewing circles in the area, so the tavern will have to do."

"She isn't the daughter of a pirate, is she?" asked George.

Duncan looked at him then as the gulls continued to circle overhead.

"If you so much as touch her . . ."

George lifted his hands, palms turned out.

"I'm a gentleman," he said.

Duncan made a sound that George belatedly realised must have been a guffaw.

"Gentleman or no, I'll slice you from your balls to your throat," said Duncan, straightening his face.

George made an exaggerated movement to check his pocket watch, an action that declared his lack of interest in the threat just issued. He didn't doubt that Duncan would hurt him if he felt the need. And he very well might feel the need. Despite this fact (or more likely because of it), George found himself warming to this man. Best to set a devil to guard an angel. George couldn't help liking the fact that Miss Lovell was so well cared for.

The Sloop Inn was a lot like The Old Inn, only filled with

A Baron's Son is Undone

more fishermen and consequently the smell of fish. It wasn't to be helped, thought Sophie. This was how people earned a living.

She could not believe that Mr. Pemberley was sitting down for lunch with her. It was just the two of them if you didn't count Duncan who was glaring at them from his stool at the bar. Mr. Pemberley did not seem quite so dangerously appealing with all his clothes on today which was just as Sophie liked it. She had placed all her unwanted thoughts of licking his chest into the naughty corner of her mind—they were to sit there and think about what they had done in an effort to avoid repeating poor behaviour.

Sophie loosed the ribbon of the bonnet she had just purchased at the milliner's. As she removed it and placed it on the chair next to her, she could feel Mr. Pemberley's questioning look.

"Why the bonnet?" he asked. "I haven't seen you bother with one before."

"I'm practising," she said with a smile, "to be a lady."

"Ah," said Mr. Pemberley. "May I make a suggestion?"

"By all means," said Sophie.

"Bonnet or no, if you spend your evenings with women of ill repute and brawlers—"

"—Let me stop you there," said Sophie putting up her hand with a laugh. "I'll not give up my evenings out in order to make myself look respectable. The bonnet will have to suffice."

"I hear you're living with Miss Byrd," said Mr. Pemberley.

Sophie wasn't sure what to say to this. He was clearly prying, and she would have to step lightly.

"Yes, she is hosting me for the summer."

"You know her?"

A Room Made of Sky

"Clearly."

"You like her?"

"No." Sophie wanted to talk about something else.

"Why would your father leave you with someone you don't like?" asked Mr. Pemberley.

"Because, Mr. Pemberley," said Sophie with some indignation at his line of questioning, "my father does not like *me*."

That stopped him short. Also, their food had arrived. Fish pies, browned and crisped to perfection. A tankard of ale for Mr. Pemberley and watered-down wine for herself. Her words hung over them like the lingering sound of a bell as the waitress fussed over their plates and cutlery.

Mr. Pemberley was staring at her now over his pie, and Sophie wondered if she should have come at all. What could possibly be the outcome of all this? She could never reveal herself to him. That whole episode felt so shameful. What man could want someone so far beyond ruined? And did she, in fact, want him? Sure, she liked him. Spending time in his company was like inhaling a drug that left her feeling all tingly and breathless. But if he touched her in that way . . . She knew from experience she wouldn't like it. Then what? How to recover from that?

Mr. Pemberley stabbed into his pie with a fork, and a wisp of steam rose up from his crust.

"If your father didn't like you, he wouldn't have sent Duncan," said Mr. Pemberley before taking a bite.

Sophie watched him chew with some irritation. He had managed to pique her ire with his questions and comments in the same way a small boy might have provoked her by poking her repeatedly and unnecessarily with a finger.

"This is unbelievable pie," said Mr. Pemberley. "You should

A Baron's Son is Undone

try yours."

"Duncan is here," said Sophie, trying to keep her voice steady and her anger contained, "because I am a possession, and I must be kept in tact."

As soon as she said it, she knew she should not have. She had wanted to correct his arrogant assumption. But her words sounded so . . . so . . . self-pitying. She couldn't retract the statement, so instead she gave a short sharp laugh as if it might all be some sort of joke, something to dismiss.

Mr. Pemberley did not join in her laughter. Instead, he put down his fork and leaned back in his chair. His eyes met hers.

"I'm sorry."

He said it with convincing feeling, and Sophie felt herself blushing. She didn't want him to be sorry for her—far from it.

"I don't know your circumstance," he continued, "so I shouldn't argue. But if you don't mind me offering just one more opinion."

She did mind, but he was going to offer it anyway. He leaned forward and dropped his voice to a whisper.

"I would wager one hundred shiny guineas that whatever your father's motives, Duncan himself is here because he truly cares for you."

Mr. Pemberley pinned Sophie back in her chair with his storm cloud eyes, and the truth of his words washed over her like a warm wave leaving her feeling both drenched in this new realisation but also strangely at sea. She looked to the scar-faced man sipping his drink at the bar. She had known him since childhood. He had flitted around the edges of her life like a gruesome yet strangely comforting shadow.

"He's the only one," she said with wonder.

A Room Made of Sky

She hadn't realised she had spoken out loud, and when she turned back to Mr. Pemberley, he was looking at her in a way that made her feel embarrassed.

"Eat." He said it almost angrily.

The rest of the meal was spent in silence. How had the conversation gone so terribly wrong? She supposed she would eat her fish pie and then excuse herself from the outing to the glass shop. Duncan would be only too pleased to head home early. At least someone would be happy.

When they had finished their lunch, Mr. Pemberley settled up their bill at the bar. Sophie could see him speak a few words to Duncan who did not respond. When he returned to their table, she thought to make her excuses.

"I don't think I will accompany you to the glass shop after all," she said. Her heart felt so incredibly heavy in her chest. She wanted to go home and cry.

"What are you talking about?" asked Mr. Pemberley in a clipped tone. He looked furious, and his bruised and damaged face only added to the effect. "You're staying with me this afternoon."

Sophie didn't know what to say to that. Mr. Pemberley reached down, picked up her bonnet, and handed it to her.

He did not speak a word to her for the entire walk over to the glass shop, but he did cast surreptitious glances her way. She noticed Duncan watching Mr. Pemberley with the look of a dog eyeing a stranger who has come much too close to the gate, so she was surprised when Duncan remained outside as she and Mr. Pemberley entered the shop. A bell tinkled as the door swung open, but no one came to greet them.

"Oh!" said Sophie looking around as she pressed one hand to her heart.

The walls of the room were painted a pale eggshell blue which made her feel as if she were standing in a room made of sky. Delicate white shelving lined three walls. Sophie stepped up to a round white table in the centre of the room. It was covered in the tiniest glass flowers of every shape and colour, each one no larger than a lady's fingernail. Some lay with their faces beaming up as if they had blossomed from the table itself, others had transparent green stems and were settled in various miniature vases made, as Mr. Pemberley had said they would be, out of strands of netted glass.

"Mr. Pemberley." Sophie wasn't sure why she said his name.

She turned slowly and stepped towards a shelf by one of the walls. She felt as if her mind were a sparkling and bubbling thing, bouncing and dancing from one tiny magical creation to the next. Birds and frogs and butterflies and tiny translucent pink pigs.

"Horses!"

She smiled. They were such fragile things made of un-coloured clear glass. She could easily fit a herd in the palm of her hand. Manes flowing out behind them. All of them were created mid-stride, running wild as if no one had ever put a saddle to their backs. Sophie reached into the midst of the crowd of horses racing across the shelf and gingerly plucked one up. She turned to Mr. Pemberley.

"It's a unicorn," she said. "I think there's only the one. Hidden among all those horses. How very clever!"

"And you were going to go home," said Mr. Pemberley in a scolding tone. "You must have more trust in me next time."

A Room Made of Sky

The man did like to berate, thought Sophie. But somehow she didn't mind just now.

Next time. She couldn't believe he wanted to see her again after her self-pitying display at the tavern.

"Show me," said Mr. Pemberley stepping forward and reaching out his hand.

She placed the unicorn in the centre of his palm, and doing so, her fingers brushed his skin. Sophie quickly glanced up to his eyes which were already gazing at her face.

"Don't worry," he said. "It was *my* promise. Not yours."

Was he referring to his pledge not to touch her? Was he inviting her to touch him? Sophie gave him a nervous smile as he lifted the unicorn up to his eyes.

"Perfect," he said. "What else do you think would suit?"

"What does your sister Grace like?"

"She likes fairytales of all sorts and dogs, but most of all she likes being right," said Mr. Pemberley.

Sophie laughed. "Well, then, the unicorn is the perfect gift." She paused and looked around. "There are also several fairytales that involve swans," she said crouching down to a low shelf and plucking one out of the midst of a flock of colourful waterfowl.

She handed the elegant bird to Mr. Pemberley, and her fingers skimmed his palm once more. This time on purpose.

"An excellent choice," said Mr. Pemberley, locking eyes with her. "I knew it would be a good idea to have you with me."

Sophie tore her gaze from his before he could see her blush.

"I wonder where the owner of the shop could be," she said looking around. "We should ask him if he has any dogs."

Mr. Pemberley chuckled.

"He's right over there," he said tilting his head towards a

A Baron's Son is Undone

large window and some shelving on one side of the room.

"Where?" asked Sophie furrowing her brow.

She stepped towards the window. Finally, she noticed the man. He was sat at a little white table right beside the window and behind the white shelving. He was quite small himself, his white-haired head bowed low over his work. He had a rod of glass that he was melting over the flame of an oil lamp. As it melted, he turned the rod to create shapes in the glass while pinching and twisting it in places with a long pair of tweezers. To Sophie's amazement, a small songbird appeared at the end of his rod of glass. The old man put down his tweezers and picking up a pair of dainty pliers, he used them to clip the songbird from the rod and set it free.

"Hello," said Sophie.

The man looked up. Eyes as pale as the blue walls of his shop.

"What you've created here is quite marvellous," said Sophie. "I've never seen anything like it."

When the man didn't respond but instead bent to work over his flame once more, Sophie added, "We were wondering if you have any dogs."

At this, the man pointed across the room to a little table in the far corner.

"Much obliged," said Sophie with a smile.

She lifted a quizzical look to Mr. Pemberley's face and found him grinning at her. He gave her a wink which, *oh no*, sent her legs aquiver as she crossed the room to the little table of dogs.

"What kind of dog does your sister have?" she asked.

"The ill-trained sort," said Mr. Pemberley. "The kind that begs for scraps from the table and eats your very best shoes."

A Room Made of Sky

Sophie didn't look back at the man, but she smiled to herself. He could be quite funny sometimes. She stepped up to the little table and took her time surveying the various dogs. Eventually, she felt the heat of Mr. Pemberley's presence close behind her. He reached around her body and picked up a tiny beige dog that looked very much like a pug. He wasn't touching her at all, but he was so very near, and she felt enveloped in his warmth. She could sense him leaning his face in close beside her head as he presented the dog to her. His warm breath tickled the sensitive skin behind her ear which sent a shiver rippling through her entire body. Sophie tried not to breathe, fighting with all the sanity she could muster against the wild thumping of her heart as she attempted to bring the stupid organ back into a sensible rhythm. She reached for the little dog he offered up in his open palm. Mr. Pemberley leaned in even closer now. When he spoke, his voice was a rumbling purr against her ear.

"Her name," said Mr. Pemberley in a low and thrillingly seductive tone, "is Potato."

It took a moment for his words to register.

"Hah!" Sophie's laugh bubbled up to the surface and burst forth into the little shop. It ricocheted off the pale blue walls causing the shop-keeper to look up from his work. "Oh now, what are you saying, Mr. Pemberley?!"

She found herself laughing again as she turned to face him. He was standing so very close, and she had to tilt her face up to look into his.

"Her name is Potato," he said holding back a smile and attempting a look of innocence.

This time he spoke the words in a regular tone of voice. *He had known full well what he was doing previously, and he'd known*

A Baron's Son is Undone

it would be funny!

"Are you christening the glass dog?" asked Sophie with some amusement.

"No," said Mr. Pemberley seriously. "Do you think I would name a dog Potato? I'm a grown man for Heaven's sake." He made a show of looking offended. "Potato is the name of Grace's pug."

"Because she looks like a potato," said Sophie grinning. "It makes sense."

"Of course it makes sense. She's a sensible girl—"

"—who will love you forever when you bring her such magical gifts from the glass-maker in Porth La," added Sophie.

Mr. Pemberley didn't respond, and Sophie wondered if she had spoken with too much familiarity. She couldn't help it. He felt familiar. Like she had met him once long ago and they were just now making a reacquaintance. The way he checked his pocket watch and kept to a schedule, the way he complained about his ruined shoes, the way he went out of his way to find a gift for his little sister—it all made Sophie feel very comfortable. Which was good because there was a side to Mr. Pemberley that left her feeling considerably less at ease—the side that picked fights in taverns and tackled her on the beach, the side that took charge of the moment in altogether unexpected ways. Sophie dropped her gaze from his eyes to his split lip and up to his bruised cheekbone.

"You don't think my face looks as pretty today," said Mr. Pemberley.

"That's not . . . I wasn't thinking . . ." spluttered Sophie, caught off her guard. She took a breath. "You think a lot of yourself, don't you?"

"*You're* the one who said I had a pretty face," said Mr.

A Room Made of Sky

Pemberley. He was still so close, and Sophie hoped he would not step back.

"Facts are facts," said Sophie without breaking eye contact. Her confounded heart was starting up again.

"I didn't think you would come today," said Mr. Pemberley. "After seeing me the other night. Not exactly the behaviour of a gentleman."

"But you forget, Mr. Pemberley. As you pointed out earlier, I enjoy the company of interesting women and brawlers. So it should have come as no surprise that I would meet you here as planned."

At that, Mr. Pemberley smiled his ridiculous, mind-melting smile.

The door bell tinkled, and Duncan poked his shiny head into the room made of sky.

"Are we done in here?" he asked. "It's starting to rain."

"Look, Duncan!" Sophie flew to his side and pulled him into the shop by his arm. She lifted a small glass dove from a shelf. "Have you ever seen anything so enchanting?"

Duncan glanced at the dove before shifting his gaze to Mr. Pemberley who shrugged his shoulders boyishly.

"It's all to the scale of a flower fairy," said Mr. Pemberley.

"A flower fairy?" repeated Duncan looking around him as if searching her out.

Sophie laughed and tugged Duncan on a tour of the room as Mr. Pemberley wandered over to the glass-maker to pay for his items. When Sophie finally turned towards Mr. Pemberley once more, she caught him watching her with Duncan. He had a disconcerted look on his face, and he was pulling a hand through his thick blonde hair.

"Are you all right, Mr. Pemberley?" she asked.

A Baron's Son is Undone

"Me? Yes," he said distractedly as he swivelled his gaze to the shelf beside him. He reached out a hand and rearranged a group of glass elephants so that they were all lined up trunk to tail.

Five

Costumes

Several days later, George sat at breakfast in The Old Inn gazing down at his sausages and muffin. He picked up his fork and moved the sausages around the plate as his mind churned over the time he had spent thus far with Miss Lovell. There was something about her that he recognised, that touched him in a familiar way. Reviewing all of their encounters in his mind, he noticed that it had been there from the very beginning in their unfortunate first encounter at the tavern.

He had been tense and frustrated that night, and his behaviour towards her had been incredibly rude. *Propositioning her!* She had not responded as expected, by taking offence or having her man Duncan see him off. No. She had held Duncan back with a hand, and there was also a look in her eyes before she spoke to him—as she spoke to him. *What was that look?* She had picked up his assumption and taken

A Baron's Son is Undone

it one step further, telling him that her services were much too dear for the likes of him. *The likes of him! Hah!* It came to him then in a flash. What he recognised in Miss Lovell was a willingness to play! Could that be it? He thought about how she had held him up at gun point to answer a personal question. Who else would do something like that? The way she stepped in time with his innocent act in an attempt to fool Duncan about their date in Porth La. And simply the pure delight with which she engaged with him in the glass shop. The way she was with him, the way she *played* with him made him feel so wonderfully . . . light.

But there was something else about her that pricked at him. Her willingness to play was startling for the simple reason that he could also see a halo of sadness resting above her head. It tinged all her words and actions with a kind of poignancy that made him ache. He knew she was hiding here in the same way that he was hiding here. To escape some unpleasant truth.

"Penny for your thoughts," said Maddy as she filled up his coffee cup.

"Do you have any terrible truths that you've hidden away?" asked George as he looked up into Maddy's wrinkled face.

"Aye," said Maddy, "We've all got at least one." She leaned in close. "Best not to pay it too much attention, or you'll squander all your life's minutes feeling all shameful and wondering what if."

George nodded ruefully.

"You should put some sugar in your coffee this morning, Mr. Pemberley. Start the day with something sweet."

She wandered off to the kitchen and returned with a bowl of sugar and a pot of jam.

"There," she said placing the items down in front of his

plate. "Don't be worrying yourself when you're on holiday, Mr. Pemberley. It's a second Wednesday, so you'll be wanting to attend Almack's tonight." She gave him a grin. "You can gamble all your cares away."

"Not sure if that's the healthy thing to do," said George.

"Oh aye, but it's perfectly healthy to let Tom pound the cares out of your face with his fist."

She was smiling sweetly at him, so it took George a moment to recognise her response for the clever rebuke that it was.

"We all have our vices," said George. "At least mine is entertaining."

"It is that," said Maddy with a laugh.

George ate his breakfast and contemplated the evening at Almack's. Mr. Harris had said Miss Lovell would be there. George hadn't seen her in days, and they had made no plans to meet up when last they parted. At the same time, he wondered if it was a good idea to keep teasing himself with Miss Lovell. For one thing, he didn't really know who she was. For another, she didn't know who he was (and still wouldn't even if he told her his real name). As much as thoughts of this woman plagued his every waking minute, George knew that there were some things he could never have. A genuine human connection based on honesty and trust was one of those things. Some truths could not see the light of day. Too much rested on them remaining hidden. Each time George considered the idea that his father or sisters might one day know he was no son at all and only half a brother, it was as if his soul took a blow that knocked it completely off balance. He had tortured himself in this way so often over the years that by now his spirit was quite bruised and devastated. He thought it possible that just one more solid punch would destroy it.

A Baron's Son is Undone

George drank his coffee and ate his breakfast as a vice tightened around his temples. He was feeling so completely lost to himself this morning that he had not even written up a schedule. The tension that normally twisted about him like an insistent python had returned. And since there was no one to goad into a fight after breakfast, he resolved to walking along the cliffs for as long as it took to feel somewhat restored. He ended up doing so for several hours at a brisk pace—into the wind one way and rain slamming down on his head the entire way back.

"Mr. Pemberley!" said Maddy as he burst through the door of the inn late that afternoon. "You'll catch your death."

George hadn't the energy to respond, so he simply headed for the stairs as Maddy clucked along behind him.

"I'll have a hot bath sent up," she said.

George gave her a nod before retreating to his room.

After a bath and a steaming spiced concoction that tasted like it was mostly whisky (Maddy's special brew), George threw himself onto his bed and fell into a restless sleep.

Waking up was a disorienting experience. His room was dim, lit by a pale grey light shining thinly through the curtains. He reached across the bed and fumbled in his wet jacket for his pocket watch. It took him a moment to comprehend that the eight o'clock declared on its face was not in fact the next morning. It was still the same day. Wednesday evening.

Almack's.

The strained sounds of a fiddle twined about his room, and the murmur of what could only be a significant crowd in the tavern below had the effect of drowning out his own unpleasant thoughts. Should he go downstairs? What else was he doing? He certainly needed something to eat. George

Costumes

took the time to comb his hair, and after deciding there was no reason for him to shave, he shaved his jaw carefully anyway. He took his time dressing, choosing one jacket and then dispensing it for another less formal affair. Examining himself in the mirror, he wondered what Miss Lovell might see when she looked at him. He knew she did not see a baron's son which gave him some semblance of relief. She had seen him after the fight with Tom. Blood and dirt and bruises with no apparent purpose. A common ruffian.

What does she really think of me? he wondered.

As George descended gingerly down the steps to the tavern, the laughter and conversation grew to a roar. The fiddle rose above it all, its tune bobbing and dancing like a fishing boat on a rather lively sea. George stopped on the second-last step and scanned the room. Whatever Mr. Harris had said about baccarat and hazard, this wasn't it. All the tables and chairs had been shifted up against the walls, and the usual demographic of working men was now liberally sprinkled with women of all ages. Several revellers were actually dancing a country dance in the middle of the room! George's gaze found Miss Lovell in the same way a compass finds true north. His eyes rested upon her form with an odd sense of relief. She was wearing a red dress. Just like her others, this one had long sleeves and a high collar, but it fit her to perfection, hugging every curve. The colour set off her ebony hair and determined features in a way that had George thinking of his sister Patience. She was an incredibly talented artist, and he knew that if she were here, she would be begging to paint a portrait of Miss Lovell in that dress. George smiled to himself sadly. He truly missed his sister.

George watched as Miss Lovell lifted the bonnet she had

A Baron's Son is Undone

purchased in Porth La and placed it on Winnie's head. Winnie was laughing. Someone handed her a knife, and she tried to use it as a mirror. Miss Lovell stepped back and turned. When she saw him across the crowded room, she became still. George lifted a hand, and she hesitantly mirrored him. He came down the last two stairs as she approached him through the crowd.

"Mr. Pemberley," she said.

"Miss Lovell." He gave her a little bow.

"Almack's," she said, half turning to the room.

"Indeed. Yet Mr. Harris led me to believe it would be an evening of games rather than dancing and socialising."

"The games are later," said Miss Lovell. "Most of the women leave after the dancing."

"But not you," said George.

"Not me."

"You like a game," he said.

She simply stared at him.

"And where is your man Duncan?" George lifted his gaze out over the room once more.

Miss Lovell stepped up beside him and turned so that they were both facing the room.

"There he is," she said pointing with one hand as she grasped George's arm with the other. "He likes to find a strategic position. No one at his back. A line of sight to the door." She laughed.

George could barely focus on her words as his stomach involuntarily tensed. He looked to her hand which was holding him, then across the room to Duncan who was (as he suspected) watching him with his usual murderous expression. The country dance had come to an end, and the dancers had

Costumes

dispersed in search of drinks, all ruddy-faced with their efforts and the heat of the room.

"Miss Lovell," said George carefully. He looked again to her hand which was still on his arm. She immediately removed it. "Normally, I would request that you save the next waltz for me, but there is the pesky matter of that promise."

"Oh." Miss Lovell dropped her gaze to the floorboards. After a second, she looked up again. "Normally?" she asked. "You do this often then?"

What was she asking?

"Dance, you mean?" asked George.

"Yes."

"It was a poor choice of words," he said. "I rarely dance."

"We will make a poor coupling then," said Miss Lovell. "I've not had much experience dancing."

"I will guide you," he said. "You won't even have to think."

"Not thinking sounds nice."

"Mmm," said George.

Sophie didn't know what was happening to her as Mr. Pemberley's low murmured vibration rippled down through her entire body to her toes. The simple fact was that she would very much like him to touch her. A dance would be nice and contained. There would be no further expectations, touching-wise. It was as safe as any form of touching was likely to be. Even Duncan could not seriously make too much of a fuss.

"I will release you from your promise for the next waltz," she said.

His eyes flared from grey to black as he registered her words.

A Baron's Son is Undone

Then he looked across the room to Duncan.

Leaning in close, he said, "I'd better make sure I won't be sliced open for the pleasure."

And with that, he set off through the crowd. Sophie watched as Mr. Pemberley approached Duncan who gave him his most surly glare. They exchanged a few words, and Mr. Pemberley returned momentarily.

"Duncan sends his regards," he said with a boyish grin. "He says he would be thrilled to see us dance."

Sophie laughed as she smacked Mr. Pemberley playfully on the shoulder. As soon as she touched him, his amused expression turned serious. He was looking at her with so much undisguised affection, she felt compelled to look away.

He certainly would not look at me like that if he knew, she thought. *But he need not know. It's only a dance.*

Sophie found she could not leave Mr. Pemberly's side. She didn't want to be anywhere else. He hadn't eaten all day, and Maddy was kind enough to bring him a platter of meat and fruit and bread and a tankard of ale. They sat at one of the tables by the wall, and Sophie found herself conversing animatedly as Mr. Pemberley ate.

"Are you sure you wouldn't like a bite?" he asked partway through his meal. "The sliced apples are especially crisp."

She looked at his plate, then up to his eyes which were twinkling merrily with the mischief of the question. To eat off his plate—it was quite unthinkable!

"Are you always so misbehaved?" she asked.

"No," he said. "Only with you."

They looked at each other for several long moments, and then Sophie reached across the table and plucked a slice of apple from his plate. She kept her eyes on his as she took a bite and chewed.

"They are quite nice," she said.

"Mmm." That resonant sound again. It sent a wave of pleasure coursing through her.

Sophie reached for another slice of apple as if she had eaten from his plate a thousand times before. Mr. Pemberley leaned back in his chair and watched her, a thoughtful look upon his face.

"You gave Winnie your bonnet," he said.

Sophie swallowed. "I bought it for her."

"Why?"

"Because she needed a lift," said Sophie. "She needs to feel like a person."

"Most people would say she's just a woman of ill repute," said Mr. Pemberley.

"Most people would be wrong," said Sophie. "Nobody is just anything. Duke, inn-keeper, waitress—these are simply roles that we play. The real person has nothing to do with the costumes she wears. If you shed all those layers of presentation, what you are left with is a naked human soul, something quite brilliant and unique if I'm not mistaken."

Mr. Pemberley swore softly under his breath, and Sophie wondered if she had said the wrong thing. He shoved his plate aside and leaned forward over the table.

"Do you speak like this to everyone?" he asked.

"No," she said.

Just to you, she thought.

"Who are you?" he asked in a low voice.

His eyes bore into hers, and although she knew what he was asking, she could not give him the answer he wanted.

"If you had been listening, you would know," she said. "I am

A Baron's Son is Undone

a naked human soul—brilliant and unique. I suspect the same is true of you."

She held his gaze defiantly.

"Naked," he said, and Sophie felt heat rise up from her neck to her face.

Mr. Pembeley gave her a lazy smile.

"I do believe it's time for that waltz." He held out his hand.

Slipping her bare hand in his, they both paused there at the table once they were joined together. Seconds passed.

"I think," said Mr. Pemberley finally, "the dancing will require that we rise from our seats."

"Oh. Yes."

He led her out onto the dance floor where several other couples were arranging themselves. Mr. Pemberley kept her one hand in his as he reached down to place his right hand firmly on her waist. Sophie stretched her free arm up to grasp his shoulder.

"You should know that you look a vision in that dress," he said. The compliment startled her. "In any dress," he added. "But beauty doesn't last, so it is a fine thing to know that it is only a costume. I think I see you more clearly today."

"I . . . well . . . Mr. Pemberley," she stammered.

Sophie realised the strains of the fiddle had been silenced. She looked around. Everyone was still. They were all looking at Duncan, and he was watching them. She looked up to Mr. Pemberley who, realising what was happening, released her hand to face Duncan and give him a small bow. The room held its breath. Duncan made them all wait as he stared Mr. Pemberley down with an expression that suggested he had eaten something that had disagreed violently with his stomach. Eventually, he gave Mr. Pemberley a nod. It was the

Costumes

barest of gestures, almost imperceptible, but a murmur arose slowly about the room, the violin picked up its tune, and Mr. Pemberley turned back to grasp Sophie's hand.

"I daresay Mr. Harris probably thought a murder was about to be committed. And Maddy had only just washed the floors."

Sophie found herself laughing.

"Duncan would never murder you in front of me," she said. "He would find you later . . . in a dark alley. He's thoughtful like that."

"Indeed," said Mr. Pemberley. "I'll keep that in mind."

As the dance started up, she noticed that he was careful not to pull her in too close. Their bodies remained at a respectful distance, and while Sophie was grateful for Mr. Pemberley's gentlemanly behaviour, several unwelcome and altogether wicked thoughts arose in her head, each one of which had to be immediately banished to the naughty corner of her mind. *Why was she even thinking these things?* They truly did frighten her.

"Are you all right," asked Mr. Pemberley as he spun her methodically through the steps.

"Yes," she lied.

"Is it too much?" he asked.

She looked at him questioningly.

"Being touched."

Sophie was momentarily stunned by his perceptiveness. She didn't know how to respond.

"We can stop dancing if you like," he added. "And I could order another plate of food for you to eat from."

Sophie gave him a soft smile. He really did know how to ease her tension.

"I should like to finish the waltz," she said.

A Baron's Son is Undone

"As long as it's something you would like," said Mr. Pemberley as he gently spun her across the floor.

"It is," she said.

They continued dancing for a few bars of music before Mr. Pemberley spoke once more. It took him some time to form the words, as if he were struggling with them.

"In the interests of shedding costumes, I should probably tell you that my name isn't Pemberley. It's Pemberton. George Pemberton. Although I suppose that is just one more costume." One side of his mouth quirked up ruefully.

Sophie faltered a step as she took in this information.

"You have been lying."

Her eyes met his, and Mr. Pemberley—Mr. Pemberton now—bowed his head down towards hers, an intimate gesture.

"I didn't think it would matter. You see, I simply did not want to be recognised. I have an aunt and uncle living nearby. If they knew I was in Cornwall, they would not have left me in peace, and peace was what I was seeking."

"And now?"

"And now I seek your good opinion."

"Why?" asked Sophie.

"Because," said Mr. Pemberton, "you are the most brilliant and unique soul I have ever met."

Sophie had to look away from the intense gaze of his eyes. She was not used to this sort of positive attention. She felt much more comfortable being harangued and condescended to by her Aunt Margaret.

Costumes

George held his breath as the dance came to an end. Miss Lovell's talk of naked human souls had skewered all his reasonable inclinations to the wall. *Who says things like that? Who the hell was she?* He honestly didn't care. A pirate's daughter. A Caribbean heiress. An apple-seller wrapped in rags. Her spirit outshone any disguise.

What he wanted . . . God, it sounded so . . . If someone else were to say this to him, he would want to vomit into a bag . . . but the truth of the matter was that he wanted Miss Lovell's brilliant light shining on him and him alone.

He had the impulse to press his hand back nervously through his hair, but both hands were currently occupied with Miss Lovell. The last strains of the violin faded, and while George released Miss Lovell's waist, she kept one hand to his shoulder and the other hand clasped in his. He watched her amber brown eyes glinting in the lamplight.

"Miss Lovell," he said.

She lifted her hands from him and darted a glance towards Duncan.

"I don't think . . ." she said. "I mean to say . . . you wouldn't like . . . that is . . . I think you're mistaken, Sir."

She looked agitated.

"Mistaken about what?" he asked.

"About me," she said stepping briskly back to their table by the wall, her red skirt rustling. He followed close behind, and when she turned around to speak again, she nearly bumped into his chest.

"Sorry," he said stepping back.

"Why are you saying these things?" she asked him. "Why couldn't we just dance?"

"I've upset you," said George. The muscles of his chest and

A Baron's Son is Undone

belly constricted making it difficult for him to breathe. He felt ill. What a complete fool he was! He had seen that she was skittish, and even so, he'd gone and all but declared himself to her like a besotted fool.

"Mr. Pemberley . . . Mr. Pemberton . . ." Her words trailed off as a sudden realisation lit her face and caused her mouth to form a perfect O. "Are you the baron's son?"

George closed his eyes and pressed a hand up over his forehead and then through his hair. His father had his fingers in so many pies, his name attached to so many social causes, that it was impossible to go anywhere without the name Pemberton being recognised. He took a deep breath.

"Yes," he said. "Does it matter?" he added.

Her answer buoyed him: "I suppose not," she conceded. "But what are you doing . . ." she looked around her, ". . . here . . . with me?"

George shrugged. "It's like when I find myself picking a fight in a tavern. I don't know why, but I do know it's necessary. At least when I'm fighting . . . when I'm here with you, I'm not pretending."

It was Miss Lovell's turn to swear quietly under her breath. Despite the desperate nature of the conversation, George had to smile at this.

"You can swear out loud with me," he said. "No pretending."

She looked a smidge embarrassed, and George had to fight to keep his hands at his sides. His mind flapped about, looking for a way out of the awkward situation he had created with Miss Lovell.

"How about we start over?" he asked.

"Pardon?"

"Start over," repeated George. "Let me introduce myself. My

Costumes

name is George Pemberton, son of Lord Pemberton, visiting from London."

He held out his hand. She looked at it suspiciously, then up at him. Gradually, her wariness dissolved before his eyes. He could actually see the muscles in her face relax and her shoulders fall ever so slightly. She took his hand, and he gave a small bow.

"Never mind about the waltz," said George lifting himself back up to his full height.

He pulled out his pocket watch and checked the time. It was a movement that was as much about calming himself as it was about calming Miss Lovell. The weight of the silver fob in his hand made him feel anchored in both place and time, a solid presence. He was real. Miss Lovell was real. The fiddler was fiddling. And he could most definitely salvage the evening.

"When do the games begin?" he asked, and he was gratified to see her eyes light up at the question.

Six

A Game that Matters

At eleven o'clock that evening, George watched as the tavern was transformed in short order from a ballroom into a festive gaming hell. The tables and chairs were pulled back out into the centre of the room. Hazard, baccarat, whist—Mr. Harris had been telling the truth. Ale flowed freely, and there was an elevated buzz of excitement about the place. Most of the women did leave, but a few remained, Winnie and Miss Lovell among them.

"Pints are half-price on second Wednesdays!" boomed Mr. Harris as George approached the bar. "Not that you would care!" he laughed. Mr. Harris leaned towards George across the counter, his face blooming red. "So you're the chosen one, are you?" he asked.

"Excuse me?"

"You get a pass from Duncan," said Mr. Harris.

"It was only a dance," said George.

A Game that Matters

"Only a dance, my foot!" said Mr. Harris sliding a whisky across the bar to George.

George gave Mr. Harris a grimace and lifted the glass of whisky from the counter. He turned and scanned the room. Miss Lovell was already playing hazard at a table with one other lady and two men. She was clearly doing well and trying not to look too pleased about it. Duncan watched from his post by the wall across from her.

George strode over to Duncan and offered him the whisky, but the man put up a palm and shook his head.

"I'll not be drinking while I'm working," said Duncan.

"Fair enough," said George taking a sip from the glass.

He turned to stand with Duncan, and they both watched Miss Lovell cheer as the two dice she had thrown wobbled to stillness on the table.

"Are you a gambling man?" asked Duncan.

"Never," said George. "It leaves too much to chance. I much prefer to strategise a win."

Duncan grunted.

"But Miss Lovell obviously likes a bit of chance," said George.

"That's not it," said Duncan gruffly.

"What's not it?" asked George.

"It's not really the gambling, the chance. It's the game she likes," said Duncan. "She's always been lacking a bit of fun. Growing up, she had no one to play with. No siblings, very few visitors. It never stopped her though. She would play on her own. Cards, spillikins, chess, some other games she invented herself."

"You were there when she was a child?" asked George.

"Not like this," said Duncan. "Not responsible for her every

A Baron's Son is Undone

day, but I was around."

George and Duncan watched Miss Lovell for some time as a silence settled between them.

"There was a party once," said Duncan not taking his eyes from Miss Lovell.

Heaven's alive! thought George. *He had not heard this man speak so many non-threatening words in a row!*

"At the country house," continued Duncan. "Her mother had insisted children were invited as well. Sophie—Miss Lovell—managed to corral all the children into a back room where she taught them a game of dice. Her own rules, mind you. They ended up wagering what they had—hairpins, ribbons, the silver buttons pulled clean off some little boy's new coat."

At this, Duncan actually chuckled.

"By the end of the afternoon, every little girl had her hair in disarray on account of missing pins and ribbons, and that little boy's mother was in hysterics over his coat. When Miss Lovell's father found out what had happened, he was none too pleased."

"Her father is not a tolerant man," said George.

"Her father takes himself very seriously," said Duncan.

"I've heard that said about pirates in general," replied George.

Duncan fixed him with a glare.

"Why did you give me leave to dance with her?" asked George as he leaned back against the wall.

Duncan paused a few beats before speaking.

"The stupid glass shop," he said finally. "It made her happy."

George grinned. "It did, didn't it?"

"Flower fairies," said Duncan shaking his head. "Where did you get that from?"

A Game that Matters

"I have sisters," said George. "I know all about flower fairies and daisy chains and the latest fashion in ballgowns. To be honest, it's never come in useful before."

Duncan gave another grunt. Just then, the door swung open to reveal a tall man finely dressed in a wine-coloured waistcoat and dark brown jacket. His auburn hair lifted up on a breeze which had blown in through the open door. Behind him was another man, less finely dressed, who followed him into the tavern.

"For fuck's sake," said Duncan standing up a little straighter.

"Not a friend of yours, I trust," said George.

"Nicholas Hatcher," said Duncan. "I thought he'd left town. And he's brought another man with him. If something happens, I'll thank you to take Miss Lovell safely home." He pinned George with a look. "And that's *all* you will take."

George downed his whisky. The night had just become unexpectedly interesting.

"If it comes to it, Duncan. *I'll* deal with Hatcher and *you* can take Miss Lovell home. How does that sound?"

Duncan made a sound that might have been in the affirmative.

"What's he done?" asked George.

Duncan did not respond. The two of them watched as Hatcher cut a line through the room straight for the hazard table. Miss Lovell looked to him as he stepped up beside her. She smiled.

"Mr. Hatcher, how nice to see you. I won again," she said looking down at the dice on the table. "Sixes and sevens—just like last time."

"You look lovely tonight," said Hatcher placing his hand on the back of her chair. "Red suits you."

A Baron's Son is Undone

George immediately felt his hackles rising. He took a step forward, but Duncan halted him with a hand to his shoulder.

"Double or nothing," said Hatcher to Miss Lovell. "On a game of whist."

She laughed as if to dismiss him. But then George saw her take a surreptitious glance across the room towards Winnie who was showing off her bonnet to another lady in the corner. Sophie looked back up at Hatcher.

"All right," she said. "How much did I take from you last time?"

Hatcher's face pulled itself into a grim smile.

"A lot."

"Forgive me," said Miss Lovell, "I'm not terribly good with my times tables. What is double 'a lot'?"

"She's humorous for a woman, isn't she?" said Hatcher to his man. "That's one of the reasons I like her."

Hatcher took the time then to swivel his head towards Duncan. He raised a hand, but Duncan remained stony-faced and unresponsive.

"I'll need a partner," said Miss Lovell looking around the room. "It seems you already have one."

"This is my associate Barnaby," said Hatcher introducing his friend.

"Mr. Barnaby, glad to make your acquaintance," said Miss Lovell. "I hope you like losing."

For all that he had a bad feeling regarding what was about to happen, George was enjoying watching Miss Lovell in her element. She was goading them, and he did so appreciate the art of provocation.

She is like me, he thought. *A lady can't pick a fight in a tavern. This is the next best thing.*

A Game that Matters

George's realisation was a momentary thing, like a flash of sheet lightening illuminating the room with Miss Lovell in the centre, her dress a blaze of red fire.

Nicholas Hatcher was the lowest form of human scum. Unfortunately, he was also a naked human soul, brilliant and unique. *Hah!* Sophie's own words came back to admonish her for being so dismissive of his person. She attempted to cultivate some empathy for the man in front of her. Perhaps he had a troubled childhood, or maybe he had loved and lost someone so dear that his heart had shattered into a million sharp-edged pieces which were gouging his insides into a bloody mess.

She looked up at the handsome man as he grinned down at her, his arm possessively placed on the back of her chair.

A sad past wouldn't excuse his actions, but it might explain them. To the locals, he was an unavoidable evil—a conduit through which the smugglers must by necessity pass. And almost everyone in Cornwall was a smuggler or benefitted from the money a smuggler brought in. It was that or spend your days in darkness, coughing up dirt down the bottom of a mine. Nicholas Hatcher knew this, and he squeezed the locals for as much of their profits as he could. He had ships and men and not a great many scruples. If anyone could be called a pirate, it was him.

"Excuse me, gentlemen, I must rustle up a partner," said Sophie.

She glanced over at Duncan and found Mr. Pemberton standing with him by the wall and looking positively feral

A Baron's Son is Undone

for some reason. She watched as he pulled a hand through his lovely hair so that it stood all askew. He then took a step towards her, but she gave a small shake of her head, and he did not approach further.

Where had Tom got to? Sweeping the room with her eyes, she eventually found him at the bar taking a sip from a tankard of ale.

"Tom!" She paced towards him. "Will you be my partner for whist?"

She knew what his answer would be.

"I'll not be partnered with a woman," he said loudly, taking another sip of his ale. The foam had collected on his upper lip, and he wiped it away with the back of his hand.

"It's a big pot," said Sophie gesturing to Mr. Hatcher.

"Oh?" Tom looked over to Mr. Hatcher and lifted his eyebrows. "What would be my cut?" he asked.

"Ten percent," said Sophie with the straightest face she could muster. Inside, her stomach was doing a flip. "I'm the one putting up the money," she reminded him. "You have nothing to lose."

"Twenty," said Tom.

Sophie placed her hands on her hips and gave him a scolding look.

"You think a lot of your card skills," said Sophie.

"That's why you've asked me, isn't it?"

Sophie counted out three long breaths. She needed to look like she was considering things.

"Fine," she said. "Twenty."

She and Tom joined Mr. Hatcher and Mr. Barnaby at one of the card tables. Sophie noticed with some alarm that Barnaby was already shuffling a deck. It wouldn't do to have him

A Game that Matters

dealing.

"Money up front," said Hatcher, placing a heavy purse on the table.

Sophie smiled sweetly at him.

"I have my winnings from tonight, but you will have to excuse me while I borrow the difference."

"Is your guard also a bank?" asked Hatcher with some amusement. He spun around in his chair to look at Duncan.

"Let's hope so," said Sophie.

She wasn't entirely sure how much money Duncan carried on his person, but he was never short to pay for anything she might need. Up until now, that had only consisted of meals out and the occasional glass of sherry.

"Duncan," she said, "how many guineas do you have with you?"

"You jest," said Duncan. "Who in their right mind carries around guineas?"

"How many do you need?" asked Mr. Pemberton reaching inside his jacket and pulling out a leather wallet.

Sophie was struck momentarily speechless as she stared at Mr. Pemberton.

"What is it?" he asked.

"You would lend me several guineas?"

"To see you take that man Hatcher at cards? It doesn't bear questioning." He smiled, but his face had a concerned look about it. "You know him?" he asked more quietly, leaning in towards her.

"We've played before," she said. "He pays me a lot of attention when he's here."

"I don't doubt it," said Mr. Pemberton looking past her to the card table. "How is he with losing?"

A Baron's Son is Undone

"He doesn't like it, but he paid up last time. To be seen defaulting on a wager would cause the worst kind of gossip. He has a reputation to uphold among the locals. He wants to be respected."

As Sophie took her seat at the card table across from Tom, she met his eyes. She had never before played a game that actually mattered. In fact, she had never before done anything that actually mattered. Closeted at home for much of her life, she had spent her days simply passing the time. Not that it was her fault—it's not as if she had any say in the situation. But women like Winnie had been out here all along. Strong women confronted with hard choices. Winnie did something that mattered every day, and Sophie's heart had been breaking for her since that first conversation six weeks back.

"You're buying me a drink?!" asked Winnie incredulously. Then, "You want me to sit at your table? Do you know . . . ? To be seen with . . ." She looked around the tavern. "Your reputation would take a blow, Miss," she said quietly.

"We're the only two women in the tavern," said Sophie. "I'm starved for conversation, and my reputation has already taken a blow from which it is unlikely to recover." She gestured to the chair opposite her.

Winnie shook her head in disbelief as she took the seat offered.

"Sherry's not really my cup of tea. Maddy knows I'll have a gin," said Winnie as the old woman stepped up to take the order.

"Gin? Yes, I'll have a gin as well, Maddy," said Sophie, thinking she might enjoy being unconventional. A man's drink sounded so daring.

They had fallen easily into conversation and laughter. When

A Game that Matters

Sophie's gin arrived, she took a large sip of the fiery liquid and nearly died coughing and spluttering as Winnie rubbed her on the back and chuckled.

"If that doesn't put hairs on your chest by morning, I don't know what will."

"But I don't want hairs on my chest!" declared Sophie laughing. "How will I ever find a husband?"

Winnie swept her gaze across the men in the tavern and leaned in.

"You'd be surprised at some of the peculiar predilections of even the most upright gentlemen."

Sophie put a hand to her mouth to hide her smile. This was turning into a very indecorous conversation indeed. It didn't take long, however, for Sophie's smile to fall.

"How do you do it?" she asked. "I don't mean to pry, but it seems to me a difficult form of employment."

Winnie's face hardened.

"Needs must," she said quietly. "I thought it would only be for the summer holiday season. That was last year. But my brother had been awful poorly. Hard to pay a physician's bills on a miner's wages. My da works hard, but Benjamin would be dead by now if I'd not taken matters into my own hands. I told my family I'd taken up service in a fine house for the summers, though I have a feeling they know the truth. Benjamin is better now, but the bills have piled up, and the creditors have been threatening my father with debtor's prison."

"Sweet Lord," said Sophie. Her own problems seemed of such little concern in this new light.

Later that night, lying in her bed and staring up at the pale canopy above her, Sophie considered her pin money. She would give it all to Winnie, but it would not be nearly

A Baron's Son is Undone

enough. Her father had so severely restricted her pin money since the unfortunate event that her allowance barely paid for a few ribbons each week. She had not brought with her any expensive ballgowns she might have sold as she had not expected to attend any functions during her exile to Cornwall. And none of the jewellery she had ever worn actually belonged to her. It all belonged, as her father liked to remind her, to the estate, and was kept under lock and key when not in use. Her father had sent her to Cornwall with nothing because to him she *was* nothing. She didn't own things. She was one of the things that someone owned.

In the tavern, Sophie turned her head to watch Mr. Barnaby shuffle. He riffled the cards together and bent them upwards into an arch that rained itself down into a neat little pile in his hands.

"I don't think so," she said. "We'll need a neutral dealer."

"My, aren't we a suspicious nelly," said Mr. Hatcher. "Have a little faith, Miss Lovell. We are respected men of business."

"So is Tom," said Sophie. "Let him deal."

She watched Mr. Hatcher make the various mental adjustments required to consider Tom 'a man of business'.

"A neutral dealer then. Mr. Harris!" he called. "You can hold the money behind the bar as well."

"Right-oh, Mr. Hatcher! Looks like it's going to be quite a game!" beamed the inn-keeper, though Sophie saw his smile falter as he turned towards the bar with the money in his hands. He returned to deal out the first hand.

Duncan didn't look at George as he spoke but kept his eyes

A Game that Matters

fixed on the card table.

"Miss Lovell and Tom will be cheating," said Duncan. "She doesn't think I know, but they've been cooking this up for weeks on the off-chance Mr. Hatcher returned."

"Excuse me?" said George.

"It's not really cheating if everyone's doing it," said Duncan.

"Hatcher is cheating too?" asked George.

"You bet your blue blood he is. How else do you think he's going to win his money back?"

"This doesn't feel safe," said George. "Why would you allow it?"

"She's been safe all her life," said Duncan. "Safe and miserable. You should have seen her the first time I brought her to the tavern. Her face. It was like I had presented her with the moon, but it was just a smattering of common people and a chance to converse . . . and then when she found out about second Wednesdays—a chance to play. I'll not let any ill befall her," said Duncan. "But I'll not wrap her in cotton either."

George thought of the many ways he had restricted his sister Patience's life before her marriage. All he had wanted was to keep her safe, her reputation in tact, but now he wondered if in the process, he had made her miserable as well. He looked over at the scar-faced man beside him who was staring straight ahead. George had been right with his earlier assumption. Duncan had been given a job to do, but he wasn't here for the job. He was here for Miss Lovell.

"Do you love her?" asked George.

"For Christ's—what kind of question is that?!" asked Duncan glancing his way then quickly back to the card table.

"I need to know," said George.

A Baron's Son is Undone

Duncan was quiet a long time, and although George wanted to hear his answer, he knew badgering the man would be to no avail. Instead, George turned his attention to the card table and eventually lost himself in the game of whist as it progressed.

How on earth could they all be cheating?

At first, he couldn't see anything that was an obvious giveaway. There was no table talk whatsoever, and no one as far as he could see was kicking anyone else under the table. As time passed, certain innocuous actions repeated themselves. Occasionally, Miss Lovell would adjust one of the cuffs on her sleeve or slide an errant lock of hair behind her ear. Mr. Hatcher had a periodic habit of placing a hand to his chin as if in thought over the cards in his hand. Tom sipped from his tankard of ale every so often and wiped his mouth on only some of those occasions. Mr. Barnaby was the worst offender in that he was the most obvious—clearing his throat and vigorously scratching his head.

"They're using small gestures to communicate with their partners, aren't they?" asked George quietly.

It was a while before Duncan responded. He appeared deep in thought.

"I loved her mother," he said.

It took a moment for George to process this statement. Duncan was turning out to be full of surprises.

"You had an affair?" he asked.

"I didn't say that," said Duncan. "Sophie's mother was faithful to a fault. She would have never."

"But you loved her."

"Not in the way you're thinking. She was thrust into an unhappy marriage. I looked out for her—that's all."

A Game that Matters

"And by extension, you love Miss Lovell," added George. He wanted to be absolutely clear on this point.

"As a daughter or a niece," said Duncan keeping his eyes on the card table. "Mr Pemberley, you'll want to be advised that both of these men are likely carrying knives."

"Pardon me?"

"Tom and Miss Lovell are about to win," he said in a calm and even tone. "There will be a lull before it all kicks off. I suggest you make your way to the bar and convince Mr. Harris to hand over that money right now. When I put myself between Hatcher and Miss Lovell, I would kindly ask you to get her upstairs and behind a locked door. Tom will take Barnaby."

"Miss Lovell said Mr. Hatcher paid up last time," said George as the adrenaline began to drip into his limbs. He hoped that Duncan was making a fuss over nothing.

"That was last time," said Duncan grimly. "A man can only be humiliated by a woman so many times before he feels the need to assert himself."

George nodded at this assessment. Two humiliations would indeed be one too many. He pulled out his pocket watch and attempted to slow the beating of his heart to match the ticking of the second hand. When he had brought his body into some semblance of order, George spoke once more.

"I thought *I* would take Hatcher, and *you* would escort Miss Lovell home?"

"It's a nice thought," said Duncan, "but I have a feeling you're not as good with a knife as you are with your fists. And to be honest, I'm not entirely certain how accomplished you are with those."

They both turned their heads towards the card table as they

A Baron's Son is Undone

heard Miss Lovell laugh. The entire room had gone silent. Several men and women took the opportunity to step out into the damp darkness, making for home. George lifted his empty whisky glass to Duncan and casually made his way to the bar.

"Refill please," he said to Mr. Harris whose face had gone completely white. George leaned over the bar. "Best give me the pot for safe-keeping," he said quietly. "Don't worry yourself, Mr. Harris, I'll pay for any damage caused to your establishment this evening."

Mr. Harris looked over at him as a hesitant smile cracked through the tension of his face.

"Kind of you, Mr. Pemberley," he said sliding the purse of money across the bar. George's body was blocking the transaction being viewed from the vantage point of the card table. He heard a chair sliding back over the floorboards.

"So sorry, Mr. Hatcher," said Miss Lovell.

George slipped the purse into his jacket and turned at the bar. He watched as Hatcher wiped a stiff hand down the sleeve of his brown coat as if to dust himself off. His face was set in a smile that did not reach his eyes.

"You cheated," he said icily. "You set it all up with this man from the start." He looked over at Tom who cracked his thick neck to one side.

"*You* cheated," said Miss Lovell standing. "But *I'm* not complaining. I'd say it was a fair game."

Mr. Hatcher stood then, face flushed, his chair clattering to the floorboards behind him. He reached for the knife at his belt.

"You foreign slut!"

George sprang forward to pull Miss Lovell away from the

A Game that Matters

table as Duncan spun Hatcher to face him. Tom had Barnaby's head smashed into the table before anyone could blink.

Seven

Brilliant and Unique

"Foreign!" said Sophie with indignation as Mr. Pemberton hastened her up the stairs. "He called me foreign!" The word shocked her in a way she couldn't quite comprehend. Was that how people saw her? It seemed so absurd.

"He also called you a slut," said Mr. Pemberton helpfully as he fumbled for his room key.

"Do you think Duncan and Tom will be all right?" she asked as he gestured her through the open door and handed her the purse of money.

"I'm about to go find out," said Mr. Pemberton giving her the room key. "Lock the door."

"What?"

"Sophie, don't let anyone in," said Mr. Pemberton as he shut the door. His steps retreated quickly down the hall.

He called me Sophie, she thought as she twisted the key in the lock and turned to take in his room. Everything was in precise order. A spare set of shoes sat together near the door. A black jacket hung neatly over a chair by the writing desk where a leather-bound book and a pen lay side-by-side in perfect parallel. The room even smelled like him, all foresty.

Foresty isn't a word, thought Sophie. *I'm being foolish.*

She sat down on Mr. Pemberton's bed and smoothed her hands over the grey coverlet. Mr. Harris obviously chose colours that would show the least wear.

We did it, she thought. *But at what cost? If Duncan is hurt on my account . . .*

Sophie paced to the open window, but the world was a wall of black. No moon. The occasional flutter of a bat nearby as if the darkness itself had taken wing. Eventually, she heard the tavern door open and quick steps upon the gravel. It was sometime later when Mr. Pemberton knocked at the door. When she opened it, he was standing before her ashen-faced.

"Duncan!" said Sophie.

Mr. Pemberton didn't say anything for a moment.

"He's been stabbed. There's a lot of blood."

Sophie tried to walk past him, but he blocked her with his body.

"Move, Mr. Pemberton!"

"It's not a sight for a lady," he said.

Sophie tried to push him out of the way, but the man was as stubborn and immovable as granite. *His body was so unbelievably hard.* She had the unwelcome impulse to touch him again, to drag the flats of her hands down his chest. Maybe she *was* a slut. Sophie felt anger bubbling up inside her—anger with herself. She turned her accusatory thoughts against Mr. Pemberton instead.

A Baron's Son is Undone

"You said you wouldn't touch me," she said.

"I'm not," said Mr. Pemberton calmly, "I'm simply choosing not to move."

Sophie was feeling desperate. Duncan needed her! Perhaps she could satisfy an impulse and call it strategy. She reached up shyly and touched Mr. Pemberton's well-shaven cheek, then slid her fingers down and across the wound on his lip. She watched as Mr. Pemberton's grey eyes widened in surprise. He did not reach out to touch her, but his body appeared to relax, and it was then that Sophie shoved her way past him and flew down the stairs.

"Duncan!"

He was lying on the floor by the card table in a pool of blood. Maddy and Tom were kneeling over him with some stripped sheets in hand.

"Lift him carefully on that side," said Maddy to Tom.

Sophie watched in stunned silence as they methodically tied him up in linen to staunch the flow. When they had finished, Sophie knelt down beside poor Duncan in his pool of blood.

"Is he . . . ?"

"He's breathing," said Maddy quietly. "But his heart rate is very low. We'll see how it goes overnight."

"Sorry," said Tom.

"It's not your fault," said Sophie. "It's mine."

"The fault lies with the person who stabbed him," said Mr. Pemberton softly as he crouched down beside her. "And with him alone."

Sophie looked at him questioningly.

"It appeared it might be murder," said Mr Pemberton, "so Hatcher fled without putting up any more of a fight. His man Barnaby is still with us."

Brilliant and Unique

Sophie followed Mr. Pemberton's gaze to the card table where Barnaby was passed out in his seat, his head resting on a disorderly pile of card tricks.

"He needs a bed," said Sophie placing her hand to Duncan's cool forehead.

Mr. Harris set Duncan up in the kitchen with a cot. They did not want to risk man-handling him upstairs, and the kitchen was nice and warm. There was also easy access to water with the pump being just out back.

"I'll escort you home," said Mr. Pemberton to Sophie when Duncan had been settled.

"No!" said Sophie, alarmed at the prospect. "I won't be leaving him!"

"You'll need to sleep," said Mr. Pemberton. "We'll watch over Duncan for you."

"I'll sleep on the floor by his cot," said Sophie. *"I'll* watch over Duncan. He's mine anyway." She knew it sounded an odd thing to say, but it was true. He was her Duncan, and she wouldn't be leaving him.

In the end, she took the first shift. Mr. Pemberton sat with her because, as he said, "Duncan would want me to keep an eye on you." Maddy showed up several hours into their vigil with a bottle of whisky.

"We didn't have time when we bandaged him, but just to be safe. . . No, don't unwrap the linens! He may start bleeding again."

She poured the whisky over the bandages where they tied the wound, soaking them through.

"I've set you up with your own room," said Maddy to Sophie. "End of the hall on your right." She handed over a key.

"Thank you, but I think I'll stay here," said Sophie.

A Baron's Son is Undone

"No need," said Maddy putting a hand to Duncan's chest and lowering her cheek to his face. "His heart rate has picked up. His breathing is strong. I'll sit with him. You get a few hours sleep, and I'll not be surprised if he's stirring by morning. You won't be any use to him if you haven't slept."

Sophie was practically keeling over with tiredness and heartache, so she allowed herself to be escorted upstairs by Mr. Pemberton. He lit the way to the end of the dark hall with a lantern. There, he took the key from her hand and unlocked the door of her room. Pushing it open, he stepped inside and placed the lantern on the bedside table. He had been silent for hours. No attempts to engage her in conversation. No platitudes or 'there-theres'. It was his simple presence that stood for itself. He had not left her side all evening, and she didn't want him to leave now.

"I'll check on you in the morning," he said quietly, concern lacing his features.

Sophie could feel a swell of emotion rise up inside her. She wiped a tear away with the back of her hand.

Mr. Pemberton closed the door and took a step towards her.

"Touch can be comforting," he said. "Would you grant me permission to comfort you?"

Sophie wiped away another tear. She nodded.

Mr. Pemberton stepped up to her and cradled one side of her face in his warm hand. It did feel nice—soothing. Using his thumb, he gently wiped away another tear. Sophie found herself reaching her arms around him. She wanted him closer. She wanted to feel enveloped in his foresty scent. Mr. Pemberton obliged by wrapping her in his arms and pulling her into his chest. She gave a small hiccuped sob, and he used

Brilliant and Unique

a hand to stroke the back of her head. They stood there like that in the middle of the room for so long that eventually Sophie felt her legs give way. Mr. Pemberton caught her up in his arms and carried her over to the bed where he laid her down. He knelt at the foot of the bed to remove her shoes slowly one by one.

"I will check on you in the morning," he said standing.

"Don't go," said Sophie sleepily reaching out an arm towards him.

Mr. Pemberton stood staring down at her for several seconds before he took a seat at the edge of the bed. He stroked a hand up over her brow, and Sophie closed her eyes.

"Hold me again," she said rolling over to face the wall.

She felt the mattress shift as Mr. Pemberton lowered himself to lie down beside her. He curled his entire body into hers and reached around her with one arm. The weight of his arm over her ribs was absolute heaven, a solid male presence which, remarkably, she did not fear.

"You must think I'm a silly woman," she said quietly. "Risking all this violence for a game."

Mr. Pemberton said nothing. She could feel his breath hot on her neck. The flickering light from the lantern danced across the walls of the room.

"But it wasn't just a game," she continued. "Tom and I . . . We wanted to do something for Winnie. So she doesn't have to . . . Some women . . . I don't know how they do it. The world isn't a fair place."

Mr. Pemberton pulled her in closer, her back to his chest. She felt him burrow his face into her hair.

"The most brilliant," he said. "The most unique."

Sophie fell asleep.

A Baron's Son is Undone

George woke early just as the sun was beginning to lift its own head from slumber. He had not slept so well in a very long time—perhaps, since he was a boy. Miss Lovell was nestled against him like a puzzle piece, she fit so neatly into his embrace. Her round little bottom was pushed up against his groin in the most pleasing manner, and George noticed that his body had already responded to her presence before he had even opened his eyes. His cock was as hard as it had ever been, straining to be released from his trousers and pressing itself against Miss Lovell's soft body.

Good Lord, thought George. *I will have to marry her.* He smiled to himself. The prospect did not seem like the worst event that might befall him. He slowly extricated himself, having some difficulty in pulling his arm free from Miss Lovell's tight grasp. He drew the covers over her and made for the door.

Downstairs, Mr. Harris was grinning at him from the bar.

"He's alive!" boomed the inn-keeper. "Mad as hell, but he's alive!"

George found Duncan sitting up in his cot in the kitchen.

"I told you to take her home!" he said angrily. "And now I hear she's spent the night all alone at the inn. It's not appropriate, and you know it."

"The whole situation wasn't appropriate," said George. "You knew that from the start. If you don't want to wrap her in cotton . . . By Heaven, Duncan, anything could have happened! To her! She wouldn't leave you, you know. Stayed up half the night holding your hand. She was quite distraught."

Duncan went quiet.

"I'll fetch her for you," said George.

When George entered Miss Lovell's room, she was still lying

Brilliant and Unique

in bed curled towards the wall. She stirred and rolled over, opening her eyes. When she saw him standing there, she flushed crimson.

"Oh. Mr. Pemberton."

"I think calling me George would make more sense at this point," he said in the most matter-of-fact tone he could muster. His voice sounded to him like it was coming from somewhere far away. "I've come to tell you that Duncan is alive and well if you would like to see him."

Relief flooded Miss Lovell's—Sophie's—face. She sat up and put a hand to her head.

"Are you all right?"

"Just a little dizzy. I'll be fine."

She rose and stepped up close to George but didn't meet his eyes. He held his breath.

"About last night," she said. "I can't imagine . . . I mean I don't know what came over . . . It's not how I usually . . ." She paused and looked up. Her eyes were shining with unshed tears. "Thank you," she said. Glancing down at her feet, she continued: "Your touch was comforting."

"It could be more than that," said George carefully. He knew he needed to tread lightly here. There was something about her that seemed injured.

Sophie looked back up to his eyes.

"Like I said before, it's all a masquerade. I'm sure you would change your mind once the mask came off."

"What mask?" asked George. He so desperately wanted to pull her to him. To kiss her into a stupor. Peel that red dress down from her shoulders. It was all he could do to remain with his hands at his sides.

"The Miss Lovell mask," said Sophie. "The pirate's daughter

A Baron's Son is Undone

mask. I'm not . . . The truth is I've just been hiding, but it has been . . . This summer, Duncan has given me so much. And meeting you . . . well, I never expected . . ."

"If not Miss Lovell, what should I call you?" asked George.

She wiped away a tear.

"You'll think my name is funny, but it's not," she said.

"Try me," said George. His heart was thrumming against his chest.

"Lady Byrd," she said with a half smile. "Sophia Byrd. Daughter of His Grace the Duke of Somerset."

George didn't laugh. It wasn't funny. He knew the Duke of Somerset through his father's activities in Parliament. The man was a pillar of ice. A memory came back to him then, clear as crystal sitting in the sun. George could hear his sister's voice in his head—Patience speaking with their mother in the yellow drawing room of the London house.

"What an awful business! That poor girl. The gossip sheets make it sound like she's some kind of witch."

"A murderess," replied his mother. "Maybe she is."

Patience fixed her mother with an angry look.

"Did she use a spell, do you think?" asked Patience insincerely. "Mother, really! Sometimes!"

Patience rose and stomped out of the room. George's mother looked over to him where he was balancing several accounts at a table in the corner of the drawing room.

"She's always so emotional," said Lady Pemberton. "I appreciate your level-headedness, George. You're my only sensible child."

"Pardon?" said George looking up from his numbers.

George found himself staring at Sophie, his mind churning through every scrap of information he had ever come across

Brilliant and Unique

about the Duke of Somerset. George didn't read the gossip sheets but often heard people talking about what had been written. The duke's daughter had not been given even one Season. No mother. When she turned twenty-two, a marriage had been arranged with a Lord so-and-so. A much older man. The marriage had been annulled soon after. Lord so-and-so had died in their bed on the wedding night. The gossip columnists had gone to town. Every lurid detail, true or imagined, ended up in print. The duke's daughter had retreated to the country estate and was kept out of society for the next year. And now, here she was in front of him, exiled to Cornwall with a scar-faced man to live with her aunt for the summer.

Sophie tried to step past him to the door. George blocked her way as he had done the night before.

"No pretending with me," he said. "Were you . . . injured . . . on your wedding night?" He could not believe he was asking her this question.

A long silence settled between them.

"Yes," she said finally, fixing him with a look that wrenched at his heart. George watched her clasp her hands together to stop them trembling. "He had promised he wouldn't. It was a marriage of convenience, a business arrangement between him and my father. We need not be man and wife, not really. He had several mistresses and an heir from a previous wife. There was no need."

"He forced himself on you," said George. It wasn't a question.

Sophie just looked at him.

"I didn't kill him," she said. "He collapsed on top of me, his face all red and puffy."

A Baron's Son is Undone

"Dear God. Sophie, I'm so sorry."

Turning away from him, she walked over to the ceramic wash basin, poured out some water from a pitcher, and splashed her face. He handed her a small grey towel.

"I need to see Duncan," she said placing the towel down and patting her hair. It was a mess. Her plaited crown was in tatters, and strands of hair were falling down towards her face. She looked so heart-achingly gorgeous that George had to look away. When he looked back up, she was stepping out of the room in her crumpled red dress.

George sat down on the bed and put his face in his hands. He took several long breaths to settle himself. Then he stood and strode quickly to his own room. Sitting down at the writing desk, he penned a quick letter to Patience. She would be the only one to properly understand. She was the only person he could absolutely trust.

Later, he found Sophie downstairs in the kitchen with Duncan.

"Drink some tea," she said, handing him a steaming cup. "You must be parched."

Duncan grimaced as he shifted himself up in the cot. He accepted the cup with two hands.

"You're a good girl," he said, "I only wish I had a treat for you."

George watched Sophie's face break into the widest smile imaginable. She leaned forward and wrapped her arms around his neck. Duncan held the tea out to the side and gave her a little pat on the back.

"What's this for, then?" he said gruffly, but George could see from his eyes that she had touched him to his core.

"Oh, Duncan," she said. "I never would have forgiven myself

Brilliant and Unique

. . ."

"It's all right," he said, patting her hand. "Your mother would be proud."

"My mother?"

"She always wanted you to have an adventure. At least one. She didn't want you locked away in that house. You did the right thing for Winnie," he added.

"You knew?"

"What kind of guard dog do you take me for?" he asked with mock affront. George was startled to find Duncan's gaze directed suddenly his way. "Mr. Pemberley," he said. "Thank you for taking care of Sophie last night."

"Yes," said George running his hand through his hair. "About that."

"His name is actually Pemberton," said Sophie.

"I know," said Duncan, his eyes still fixed on George. "I've been making enquiries."

George steeled himself. This matter was weighing on him, and it needed to be settled right now so that he could rest easy.

"She told me who she is," he said. "You can't take her back to her father."

"I know," said Duncan sipping his tea. "Any ideas?" His dark eyes pierced through George. They both knew there was only one idea that would work.

Sophie's head swivelled from one man to the other.

"I'll marry her," said George. He swallowed hard. "Here in Cornwall. No need to alert everyone by asking the Archbishop for a special licence. If we stay for the next three weeks, the bans could be read in a church nearby. It could all be sorted before we return." He paused, thinking. "But perhaps we are

A Baron's Son is Undone

being too hasty. Do you not think the duke would accept if I offered for his daughter? I'm the son of a baron."

"Not worth the risk," said Duncan. "The man always has very specific plans. I imagine he is cooking one up for Sophie right now. Despite all that has happened, she is still the daughter of a duke and has some social value. His Grace always makes the most of his resources, and Sophie will be no exception."

"Excuse me," interrupted Sophie, the pitch of her voice lifting. "But I'll not be marrying anyone!"

George looked over at the Duke of Somerset's daughter who was sitting on a stool in a tavern kitchen wearing a bloodstained dress. He didn't comprehend what she was saying. It made no sense.

Duncan opened his mouth, but George put up a finger to hold him off. He gestured for Sophie to join him out the backdoor of the kitchen. She stepped out into the quiet early morning with him. A rather handsome brown-and-gold chicken clucked thoughtfully in the dirt near their feet. The air was sweet with the scent of crushed thyme rising up from the herb garden where a large white cat had made its bed.

"Mr. Shitter!" said Sophie when George turned to face her. She looked, for some reason, quite angry. "That's what Duncan named you from the start. And you really are! Of all the unbelievable . . . thoughtless . . . self-important—"

This wasn't going well.

George knew he often didn't do things very tactfully. Patience was always yelling at him for being overbearing and dismissive. He didn't mean to be. His urge was always to simply sort the matter at hand with speed and efficiency. Tidy everything up. Nice orderly lines. Everything tucked away in a neat little box so that he could relax. But perhaps a marriage proposal was not one of those things that required efficiency. Sophie, for her part, looked spitting mad! George reflexively reached both hands up into his hair, gripped, and pulled.

She continued to yell at him, but he found that he couldn't make out the words. His head was buzzing, and every nerve was on high alert.

This was not going well at all! He was going to lose her. For being sensible and efficient! Of all the possibilities, this one would never have occurred to him.

George released his grip on his hair. He dropped down to one knee in the dirt in front of the most brilliant soul he had ever met. Then he lowered the other knee and sat back on his heels. He bowed his head.

"What are you doing?" asked Sophie. He could hear the uncertainty in her voice.

"Begging forgiveness," said George with his gaze to the ground. He lifted his eyes. "If you agree to be my wife, I will honour you, Sophie, every day of my life. And you need not fear . . . The whole point of this is to protect you from being married off again by your father, so you need not fear that I will touch you without your permission . . . even on our wedding night." He swallowed, but a lump had lodged itself in his throat, and it wouldn't be shifted.

Sophie put a hand to her mouth and took a shuddering breath.

"Why?" she asked quietly.

Sweet Lord, why do women need answers to these questions? Actions speak so much louder. George knew Sophie would prefer a flowery sentiment, but though he struggled to find the words,

A Baron's Son is Undone

they simply wouldn't come. He didn't read novels or poetry. He balanced ledgers and followed politics.

"I need you with me," said George. "You see me as I am, and I'm finding it difficult to contemplate the rest of my life without you."

That's all he had in him to give her this morning. It seemed a paltry sort of gift as far as declarations went. He bowed his head once more, closed his eyes, and waited. With each second that passed between them in silence, his nerves frayed just a little bit more. The urge to check his pocket watch was overwhelming, but he had the wise feeling that that particular action would not go down well at this particular moment.

Eight

Souls and their Salvation

Sophie wished Mr. Pemberton would pull out his silver fob to check the time. If he had a schedule to keep, she might be able to ignore the fact that he was kneeling in the dirt at her feet. She might be able to disregard the overwhelming emotion that was threatening to engulf her. No man had ever humbled himself before her in this way, and she felt altogether uncomfortable and embarrassed, as if she couldn't possibly deserve this sort of gesture.

"You say this now, but what about your family?" she asked. "I will be a stain on your reputation."

Mr. Pemberton looked up and smiled as if nothing in the world mattered.

"Is that a 'yes'?" he asked, reaching out a hand. "I'm taking it as a 'yes'."

She pulled him to standing.

"You haven't answered the question," she said.

A Baron's Son is Undone

Mr. Pemberton looked down at his trousers.

"Look what you made me do," he said. "Maddy will have to do another laundry. She's not going to like it."

"Mr. Pemberton!"

"George," he said, holding her still with his gaze.

"George," she said quietly. "You haven't answered my question."

He gave a dismissive wave.

"My family is now immune to stains on reputations. Patience is married to Lord Winter. The man's a bloody (excuse my language) war hero, and if he places his support at our backs, no one will say a peep. I've already written to Patience."

"You what?" Sophie was starting to feel irritable again. "You assumed I would say yes? Of all the arrogant—"

George put up a hand. Sophie noticed that he couldn't stop smiling.

"Is this what it's going to be like?" he asked. "Our marriage? Because I'm enjoying myself already."

Sophie wasn't sure what to say to that.

"To answer your question," he continued, "it truly did not occur to me that you would say no. I died a death in the kitchen when you refused me just now." He took a breath and gave a shake of his head. "Sophie, I spent the night in your room. You must have expected I would propose marriage by morning."

"I expected no such thing," said Sophie in a whisper.

"I will always treat you with respect," said George solemnly. "It is something you should expect of everyone."

Sophie looked down at her shoes. This man! He was not ordinary by any means. *How had she known to trust him the night before? And how had he managed to live up to that trust?*

Souls and their Salvation

Even dancing with her, he had been solicitous of her feelings, offering to end the dance if she wished. He had picked up on her wariness before he even knew who she was.

"I'll marry you," she said.

"I thought we'd already decided that," said George offering her his arm.

Sophie shook her head in disbelief and pressed her lips together to hide a smile. This exasperating man would be her husband. Somehow, it didn't seem like such a terrible thing.

When they walked back into the kitchen arm-in-arm, Duncan raised his eyebrows.

"She'll marry me," said George. "She's a sensible woman."

Duncan chuckled, then flinched and gripped his stomach. At that moment, Maddy and Mr. Harris rushed into the kitchen, nearly wedging themselves in the doorway as they attempted to pass through together.

"Miss Lovell!" said Mr. Harris breaking free of the door frame. "Circumstances are changing!"

"A driver's been sent with all your cases," clarified Maddy. "And Duncan's. There's a note." She handed an envelope to Sophie who knew what it would say before she opened it.

My dearest Sophie,

I welcomed you into my home with open arms and a generosity of spirit that unfortunately you do not deserve. It has come to my attention that you have been frequenting with commoners. Prostitutes! Working men!

Having stayed out all night, I can only assume the worst of your activities, and since I have a reputation to uphold, I can no longer be associated with you or your hired man Duncan. I am writing to your father to inform him of events. If I were him, your punishment

A Baron's Son is Undone

would be swift, and it would be severe. Scotland seems like a good place to keep you, tethered to a rock somewhere out of sight.

As always, I pray for your eternal soul and its salvation. May the Good Lord show mercy if He is so inclined.

Sincerely,

Margaret Byrd

Sophie looked up from the letter and met Duncan's eyes. It would have been devastating if not for the events of that morning.

"She prays for my eternal soul and its salvation," she said. "Also, she is writing to Father."

Duncan grunted.

"Mr. Harris," he said. "We'll be needing two rooms. There's to be a wedding."

"A wedding!" said Maddy clutching at her heart.

"Sophie has agreed to be my wife," said George. He sounded, Sophie thought, quite stunned by his own words.

"And here we all thought Duncan would gut you like a pig," said Maddy grinning.

"But Duncan's the one who ended up gutted!" laughed Mr. Harris.

Sophie felt the joke was in poor taste, but she decided to remain silent since there was nothing to be gained by bringing down the jovial mood in the kitchen.

Back in her room, it felt lovely to wash and change into clean clothes. Sophie undid her hair and brushed it out. She would not be able to do the plaited crown herself—that was a talent of one of Aunt Margaret's lady's maids—so instead she wove one long plait and pinned it up in a twist at the nape of her neck. It was a neat hairdo, if not remarkable.

Souls and their Salvation

Tom and Winnie came by later that morning, and Winnie was beside herself with gratitude. The three of them stood together in an out-of-the-way corner of the relatively empty tavern. Maddy brought over a pot of coffee and some mugs and set them down on a nearby table.

"I'll not be able to travel home with this kind of money," said Winnie sitting down and hefting the purse Sophie had handed to her. "It's likely to be thieved before I reach the half-way mark."

"I was thinking . . ." said Tom shifting on his large feet and holding his hat in his hands. "I was thinking that maybe I could escort you along the way."

Winnie looked up at him with her big blue eyes.

"You would do that for me?"

"Sure," said Tom. He fiddled with the brim of his hat. "It's possible I'd do anything for you, Winnie."

Sophie placed a hand on Winnie's shoulder and gave it a squeeze.

"Enjoy the coffee," she said. "I should go and check on Duncan."

Winnie and Tom needed a moment alone. Sophie knew Tom was not the perfect man, but it was clear that he was completely besotted with Winnie. And he wasn't afraid to apologise—they had all witnessed that. Winnie would have to decide for herself now how her life would proceed.

George had disappeared for much of the rest of the day. *Sweet Heaven, the man was efficient.* By the time supper rolled around, he had secured the services of a parson and ensured that the

A Baron's Son is Undone

bans would be read every Sunday for the following three weeks. Somehow and somewhere in this little wind-blown corner of England, he had found a solicitor who was drawing up the marriage settlement with all good haste. At supper (just the two of them at a small table in the tavern), he slid a small package wrapped in brown paper across the table to her.

"What's this?" she asked.

"Open it," said George.

She unwrapped the paper to find a tiny yellow cloth-covered box. Lifting the lid revealed a gold pendant and chain sitting on a bed of white cotton. The pendant was shaped like a heart, its centre set with a finely cut ruby.

"I noticed you have no jewellery," said George. "None that you wear, anyway."

"It's lovely," said Sophie lifting the heart from the box. "Could you . . .?"

George stood and stepped behind her chair to fasten the necklace. His fingers brushed the nape of her neck sending a shiver down her spine. He had given her a heart. It was not without meaning.

"I have nothing for you," she said as he took his seat once more. She was feeling not a little overwhelmed by his attentions.

"That's not how this works," said George. "Nothing about this, about our marriage, is transactional. I want to make that perfectly clear."

He was looking at her with an intensity and concern she could not quite comprehend. His words were not exactly romantic . . . but they were unambiguous and to the point—a lot like him.

Souls and their Salvation

"Thank you," she said, for she honestly didn't know what else to say.

That night as George lay on his bed staring up at a crack in the plasterwork of the ceiling, he could not have been more pleased. The day had gone swimmingly. Everything in order. Purchasing the pendant had not been exactly sensible—a spur-of-the-moment impulse at the goldsmith's where he had gone to purchase two wedding bands. Sophie seemed to like it. What else might she like? He would have the time to find out. An entire lifetime.

There was a gentle knock at his door.

George was wearing only a set of drawers, so he pulled on a pair of trousers and opened the door. Sophie was standing in the hall with a lantern. Her thick black hair was down, cascading over her shoulders. She was wearing a white nightdress and a shawl. Nothing else. Bare feet.

"Oh!" she said glancing to his naked chest. "I only wanted to talk. I didn't mean to disturb . . ."

"You can never disturb me," said George stepping aside to let her in. He peered out into the empty hallway before closing the door and turning to her.

"Talk then," he said with a half smile. "You know visiting me in my room is highly inappropriate."

"Oh," said Sophie, her expression bewildered. "I thought since last night . . . It's just . . . we're to be married, so . . ."

"I'm joking," said George with a grin. "You can visit me in my room whenever you like. With no fear," he added.

He watched her face soften.

A Baron's Son is Undone

"Even on our wedding night?" she asked.

"Even then," he said.

"It's the why of it I don't understand," said Sophie. "Forgive me, but what could you possibly gain from this arrangement? My father will not offer you a dowry, my reputation (despite what you say) will bring gossip, and I'm not exactly . . . fetching."

George felt himself growing angry.

"That's enough," he said. "Sit down."

He gestured to the bed. To his utter amazement, she sat down immediately, placing her lantern on the side table. He seated himself gingerly beside her. She turned herself to him which caused her thigh to slide against his.

"You're angry with me now," she said.

"No," said George. "I'm angry *for* you. There's a difference."

She looked down at his hand and placed hers lightly over it. His breath hitched in his chest as he looked down into her beautiful face. Her dark lashes swept down and up in a slow blink.

"Who says you're not fetching?" asked George in a hoarse voice. "I shall flay them alive."

Sophie laughed, and George thought his heart might burst clean out of his chest. She looked down to where her hand was resting on his and slowly drew her fingers up to his wrist, along his arm, all the way up to his shoulder. It was such a light touch, like the flutter of a butterfly wing against his skin. George kept himself still, as if any movement might frighten her off. Her hand skimmed its way up his neck to his jaw and along his bottom lip, and then she leaned in slowly and pressed her soft warm lips to his. George's heart was hammering in his chest. Though it practically killed him to do so, he allowed her to kiss him gently without responding in any way,.

Pulling her face from his, she said, "I suppose it would be all right if you kissed me back. Unless..."

"Unless what?" asked George. His breath was already ragged. He felt as if he'd run a mile.

"Unless you'd rather not," she said.

"Jesus, Sophie, what goes on in that head of yours? I'm half mad for you. If you want me to kiss you, you only have to say so."

"Truly?" she asked. "You're mad for me?"

"Mmm," responded George. He didn't trust himself to speak.

He saw Sophie's pupils bloom in the lantern light.

"And if I ask for a kiss, you won't take it to mean...? That is..."

Dear God, she was still afraid. What did that man do to her? If he weren't dead already, George would be hunting him down like the fucking vermin he was.

"I'll not take more than you offer," said George.

He was taken aback when she leaned quickly forward and pressed her lips to his once more. This time, he tilted his head in response, moving his mouth over hers, slowly, languorously, trying his best to give her a kiss she would want to repeat. He had never taken so much care with a single kiss in his life. As her mouth parted for him, he swept his tongue inside her, and she made a small sound in her throat that had him squirming in his seat. She was so unbelievably warm and sweet, he thought he might die if she stopped too soon. Carefully, he reached his arms around her—one hand to the back of her head, the other to her delicate back. He felt her soft hands

A Baron's Son is Undone

slide up his bare back, and it was nearly enough to undo him. Tenderly, he pulled his face from hers.

"Sophie," he said trying to catch his breath, trying to slow his heart.

"I didn't know it could be nice like that," she said.

Her face was flushed, and her lips were red and wet. He wanted to . . . No, best not think about what he wanted. She dropped her eyes to his chest and reached out a hand to touch him.

So it is to be an evening of torture, thought George. *Very well.*

He closed his eyes as her hand stroked across the hair of his chest. She ran a thumb over one nipple, then slid her hand down to follow the swirl of hair that whorled about his belly button.

"I'm feeling," she said, "uncomfortable in a way I have only felt when I'm with you."

George couldn't speak as she stroked her hand up his side to his armpit, down the inside of his arm. Her fingers passed over his wrist and traced a circle over his palm. She shifted herself on the bed.

"Would you hold me?"

George opened his arms, and she lifted herself to his lap. He wrapped his arms around her as she tucked her head into the side of his neck. For all that George did not want to take what was not given, he was only a man, and his body was not entirely under his control. Sophie lifted her face to his, eyes wide as his erection pressed up against her.

"Sorry," he said. Her shawl had fallen from her shoulders, and her golden arms were bare. George had the sudden urge to lick his way up from her wrist to her armpit, then take each finger in his mouth in turn.

Souls and their Salvation

Sophie twisted a little against his lap, and George groaned.

"Did I hurt you?" she asked softly.

"No," said George pressing his forehead to hers, his voice a rasp. "You could do that all night, and I wouldn't complain."

She rocked herself against him once more.

Mercy. When she leaned in for another kiss, George gorged himself on her as if she were the first real meal he had eaten in a year. She rocked against his cock as they kissed, and he responded in kind. He could feel the need building in her as her kisses became more desperate. She threaded her fingers through his hair, and he stroked his hands up her bare arms to her shoulders and neck, then down her back.

"I don't know . . ." she said breathlessly as she moved against him. "I feel as if I can't—" Her sentence broke off as she stifled a cry with one hand while she fisted her other hand in his hair. The way she was pulling on his hair hurt, and George liked it. He didn't want her to stop, but her grip soon relaxed, and he held her trembling body in his arms as her breathing settled into a calmer pace.

"Apparently, you *can*," he said with a grin.

"That was . . ." she said laughing into his neck. "I've never . . ." She shifted herself to the bed and looked down at his lap. "Are you uncomfortable?" she asked.

"Very," said George.

Sophie looked at him then with such consideration that he felt quite embarrassed.

"Show me how you would do it," she said. "How you would find your release without using my body."

George could feel himself growing even harder as she spoke, but something about the situation was making him feel uneasy.

A Baron's Son is Undone

"That hardly seems . . . No, I don't think so," he said, reaching out a hand to cup her cheek.

He couldn't put his finger on the reason for his reluctance, but he suspected it had something to do with the fact that she was likely feeling obliged. When he had given her the pendant that evening, she had immediately remarked upon the fact that she had nothing to give him in return. This seemed a parallel kind of circumstance. It was enough that she had trusted him to kiss her, to hold her, and to help her find some pleasure. He did not want her to think it was a debt that needed repaying.

"It will pass," he said looking down at his tented trousers. "Would you like a cuddle? Like we did last night?"

"That would be nice," said Sophie sliding down to lay her head on his pillow.

The movement dragged her night dress up her legs, and George swore softly to himself as he lay down beside her. This time she turned to him and threw a bare arm across his chest and one leg over his. He tried to think of his Uncle St. John jabbering on about Parliament, about sad puppies lost in the rain, and other such cock-shrinking subjects as she nestled her face against his neck, her warm breath like the rhythmic stroke of a feather across his skin. She was asleep within minutes, and George had to marvel at the blessed situation in which he found himself.

Tomorrow, he would take his bride for a picnic. He wondered where he might acquire some pasties.

Nine

A Rare Breed

George woke to find himself alone with the light of a new day filtering in through the curtains. He rolled his face against the pillow and inhaled the scent of Sophie's body that still lingered in the sheets. It was as if a faint mist of lilac had settled over the bed, and it made him think of spring.

By the time he had dressed and made his way downstairs, Sophie was already in the kitchen fussing over Duncan.

"You don't look quite so pale today," she said punching his pillow into shape so that he could sit up. "The physician should be by to check on your wounds. And we'll ask him if we can move you upstairs to a proper room."

"No fever!" marvelled Duncan. "That would be Maddy's doing," he chuckled. "It smells like she's poured the entire contents of the bar over my bandages."

When George stepped into the kitchen, Sophie looked up

A Baron's Son is Undone

to see him, then quickly made herself busy with the kettle. George watched her for a few moments, his mind completely oblivious to the fact that Duncan was also in the room. She was wearing a creamy yellow dress which made him smile. *Just wait until she sees the yellow drawing room at home.* By the time he looked Duncan's way, the man was staring at him with narrowed eyes.

Thank goodness he's incapacitated, thought George.

"Sophie showed me the pendant you gifted her," said Duncan. "It was thoughtful of you." His words sounded grudging and forced.

"I'll just . . ." said Sophie glancing from one man to the other. "I'll go help Maddy in the garden."

George followed her with his eyes as she swept out the back door. He went over to prop the door open with a stool so that he had a clear view of Sophie's whereabouts. He didn't like it when she was out of his sight—it made him feel slightly panicked. By the time he turned back to Duncan, the man's eyebrows were lifted, and there was a curious smile on his face.

"Don't overdo it," said Duncan.

"Overdo what?" asked George.

"The cotton wool," Duncan responded. "It will smother her."

George lifted the whistling kettle and poured it into a fat green teapot that sat like an enormous frog beside the stove.

"I will do what's best," he said.

He knew Duncan was right, but he didn't feel like giving him the pleasure of acknowledging that fact.

"That pendant," said Duncan shaking his head in disbelief. "She won't be taking it off—ever. You should have heard her cooing over your thoughtfulness. What *are* you? How does

A Rare Breed

a man know to do these things without a woman to guide him? Flower fairies and golden hearts—it's enough to make a person sick."

Duncan pretended to retch over the side of his cot. Then he caught George's eye, and they both laughed.

"I had a good feeling about you," said Duncan.

"No you didn't," said George. "You called me Mr. Shitter."

"Well you *are*," said Duncan laughing. "Sometimes."

"Listen, Duncan," said George seriously. "We need to make a proper plan. If Sophie's Aunt Margaret has sent a letter to the duke, he will be here soon to collect her. We need to keep her from him for the next three weeks while the bans are being read."

"Nothing to chance," said Duncan. "You like to strategise a win."

"Precisely," said George running a nervous hand through his hair and looking out to the garden through the kitchen door.

Sophie was crouched down among the greenery collecting herbs with Maddy. The white cat was rubbing itself up against her yellow skirt.

"For one thing," said Duncan, "the duke won't actually come himself."

"He won't?!" George was incredulous. This was his daughter they were speaking about.

"No, he'll send a man—someone a lot like me."

"And he'll be sending him here, since this is where her aunt knows she has been spending her time," added George.

Maddy and Sophie bustled in through the door with baskets bringing the scent of thyme and rosemary in with them.

"Maddy," said George taking her basket and placing it on

A Baron's Son is Undone

a table. "How long does a letter take to travel from here to London?"

"They'll tell you two to three days," said Maddy as she turned to Sophie to take her basket.

George took in a sharp breath.

"But my last letter to my sister in London took at least ten to arrive. Her letter took five days to make its way here. Problem is there's not a lot of mail coming and going from the area on account of the prices. It's not worth sending the mail coach through too frequently. Can you believe it cost me over a shilling to receive my sister's letter? Two days wages, Mr. Pemberley!

George looked at Duncan.

"Let's be pessimistic and say the letter arrives in five days. And then another two to three days for the duke's man to arrive," said George. He pulled out his silver fob simply to feel the weight of it in his hands, to keep from fidgeting.

"What's going on?" asked Sophie.

"Your Aunt Margaret's letter," said George. He watched Sophie's face pale as realisation dawned on her. "It's been one day since it was sent. That gives us six to seven days before someone arrives to fetch you. I'm rounding down. Let's call it five days."

"But the bans . . ." said Sophie.

George placed what he hoped was a comforting hand to her back. He said a word of thanks in his head for the fact that the bans were being read at a church several towns over. He had known a local church would be problematic since Sophie's aunt may actually hear the bans being read if she were in attendance.

"All right," said Maddy in a business-like tone, "I understand

A Rare Breed

these are important matters to consider." She turned to Sophie. "I'm also coming to understand that you're likely not the daughter of Captain Lovell."

Sophie gave her an apologetic look.

"But," continued Maddy, "it's nearly breakfast time, and I'm going to need you both out of my kitchen!" She shooed them with two hands. "You can stay," she said with a gap-toothed smile as she turned to Duncan.

George took Sophie's hand and led her up the stairs to her room.

"May I come in?" he asked. "I need to speak to you privately."

Inside Sophie's room, she closed the door and turned to him with a look of anguish on her face.

"My father will kill you," she said.

"No, he'll *send a man* to kill me," corrected George. "Not exactly the way I would avenge my own daughter's honour."

"He won't be avenging me," said Sophie. "Simply retrieving lost property."

"Hm," said George.

He had a plan, but he didn't like it. It was possibly the most ill-advised plan ever imagined.

"We're going to have to do the unthinkable," he said.

"What would that be?" asked Sophie.

George felt his face cringing with the prospect of their next move.

"We're going to have to seek refuge with my Uncle St. John and my Aunt Evelyn. No one at the inn knows my name is Pemberton, so there will be no connecting us to them."

George pushed his hair up over his head.

"I like it when you do that," said Sophie watching him thoughtfully. "It's terribly endearing."

A Baron's Son is Undone

She took a step towards him and placed her arms around his waist. Resting her cheek against his chest, she said: "Tell me you will be my husband and that everything is going to be all right."

"There's no question," said George wrapping his arms around her. "No question at all, Sophie. You must know that whatever happens, I will never let you go." As he said the words, he felt a surge of protectiveness course through him. He pulled her tightly to him and kissed the top of her head.

"We'll give Duncan a few more days to recuperate. Hopefully, he'll be well enough to travel," said George. "It's not far."

"What will we tell your uncle and aunt?" asked Sophie. "It's quite a scandal we bring to their doorstep."

"The truth," said George. "I'd be surprised if they batted an eye about any of it. They'll be too thrilled at the prospect of company."

Sophie had never heard of anyone who did not care whether or not they were caught up in a scandal. She wondered about George's relatives, but she didn't wonder for long. George was insisting she get dressed for a day out.

"There's a wind, so you'll need a jacket," he said opening her closet. "Proper walking boots. Not those flimsy slippers," he added gesturing to her shoes.

Sophie smiled. He did like to take control . . . which might seem overbearing at first glance, but it was the detail that touched her. *He thought of her feet!*

"We'll grab a bite downstairs before we go," he said. "Maddy

A Rare Breed

says there's a pastry cook-shop around the corner. They'll be selling pasties first thing in the morning."

"Pasties? Where are we going?" asked Sophie.

"To the beach," he said. "For some peace and quiet."

"Just the two of us?"

George rested his eyes on hers.

"You'd rather not," he said with some disappointment. "I should have asked. Patience says I'm always doing things like this."

"No," said Sophie taking his hand. "I'd like to go."

"Truly?" asked George looking down at his hand in hers.

"No pretending," she said. "I'd like to go to the beach with you."

She was rewarded with a smile that sent a pulse of heat throbbing down into her belly and lower still.

The night before had been . . . unexpected. She knew she shouldn't have gone to his room, but after having slept in his embrace the previous night, she felt as if she would never sleep again without his comforting body wrapped around hers. In some ways, her own body and heart were at war with her mind. She had known quite well what might happen if she turned up at his door in her nightdress, but she had told herself she only wanted to speak with him. She lied to herself by imagining it was an innocent visit.

He had been so incredibly solicitous of her feelings. So gentle and restrained, just as he had been the previous night. On the other hand, she had not restrained herself in the slightest, and now, in the light of morning, she felt rather embarrassed and ashamed about it all. *What kind of a lady does that? And what kind of a lady wants to do it again but with less clothes on?* She wondered if perhaps she deserved the kind of

A Baron's Son is Undone

thing that had happened to her before. Had she brought it on herself? Unknowingly? Being the way that she was?

Unfortunately, George continued to be a trustworthy and reassuring presence, and it was this pesky characteristic of his that was making her feel quite bothered . . . and warm—uncomfortably so.

"Pasties on the beach," said George with a grin. "As we began, so shall we continue."

"Minus one pistol," said Sophie with a half smile.

"I could teach you how to shoot, you know," said George. "A lady should be able to defend herself."

"That would be . . . Yes, I would like that," said Sophie.

She imagined his shooting lessons would be succinct and methodical. She also imagined him standing behind her with his arms over hers, showing her how to hold the gun, his breath hot on her ear as he whispered his instructions.

"You're flushed," said George with some bemusement.

"Am I?"

"Mmm."

"Don't do that," said Sophie with a small shake of her head.

"Do what?"

"Make that sound."

"You don't like it?" he asked.

"The problem is that I *do* like it," said Sophie feeling her face heat.

"I don't see how that's a problem," said George closing the space between them. "Mmmm, mmmm."

"Mr. Pemberton!"

"I told you, it's *George*." He paused and regarded her carefully. "Permission to scoop you up and press my face into your neck."

A Rare Breed

Sophie's eyes went wide.

"Permission granted," she whispered.

He was on her in a flash, whisking her up into his surprisingly strong arms. He nuzzled his face into the side of her neck and made that sound in his throat sending those delicious vibrations rippling down through every nerve of her body. The stubble of his face tickled her soft skin, and she squirmed and laughed, reaching her arms around his neck. When he lifted his face from her, she continued to laugh, pressing small kisses to his jaw, then his cheek, his nose, and finally as her laughter fell away, she found herself staring up into his serious grey eyes.

"I think we shall have a lot of fun," said George.

"At the beach?" asked Sophie.

"In our life," said George.

Sophie kissed him then full on the mouth with such force he stumbled back a pace before catching himself. It didn't take him long to respond, and Sophie wondered that he was as hungry for her as she was for him. As she pressed her tongue past his lips, she grew heavy and damp between her legs. She felt suddenly shameful in a way she couldn't understand, but that feeling was soon burned up by the heat of his mouth, the pounding of his heart, and the intensity of his eyes when he pulled away. He set her gently back down on her feet. They gazed upon one another for a long time before George broke the silence.

"One of us has to be sensible," said George. "Or we shall never leave the bedchamber."

His hair was standing on end in that way that she loved, and his cravat was all crooked. He was flushed from his cheeks down to his throat.

A Baron's Son is Undone

"I suppose you're the sensible one," said Sophie.

"Obviously," said George with mock seriousness. "It's certainly not you. You're the one who likes to wave pistols about and bait dangerous men into games of chance."

Sophie liked the way he was teasing her. It made her want to kiss him again, but she held herself back. She could be sensible if she wanted to be.

George took her on a vigorous hike along the cliffs. He carried a roll of blankets under one arm which held their pasties wrapped in napkins as well as a flask of tea. The warm wind buffeted them as they pressed against it arm-in-arm. Tall green grasses, wild flowers, and gorse to their left, and a clean drop to a perfect blue ocean on their right. The sky was as blue as the walls of the little glass shop in Porth La, and the wind had stretched a few strands of white cloud over the horizon.

"A standing stone," said Sophie breaking free of George's arm and running forward. It was a full half-man taller than herself. An irregular upright rectangle. She placed her bare hand to the purplish grey rock and was surprised to feel the heat of the sun against her skin. "It looks so cold," she said, "but feel it."

George placed his hand beside hers. They stood there together soaking up the heat of the rock for several seconds before George pulled away.

"The schedule," he said briskly. "No dilly-dallying with standing stones, as fascinating as they may be."

Sophie laughed.

"I forgot," she said. "We have important matters to attend."

A Rare Breed

"That's right," said George as he strode off at a clip. "Paddling in the surf and sitting on blankets." She hurried after him.

"Not to mention pasty eating," she called out from behind.

He turned on her with sparkling eyes.

"So hurry up, then! If we're late, I'll know who to blame."

Sophie smiled as she took his arm once more.

When they finally arrived above the perfect secluded cove, Sophie felt George tighten his grip on her arm as they descended the precarious steps to the beach. They spread out their blankets in the shadow of the cliff, and Sophie sat down to pull off her boots and stockings. When she looked up, George was watching her. He quickly glanced out to sea.

"Won't you come paddling?" said Sophie. "You'll want to take off your shoes. One ruined pair is enough I should think."

George looked down at his feet, then carefully kicked off his shoes before bending down to arrange them neatly side by side. He peeled off his stockings and tucked them into his shoes, folded up his trousers, then looked to the waves as they rolled in and up the sand.

"I brought Grace with me to Cornwall once," he said. "But I'm afraid I ruined the trip for her."

"Oh?"

"The schedules," said George. "And there was a great deal of cotton wool."

"Cotton wool?" asked Sophie.

"I had her all wrapped up in it, and I just sort of rolled her around and told her she was having a good time."

Sophie noticed he didn't look her way. His gaze was still fixed on the breakers.

"I've tried so hard," he said. "And it's made me so tired. I

A Baron's Son is Undone

imagine it's what the maid feels like—always tidying things up, trying to arrange things just so, and then someone comes along and tosses a cushion on the floor or eats a biscuit without a plate or throws a paintbrush covered in paint against the wall. And it seems like . . . when something like that happens that is out of order, it seems like absolutely anything terrible might happen. No day feels safe."

Sophie stood and slipping her hand in his, led him down to the water's edge where they let the cold sea lap at their toes.

"Who threw the paintbrush?" asked Sophie with the soft beginnings of a smile.

"Patience," said George. "But it's supposed to be a metaphor."

"I know," said Sophie. "If we continued the metaphor, don't you think it's possible that the cushion could simply stay on the floor for a few days? And maybe the crumbs will be licked up by the dog . . . and maybe that splash of paint on the wall is just what the room needed? Maybe you don't have to be the one to hold everything together."

George gave her a fierce look.

"Who would I be then?"

Sophie didn't understand the question.

"You would always be George," she said. "The fact is that no day is safe regardless of whether or not that cushion stays on the floor."

"Maybe," said George, but he didn't sound entirely convinced.

Sophie distracted her complicated man by engaging him to collect sea glass and shells and ocean-scrubbed pebbles that winked up at them from under the shifting waters. He took to it the way a small boy might, getting lost in the search for the next little wonder and periodically coming over to present

A Rare Breed

his findings to her. When he did this, he would glance up at her face like a puppy looking for approval, grinning broadly whenever Sophie displayed any sign of delight. They made a fine collection, and Sophie took some time to arrange it on a large rock for someone to find on another day, but she slipped one particularly smooth piece of blue sea glass into her pocket—a keepsake.

As they ate their pasties seated on blankets with their feet in the sand, Sophie wondered at the way George had confided in her. She had been vulnerable with him the night before, trusting he would treat her gently, and today he had done the same. Opening himself up like that, revealing his own faults—it was not something that men normally did in Sophie's experience. She was reminded of the last time they had eaten pasties on the beach. He had said then that he was tired as well. . . of the masquerade. She had wanted him to elaborate, but he wouldn't do so, even at gun point. Clearly, there was more to it than what he had acknowledged today. Sophie took another bite of her pasty and looked out to sea as a white-and-grey seagull dove head first down into the water.

"Penny for your thoughts," said George.

"They're all about you," said Sophie tearing her gaze from the sea.

He looked suddenly concerned.

"You've not changed your mind, have you?"

"About what?" asked Sophie.

"About marrying me," asked George putting down the remains of his pasty.

"That would never happen," she said. "Someone needs to take care of you since you are so very tired." She patted the blanket. "You can rest your head if you like."

A Baron's Son is Undone

George shifted himself to lie down, and she did the same, curling into his side.

"Close your eyes," she said.

He did so, and she took the time to delicately stroke his face with her fingers. *Sweet Heaven, he was a handsome man.* She followed the line of each eyebrow, drew her fingers down the sides of his jaw, along his lips, then up his cheek to follow the line of each eyelid. She could feel the muscles of his face relax under her touch.

"You're always wound quite tightly, aren't you?" she said.

"I have a lot on my mind."

He opened his eyes and turned to her on the blanket.

"Sophie," he said earnestly, "You must tell me if I ever make you unhappy. Sometimes . . . I don't mean to, but sometimes I can be . . . inflexible . . . overbearing . . . single-minded. I've also been told that I'm full of myself."

"Patience?" asked Sophie with a wry smile.

"She doesn't mince words," said George, "and she's not always wrong."

"Don't worry," said Sophie, "I'll let you know if I'm ever discontent."

"Right away," said George. "Don't sit on it and hope I will change my behaviour on my own because I likely won't."

Sophie laughed.

"That's good to know. I wonder how many prospective brides are treated to this sort of conversation before their wedding?"

"You're probably the first," said George with a smile, "I'm a rare breed."

"And not at all full of yourself," said Sophie.

Ten

Pixies and Politics

George lay in his bed fully clothed staring up at the ceiling. He cast periodic glances towards the door of his room. It was getting late, and Sophie had not come to him as she had done the night before. He wondered if he had said or done something to make her feel uncomfortable. Perhaps, it had simply all been too much for her. She had been wary of his touch not two days ago—and with good reason! Every time he thought about what she had been through on her wedding night, his chest grew tight, and a sharp pain stabbed him in the sternum making it difficult to take a breath. Perhaps after last night, she feared he would not keep his promise.

As much as he wanted to go to her and reassure her, he felt that she might take it the wrong way. She might feel as if he wanted more—and, Heaven help him, he did. Perhaps, this was for the best. Two rooms. Plenty of husbands and wives

A Baron's Son is Undone

slept in two rooms without complaint. The problem was that he didn't think he would be able to sleep at all without her now. He reached for his fob on the side table and flipped open the lid. It was going on half past one in the morning. At this rate, he would get no sleep at all.

A faint knock sounded at the door so softly he might have simply thought it the sound of the building creaking against the wind. But George's ears were tuned for any hint of Sophie, and he sprang from the bed so quickly that he made himself quite light-headed for a few seconds. The knock sounded again.

When he opened the door, she was standing there in her golden shawl and white night dress with her hair in a long black plait over one shoulder, a candle in her hand.

She's an angel, thought George. *It's a miracle she lets me touch her at all.*

"It's only . . ." said Sophie looking to him then down at her feet. "I don't want you to think . . . It's only I can't sleep." She lifted her gaze to his.

"Neither can I," said George stepping back to let her in. "It seems that everything is out of order if you are not resting beside me. Terrible things might happen, and I can have no rest."

She gave him a shy smile as he took her candle, blew it out, and set it down beside the lantern on his side table. George knew that he needed to be careful tonight, so very careful. She removed her shawl and hung it on the back of his chair. Then he lifted the covers of his bed, and she slid under, nestling her head into his pillow and looking up at him somewhat anxiously.

"Not to worry," he said. "We'll only be sleeping."

Pixies and Politics

She reached for him then, and he lay down beside her fully clothed. She snuggled in close, placing an arm over his chest, and George felt his heart expand as if it were a sponge soaking up all the warmth and aching sweetness of the moment. When he turned to snuff the lantern, he felt her hand press into his chest as if she didn't want to let him move even slightly away from her. It made him feel as if he were the most important person in the world, and he vowed to himself then and there that he would do everything in his power to make her happy.

In the morning, George found himself curled around her. She stirred in his arms and turned to face him. Looking into her sleepy, dreamy eyes, he was flooded with a feeling of overwhelming protectiveness, not to mention a brief moment of blind possessiveness.

"I'll not have you wandering the hall in your nightdress after dark," said George.

He spoke the words without thinking and winced at the way he sounded so high-handed and domineering. Happily, she didn't seem to notice.

"Then you had best come to me," she said.

His heart immediately lifted like a seagull rising up on a warm current of air. He stroked a lock of hair from her forehead and slipped his fingers down her long shiny plait.

"I imagine I could spend every evening brushing your hair," he said.

She lifted her eyebrows.

"What?" he asked.

"I doubt very much that is how you would like to spend your evenings."

George laughed, and Sophie regarded him then with an odd look.

A Baron's Son is Undone

"You're not a normal man," she said as her fingers stroked their way along the side of his neck and up to the whorl of his ear.

George willingly submitted himself to the exquisite torment of her touch.

The next couple of days passed in a blur of long walks arm-in-arm and warm nights sleeping in a tangled yet chaste embrace. Each night as she lay with George, Sophie's mind churned up the most indecent thoughts. She was desperate to repeat the amorous encounter she had experienced with him on that first night after his proposal, but she could not bring herself to ask and half-feared that if she did, she would reveal herself as a rather wanton slut.

George, for his part, remained the perfect gentleman, though she was well aware that her presence in his bed was likely as arousing an experience for him as it was for her. Each morning, she awoke to the hard length of his erection nestled against her backside, and it was all she could do not to rub herself up against him as she had done on that first night.

By the time Duncan was well enough to be moved to a room, he was insisting they leave the inn in all good haste.

"It's the fifth day," he said taking a few precarious steps across the kitchen. "Let's not press our luck."

Sophie marvelled once more at the efficiency and competence of her husband-to-be. George had them quickly packed and loaded into a hired carriage he had procured several towns over. It was a costly endeavour to bring the vehicle and driver into town, but a local man might talk if someone came asking

Pixies and Politics

questions, and that was not something they could risk.

Mr. Harris and Maddy were all smiles and well-wishes as they waved them off. George had compensated them well for their time and care, and he had offered a little extra if they would tell a tale that did not involve him. If a man came asking after Sophie, they would say she had fled north with Duncan, the implication being that they were making their way to Scotland.

As the carriage rumbled over the uneven road, Sophie felt Duncan's eyes on her. He was seated across from her and beside George.

"Two more weeks," he said.

"And a day," added George to be absolutely precise.

"These relatives of yours," said Duncan turning to George. "They will keep quiet?"

"Not as such," said George pressing a hand through his hair. "But they won't turn us in if that's what you mean. Aunt Evelyn will be only too delighted to witness a wedding."

"And your uncle?" asked Duncan. "You are confident this is a good idea?"

"I never said it was a good idea," said George. "But I have faith that my uncle will shelter us until the appointed time. It's only a matter of whether we will survive until then."

Duncan gave Sophie a look, and she shrugged her shoulders. As the carriage proceeded along its way, she rested her head against the window and closed her eyes. Duncan said her mother had wanted her to have an adventure, but if all adventures were this nerve-wracking, Sophie wasn't entirely certain she wanted another.

The three travellers settled into their silence as the carriage whisked them along back tracks and verdant fields with a

A Baron's Son is Undone

light mist settling over them. When Sophie glanced over to George, he was regarding her with a look of such tenderness, she had to look away lest Duncan see them ogling each other like fools.

As the carriage finally slowed to a halt, the soothing quiet of the countryside was broken by a woman's shouts. Sophie peered out the window to see a rather large and rambling cottage surrounded by overgrown hedges and wild flowers. A middle-aged lady wearing a rather fantastically flouncy green dress was waving her hands. A maid followed close behind her.

"That will be Aunt Evelyn," said George opening the carriage door and stepping down.

Sophie could hear his aunt from inside the carriage.

"George! It's you! But you bring death in your wake!"

"Nice to see you as well, Aunt Evelyn." said George.

He handed Sophie down from the carriage, and Duncan followed behind.

"How many have to die each time there is a visitor?" asked Aunt Evelyn lifting her gaze to the heavens.

Sophie looked at George.

"The slugs," he explained pointing at the drive.

It was covered in a smattering of shiny black slugs, some the length of two fat thumbs laid end to end. They were almost cartoonish in appearance, like enormous snails without their shells. Their heads reared up with their eyes balanced on two wavy eye stalks. Several had been unceremoniously squished under the wheels of the carriage.

"Oh," said Sophie.

Aunt Evelyn came over and eyed her up and down.

"Travelling in a carriage with two gentlemen? Not a lady's

Pixies and Politics

maid in sight? But you don't look like that sort of woman at all." She turned to George. "With those sleeves and that collar, she's dressed like a Catholic nun!"

A man's voice suddenly rumbled down from the front steps of the cottage.

"Catholic?! Who's a Catholic?!"

Sophie assumed this man was Uncle St. John. His two green eyes twinkled above a generous allotment of salt-and-pepper whiskers as he trotted down the steps to greet them. She looked to George, but he had his forehead pressed into one palm and a pained look on his face.

"Aunt Evelyn," said George composing himself. "Uncle St. John, may I introduce Lady Sophie Byrd and . . ." He turned to Duncan with a quizzical look on his face.

"Duncan will do," said Duncan.

". . . and our good friend Duncan," finished George. He proceeded to introduce his aunt and uncle as Mr. and Mrs. Worthington. "We were hoping to impose on you for the better part of the next fortnight," he added.

His aunt and uncle were silent for a moment. They looked at each other and back at George before breaking into the widest, most genuine smiles Sophie had ever seen. Uncle St. John clapped George on the back and shook Duncan's hand vigorously. And Aunt Evelyn took Sophie's two hands in hers.

"Sophie is to be my wife," said George, "but the situation is . . . complex."

"A wedding! But that is marvellous! You can explain it all over tea and crumpets," said Aunt Evelyn linking arms with Sophie. She leaned in. "I will lend you a lady's maid while you are here. And if you'd like something more fashionable to wear, you can take a look through my closet. But first, we

A Baron's Son is Undone

must say a small prayer for the slugs."

Sophie was having a hard time containing her amusement. She would be happy to pray for the slugs and eat crumpets although she was not entirely certain she wanted Aunt Evelyn as her dresser.

"I've not got anything against Catholics, mind you," she heard Uncle St. John confiding in Duncan as they walked to the front door. "I'd simply like to know if one is staying in my house."

"It stands to reason," said Duncan with a straight face.

Uncle St. John halted mid-stride.

"Yes, it *does* stand to reason, doesn't it?" he said wonderingly, as if no one had ever agreed with him before.

George explained the situation over tea as they sat around a low table in the drawing room. Duncan, of course, refused to sit. He stood to the side and just behind Sophie's place on the settee. Unfortunately, he was within easy reach of Uncle St. John who was seated kitty-corner to Sophie in an upholstered wooden chair whose legs splayed outward in a demonstration of stability and elegance. As George had predicted, his relatives were less concerned about the scandal involved and more than thrilled to simply have visitors in their home. Aunt Evelyn kept interrupting the story to offer George a different flavour of jam, and Uncle St. John appeared to barely be listening as he engaged Duncan in a parallel conversation about the "jolly sharp knife" Duncan was carrying at his side.

When George had finally finished his tale, Uncle St. John surprised them all by summing it up in one succinct sentence: "So you're all in hiding until the wedding which happens in about two weeks' time—excellent!" He turned to Sophie.

Pixies and Politics

"Welcome to the family, my dear. We will treasure you as I'm sure George does already."

Sophie felt her face heat and was relieved when Uncle St. John turned his attention to Duncan.

"And you are the hired guard gone rogue!" He laughed heartily. "Welcome, welcome, one and all. We shall have a merry time of it until the nuptials."

Aunt Evelyn clapped her hands with genuine joy.

Most people did not take to Uncle St. John and Aunt Evelyn in quite the same way that Sophie did. George watched her indulge his aunt in the most ludicrous conversations about trifle and slugs and the merits of encouraging a garden to grow wild.

"You'll not find any pixies in a manicured garden," said Sophie to his aunt as they walked arm-in-arm through the long grass at the back of the cottage. "They find order offensive."

"Indeed!" replied Aunt Evelyn. "Though I'm not entirely certain I want to attract pixies exactly. They can be terribly mischievous."

"Only if you don't feed them," replied Sophie without missing a beat. "If you leave a saucer of milk out the back door every so often, they will be quite content."

George found himself grinning as he strolled behind them with Uncle St. John at his side. St. John was harping on about Bonaparte once more.

"Left the whole place in a shambles," he said. "Europe, I'm talking about. They'll want to set things to rights."

A Baron's Son is Undone

"That is what the congress is for," said George.

"Eh?"

"In Vienna. Next month. Perhaps the month after."

"Bloody good," said Uncle St. John. "As long as those Austrians and Russians keep their sticky fingers to themselves."

"I have a feeling everyone shall be arriving with sticky fingers," said George. "It's the way of these things."

"So long as there is order," said his uncle.

"Someone's idea of order, anyway," said George almost to himself.

Sophie and Aunt Evelyn had stopped to admire a particularly rambling and thorny rose bush bursting with tiny white blooms. As he and his uncle stepped up to the women, Sophie turned her head towards them.

"If the powers that be do not contend with the forces that helped them win the war against Bonaparte, they will find themselves dealing with several rebellions in the near future," she said.

George found his mouth dropping open in surprise.

"You're collecting flies, my dear," said Aunt Evelyn, tapping him on the jaw.

"What do you mean by that?" asked Uncle St. John.

"His mouth is open," responded Aunt Evelyn.

"I was talking to Sophie," said Uncle St. John.

"National sentiments," replied Sophie reaching out to pluck a snowy rose from the bush. "We defeated Bonaparte with the help of several peoples, all of whom share a love and devotion for their common history and culture and land. They will want what is due to them, and if they do not get it as a settlement through the congress, they will eventually rebel. They will fight for it. There will be more violence."

Pixies and Politics

Uncle St. John looked at George.

"Are you hearing this, son?"

"Yes," said George as he watched Sophie lift the white rose to her nose to inhale its perfume. She looked like any other lady might in an English garden, but she was not any other lady. Not by a mile.

He felt suddenly abashed. Not two seconds ago, he had been admiring the way she could talk nonsense with his aunt, but it had not occurred to him that she could do so while harbouring an intellect the match of any man's. She would not simply be a comfort to him in his life, a person to have fun with and care for, she would also be someone he could come to for advice. He would be able to talk to her about anything. She was his . . . The word he was looking for seemed to be hiding somewhere in the dark recesses of his heart, somewhere behind a high wall of pride and manliness and duty. He struggled to find it, but as he watched his lovely bride turn her face to the sun, he managed to put a hand on the word he was looking for. He wrestled it out into the open where he could get a good look at it, and when he did so, it was with some surprise.

She was his *equal*!

Sophie stepped up to him and pressed the small rose into the lapel of his grey jacket.

"You look quite fine decked out in flowers," she said. "I could make you a crown."

Aunt Evelyn and Uncle St. John laughed.

"You should have seen him when he was a boy," said Aunt Evelyn. "Always picking daisies and playing with the girls."

George was too entranced with his bride to give his aunt the warning glare she deserved.

When they returned to the cottage, Aunt Evelyn whisked

A Baron's Son is Undone

Sophie away on a tour. George came upon her later in the day as he emerged from the drawing room. She was alone at the end of the hallway and unaware of his presence. He watched her step up to a large oval mirror that was hanging on the wall. (Aunt Evelyn always said that mirrors made the cottage seem larger.) He watched Sophie regard herself in the mirror, a sad expression settling over her features. She tugged at the cuff of one long sleeve and then raised her hand to the high collar just beneath her chin. From his distance down the hall, he couldn't hear her sigh, but he could see her chest heave up and then drop down. When she turned from the mirror, she was startled to see him watching her.

She fixed a smile on her face that seemed almost genuine.

"Your uncle and aunt have been ever so welcoming," she said as George approached her. "Duncan has been given a room near the servants' quarters so that he can recover properly. There's a maid who has changed his bandages and will not stop fussing over him. I think he quite likes the attention."

George reached for her hand.

"Is everything all right?"

"Of course," said Sophie.

"You can talk to me about anything," said George. "If there's something that is bothering you . . ."

Sophie looked into his eyes, and it felt as though she were searching there for something. Whatever it was, he would give it to her if only she asked.

"Thank you for everything," she said looking down towards her feet.

"Sophie," said George lifting her chin. "You mustn't thank me for anything. I'm the one who is grateful. You have absolutely no idea."

Pixies and Politics

She said nothing but reached out and adjusted the rose in his lapel.

Eleven

Intimate Thoughts

After a long day and an even longer dinner with his aunt and uncle, George made his way along the darkened hall with a candle to Sophie's room. The very notion that she might not be entirely happy, that she might be troubled, set him on edge in a way he could never have anticipated. After their little talk by the mirror in the hall, he found himself so disconcerted by the manner in which Sophie had brushed away his concerns that he could barely engage with his relatives for the remainder of the day. What he wanted was to know her every thought and fear and love. It was more than a want, it was a need he felt so keenly, he thought he might die if it was not sated. He needed to know her—truly know her the way one naked soul might know another. He wondered if that was even possible. Can one person truly come to know another? How else would he be able to take care of her? It hurt him to think that though they might be together, she suffered in some ways alone.

Sophie opened her bedchamber door just as he stepped up to it. As always, she was a vision in her white night dress with her dark hair tumbling down over her shoulders. George examined her face by the light of the candle. She seemed relaxed, and this caused some of his tension to ebb.

"I thought you wouldn't come," she said.

"I was waylaid by Uncle St. John and his cigar collection. I'm sorry if I smell a bit."

Sophie laughed, and his heart lifted. Perhaps everything *was* all right.

As he stepped through the door, she said, "I've never prayed for a slug before."

"We've all had to pray for them at one time or another," said George with a smile as he put his candle down on a table and looked around the room. "Aunt Evelyn gave you the blue room. That means she likes you."

"Does it?" asked Sophie looking around. "I suppose it is quite a nice room."

"Uncle St. John thinks you are too beautiful and too clever and too kind for such an undeserving man as myself. He made that clear over cigars."

"Do your relatives not read the gossip sheets?" asked Sophie. An edge had crept into her voice.

"No," said George. "They are not much for the ton and its games. They would much rather live contentedly here in Cornwall with their garden full of pixies."

"George," said Sophie sitting down on the bed. Her tone had now changed in a way that shifted all his nerves to high alert. The good humour had faded from her face. Everything was *not* all right.

A Baron's Son is Undone

"Yes," he said carefully. He wasn't certain if he should sit down beside her just yet.

"Do you think I dress like a Catholic nun?"

Was that all she was worried about? He relaxed ever so slightly.

"I don't care how you dress," said George because it was the truth.

"You don't?"

"Not a whit," said George. "It's all just costume, remember? I only care for the shining soul beneath it all."

"Truly?" asked Sophie, sounding relieved but still looking pensive. She looked down at her lap where her hands were clasped nervously together. "I hadn't thought about it properly before, but I suppose I changed how I dressed after . . . after all the bother with the gossip sheets. The way they wrote about me, it made me feel as if it had all been somehow my fault. And maybe it was. Maybe I lured that man to his death."

"What?! No!" George quickly sat beside her and took her shoulders in his hands. "Sophie, listen to me carefully. None of that was your fault. And it certainly had nothing to do with how you were dressed."

"It's just . . ." said Sophie. "I feel ashamed of it all. Father wouldn't even look at me after it happened."

George felt suddenly out of his depth. She felt at fault. It made him so angry he could barely think straight.

"Listen to me, Sophie," he said releasing her shoulders and running both hands through his hair in an effort to calm himself. "You have nothing to be ashamed of. You are an angel, and any man would count himself lucky to be given the opportunity to worship at your feet." He took her face gently in both hands. "Do you understand me?"

She nodded quietly, her face still in his hands.

Intimate Thoughts

"But I'm also ashamed of my thoughts," she said. "I'm not the angel you think I am."

"What thoughts?" asked George.

Her face grew red in his hands.

"Thoughts about me?" he asked, hope rising like a warm tide in his chest.

She nodded.

"Those are nothing to be ashamed of," said George. "I have similar thoughts about you."

"You do?"

"These days, I find it hard to concentrate on anything else," said George with a smile.

Her face softened, and she took his hand.

"They're ever so wicked," she said looking up at him from under her lashes. "Sometimes I'm shocked by the workings of my own mind. It seems somehow wrong."

George shook his head and laughed. He pulled her into an embrace.

"I'm to be your husband," he said. "Whatever your thoughts, you can tell them to me. And they're not wicked—they're intimate, Sophie. These are intimate thoughts. I should be honoured to be the object of your attentions."

George was holding Sophie to him, and she gently rubbed the side of her face against his. He could feel her inhale the scent of his skin just in front of his ear. She pressed herself to him and simply allowed herself to be held quietly for several minutes. George schooled every impulse in his body, allowing her the opportunity to make the first move . . . or not. He could wait.

Sophie eventually broke the silence.

"One recurring thought," she said in a low hesitant murmur

A Baron's Son is Undone

by his ear, "is that we wear entirely too many clothes to bed."

This was happening fast. George tried to slow the pounding of his heart. He could already feel his cock rising to the occasion.

"I have thought as much myself," whispered George.

Sophie pulled away from him and proceeded to unbutton the front of her nightdress. She worked her way methodically down the buttons one by one until her dress fell open to reveal the plump swell of her breasts, the shadow between them. She pulled her dress first from one shoulder and then the other until it pooled at her waist, but she didn't meet his eyes. She was gazing down at her lap.

"Sophie," whispered George.

"I should like to feel your skin on mine," she said shyly, "so that there is nothing between us."

George pulled his shirt up over his head.

"Your wish is my command," he said, and saying the words, he realised they were true and would be so for the rest of his life.

She reached for him, and as she did so, he reached for her as well. His heart was racing, and his mind was practically blank, his brain having sent all its blood down to his groin. He struggled to regain control of himself. This would be no rough and urgent coupling, no matter how welcoming she appeared. He was here to worship her, and he would do just that.

"Let me touch you first," she said, stroking her fingers down from his collar bone and over his chest.

Good Lord.

It was an unexpected request, but he could understand it. She needed to be the one in control right now. George shifted

Intimate Thoughts

himself to lie down on the bed so that she had the full run of his body. She was seated beside him, and he gazed longingly at her breasts in the candlelight, the sweet curve of her belly.

"Can I tell you another thought?" she asked as she stroked the hair of his chest.

George nodded. His cock was now straining at his trousers uncomfortably.

"Every morning, you wake with your member as it is now, quite enlarged and pressing into me from behind."

"It's involuntary," said George apologetically.

"Do you remember that night you held me in your lap?" she asked. "When I . . .?"

"How could I not?" said George. He had to close his eyes as her fingers swirled around one of his nipples and then down to the waistband of his trousers.

"Every morning, I have the urge to rub myself against you, against your swollen member in that same way, but it feels so wanton, I worry what you would think of me if I did."

"I would think nothing beyond how grateful I am that you would seek your pleasure from me," said George hoarsely.

"Can I see the rest of you?" asked Sophie looking to his trousers. "I should think we're still wearing too many clothes."

George felt entirely unprepared for how the evening was unravelling. It was one thing to kiss a woman, to fondle her breasts, and press his cock up into her. It was quite another to do what they were doing now. This slow exploration, the way she was sharing herself with him, the exquisitely raw connection that was forming—this was something else entirely.

To his surprise, Sophie stood from the bed and allowed her nightdress to fall in a white muslin puddle at her feet. George

A Baron's Son is Undone

took a shuddering breath as he drank in her glorious body with his eyes. Her black wavy hair fell over her shoulders to brush up against her tight little nipples. He shook his head slowly as if to ward off whatever it was that was happening to him. He quietly prayed for mercy though he suspected the Good Lord was not about to grant it in this particular instance. He sat up and swung his feet over the bed to unbutton the fall of his trousers.

"Let me," she said, kneeling down in front of him.

Holy hell! He might spend himself right now as she worked her way down his buttons. *Sad puppies*, thought George. *Sad fucking puppies.* It wasn't working. As his cock sprang free of his trousers, she let out a small gasp that made him feel completely deranged with longing. He had to close his eyes once more as her butterfly fingers drifted softly over his erection. She held it so lightly, he thought he might die of the need that was threatening to drown him.

"Does this feel nice?" she asked stroking him gently down and then up again.

"Mmm."

George looked up to the ceiling, then back down at the naked woman kneeling in front of him.

"Sophie," he whispered.

"Can I lie beside you?" she asked standing.

George stood shakily and dropped his trousers to the floor, then joined her in the bed. She wriggled herself up against him and groaned softly into the curve of his neck. It took all his willpower to remain impassive, to let her touch him without touching her in return. He was suffering but in the best possible way.

"I like it when there's nothing at all between us," she said reaching down to hold his cock once more.

Heaven help me, he thought.

This time she gripped him more firmly, and George rocked his hips forward instinctively. She leaned in for a kiss, and it was the warmest, most delicious and arousing kiss of his life. He pressed his tongue into her mouth, and she actually closed her lips around it and sucked. With her hand on his cock and her sucking on his tongue, George knew he was lost. Too soon, she pulled her beautiful face from his. Her hot hand continued to slide slowly up and down his erection as she spoke.

"My first shocking thought," she said huskily, "happened when we were sitting in the tavern after your fight with Tom. You were all sweaty and your chest was smeared with blood that must have dripped down from your mouth."

She looked at him, and he could see the naked desire in her eyes. George was holding it together, but only just.

"I had the sudden urge to drag my tongue up your chest to lick you clean."

She leaned in to give his neck a lick, and George's heart began thrashing itself against his ribs while her hand continued its rhythmic movement over his erection which was now exceptionally wet. He could hardly believe it when she shimmied a little further down to nuzzle her face against his chest. As her little pink tongue reached out to taste his nipple, George felt his entire body seize. He heard himself make a low guttural sound he had never made before as he spent himself in pulsing waves up and over her fist. She watched with a look of fascination as his seed spilled down the side of her hand.

"I'm so sorry," he said rolling into her and pressing his lips

A Baron's Son is Undone

to her brow.

"Why?" she asked quite innocently, reaching for a handkerchief on the bedside table and wiping her hand, then him. "I liked it."

"You did?"

"Mmm," she said smiling as she mimicked the noise he habitually made. "Somehow, it doesn't feel shameful with you. It feels . . . You make me feel . . . I don't know . . . It just seems free of pretence, as if we're completely exposing ourselves to one another. I thought it would be a frightening thing, but it's not with you."

George's heart ached to hear her words. He pulled her to him and held her in a fierce embrace. She laughed, and he could sense the ripple of that laughter through his own body and down into his soul. It was a balm for all his worry, his hurt and anguish, and he could not understand how he had managed to live without it all these years.

Sophie felt euphoric as she wallowed in the power of the moment. It was all hers. And he was hers. She could see that clearly now.

Intimate.

He had given her the perfect word to describe her thoughts, her urges, her actions. *How one's entire perspective could shift with one simple word!* She kissed him hard on the mouth—a thank you.

"I think I've been a good boy," said George playfully when she released him from the kiss. "I submitted to your touch—an arduous feat, if I do say so myself. Could it be my turn to

Intimate Thoughts

pleasure you now?"

His eyes twinkled with a brilliance she had not seen in them before. Sophie took a deep breath. She was already swollen between her legs. She could feel the weight and the heat of it. But she wasn't ready for . . . *Could he even do it after that?*

"How will you pleasure me?" she asked quietly.

She could see him register her concern.

"With my hands," he said. "Gently," he added. Then, "I could be persuaded to use my mouth."

There was a mischievous flicker in his eye as he let those words land.

"Your mouth?!"

"Mm," responded George with a smile. "Mmm."

Sophie laughed. "You're being . . . You don't mean . . . ?"

"What don't I mean?" chuckled George stroking a finger up over the curve of her belly and skimming his palm over one breast.

Sophie liked the way he was playing with her.

"And how exactly could you be persuaded to do this?" she asked a little breathlessly as she arched her breast up into his hand.

"I would want you to beseech me," said George wickedly. His expression was devastatingly serious. "You would have to plead. At the very least, you would be required to say the word 'please'."

"I would never lower myself in that way," she replied disingenuously, for she quite expected she would do so with some enthusiasm. It was only a matter of how long she could hold out before giving in. As games went, she felt this was a good one—even if you lost, you won!

"I suppose time will tell," said George in a teasing tone. "Do

A Baron's Son is Undone

I have your permission?"

Sophie nodded.

He rose up and placed one knee between her legs. She stared at his member which, while no longer fully erect, was still somewhat swollen with lust. Then she looked to his dark eyes. They gazed at each other for a few seconds before George lowered his lips to hers, and her arms came around him. This time, he was the one in control, and he wielded his power well. His lips pressed in gently at first, then more urgently as he swept her mouth with his sweet silken tongue. As he did so, he moved his thigh deeper into the space between her legs until she could feel the crisp hairs of his leg against her soft flesh. Instinctively, she rubbed herself up against his leg, and the aching need within her expanded rapidly as he kissed her mind into oblivion. Just when Sophie found herself becoming breathless as her body rocked frantically against him with desire, he pulled his leg away gently. She shimmied herself desperately towards him, but he retreated, just out of reach. Sophie's frantic craving for his touch between her legs sent her practically blind. For a moment, she couldn't tell which way was up.

"Not yet, my petal," he said as he slipped down her body to kiss her neck, her chest. He licked his way up from the base of one breast until his mouth rested over her nipple.

"Ah, oh . . ." Sophie was momentarily distracted by the way he worked his mouth against one breast while he rolled her other nipple into a tight bud between his fingers. She squirmed.

"Oh, George . . ."

He made a low sound deep in his throat when he heard her say his name.

Intimate Thoughts

As he lifted his face to look into her eyes, Sophie felt his fingers reach down between her legs. Gently, gently, he parted her to find that special place where all sensation is gathered to a peak.

"Tell me if this is all right," he said seriously.

Sophie's lips were parted, but she had a moment where she thought she might not be physically able to speak.

Finally, she said, "Yes. I like it," and was immediately struck by how poorly the words described what she was feeling.

"Only 'like'?" asked George mischievously as he swept his fingers methodically over her sensitive bud of pleasure. She writhed beneath him, panting and clutching at his biceps.

When Sophie finally gathered up the words to respond, she did so with a sense of triumphant satisfaction: "It's nothing to write home about," she sputtered before a moan broke free of her lips.

George laughed and buried his face into the side of her neck. He licked his way up her ear and then kissed her hungrily on the mouth. His fingers were persistent as he lifted his face from hers.

"Say my name once more," he said.

She shook her head in defiance. She wasn't even sure she could form coherent words again while he was manoeuvring his fingers against her in that delicious rhythm.

"Say it," he commanded.

"George," she whispered as she wriggled against his touch.

When she spoke his name, his grey eyes flared to black. Sophie herself was nearly at her limit, but just as previously, he sensed this and pulled his hand from between her legs. She let loose an involuntary whimper when he did so.

"You're a terrible man," she said with a laugh.

A Baron's Son is Undone

"Mr. Shitter," he responded. He smiled seductively, and she could feel herself blooming again between her thighs. "I think I'm about to win this little game, my angel."

He slid his way down the entire length of her until he was sitting at the base of the bed. She couldn't believe it when he lifted her ankle in one hand and kissed the arch of her foot. He then slid his tongue along her ankle. The sensation was excruciating. Soft wet kisses were scattered up her calf as he made his way to her knee which he bit ever so gently. Sophie's breath started coming hard as he licked his way up the inside of her thigh until his face hovered in front of her sex. She could feel his breath on her. The incongruity of the situation, the sheer inappropriate arrangement of their persons was enough to squeeze a small cry from her throat.

She felt him slip a finger slowly inside her, and her body tightened around it, trying to draw it in deeper. Sophie clutched at the bedsheets and arched her back.

"You have the prettiest, tightest little flower in the whole fucking world," he said hoarsely.

His indecent words nipped at her arousal, sending it to new heights.

"George," she whimpered. "Please, please, George, I need . . ."

With his finger still inside her, he plunged his face between her legs, and she could feel him sniffing and lapping at her like a ravenous animal.

Mercy.

Sophie dug her fingers into the mattress. She arched her back and tossed her head, whimpering and pleading with him not to stop as the sensation built itself up into a fevered crescendo. As George continued to lick and suck hungrily

Intimate Thoughts

between Sophie's legs, she could feel him pressing her thighs further apart with his free hand. This had the effect of heightening every sensation so that she was sent over the edge screaming and writhing against his face with uninhibited abandon. As she shuddered to stillness, he slid up beside her.

He was flushed from face to chest, his golden hair was completely dishevelled, and she noticed his member was as hard as steel once more.

"Well," said George. "It's a good thing your room is at the back of the house."

Sophie placed a hand over her mouth.

"Was I terribly loud?"

George laughed, and she smacked him playfully on the arm.

"You really are horrible," she said with a smile.

"Sophie," said George, his face suddenly serious. "That was . . . I mean, all of it . . . You are . . ." He shook his head. "It was the most intimate experience of my life."

George lay down beside her and pulled her tightly against him. As he held her, Sophie's breath came softer and softer, and her heart rate slowed to a leisurely, languid pace. She felt so thoroughly at ease after her amorous undertaking with George, as if like a serpent, she had finally shed a skin that was ragged and old and much too tight for her wonderful new body.

Twelve

All of You

~~~~~~~~~~

Sophie floated through the next day on a cloud of contentment. It didn't matter what she was doing—drinking tea or tending to Duncan or walking in the garden—it all gave her the same delicious sensation, as if she were pressing a fork into the softest, fluffiest piece of cake knowing full well there was more to come. As the day rolled on, however, she found there were matters that would interfere significantly with the eating of said cake.

"You two seem to suit," said Aunt Evelyn out of the blue.

It was late afternoon. Sophie and the older lady had been seated in the eclectic drawing room sewing yellow-and-pink bunting for what Aunt Evelyn referred to as "the next celebratory occasion at the cottage".

"Yes," said Sophie biting her lip. It was a reflex, and she immediately wished she hadn't.

"George can't take his eyes off you when he's in the room,"

said Aunt Evelyn. "He's smiling from ear to ear all day, a bit like a madman."

Sophie could feel her face warm.

"Oh, I did not mean to embarrass you," said Aunt Evelyn quickly. "It's just . . . well . . . it's George! No one would have guessed . . . I mean, it's such a surprise . . . He seems so changed. So happy! I occasionally wonder if you are in fact a real woman of flesh and blood or simply an illusion brought on by malevolent pixies. You see, I haven't been leaving any milk for them at all! I had no idea they needed feeding."

Sophie laughed.

"I assure you, I am quite real," she said. "And I doubt very much that I have affected more change in George than he has in me."

Aunt Evelyn dropped the bunting in her lap to press a hand to her heart.

Sophie thought this might be a good time to address a certain necessary situation that had come to light an hour or so earlier.

"Aunt Evelyn," she said, lowering her voice and leaning forward. "Could I ask you . . . ? That is, I find myself in the midst of a monthly condition for which I am unprepared." She hoped George's aunt would take her meaning.

Aunt Evelyn looked at her quizzically before her eyes lit with understanding.

"Ah," she said. "Of course, of course. No need to beat around the bush with me, my dear. I've not been afflicted in that particular manner for a few years now, but I'm sure the maids can sort some supplies for you. I will have them delivered to your room posthaste."

Sophie heaved a sigh of relief and leaned back in her chair.

A Baron's Son is Undone

"Thank you. That is very kind."

Aunt Evelyn waved off her thanks with a hand before looking towards the door of the drawing room. George had entered with his uncle in tow, and Sophie felt her entire being lift as if she had been swept up and tossed gently into the air. He was wearing a dark green jacket, his cravat was somewhat loosened, and he must have recently run his fingers through his hair since it was standing impishly on end. His eyes met hers, and she could only vaguely make out Uncle St. John saying something about Bonaparte followed closely by something about national sentiments. Sophie recognised her own words being repeated, but she was still looking at George *(Good Heavens—she couldn't look away!)*.

"What do you think, Sophie?" asked Uncle St. John.

"Um, oh . . ."

"Whose national sentiments should we be taking more seriously?" he clarified.

Sophie couldn't look away from George.

"The Belgians," she answered. "The Italians, the Polish."

"Ah, yes, of course!" Uncle St. John sounded satisfied. He gave George a whack on the back. "She's a corker, isn't she?" he said. "A blooming corker just like mine."

"Oh, St. John!" said Aunt Evelyn. Sophie didn't look, but she imagined George's aunt was clutching at her heart once more.

And then George did something she could never have anticipated. He stepped up to her chair, took her hand, and kissed her fingers in the middle of the drawing room in front of his aunt and uncle. It was a fairly warm and wet kiss as far as hand-kissing went, and Sophie felt herself flushing in one grand sweep from head to toe.

All of You

"I think," said Aunt Evelyn, "that we have occupied the bride and groom quite thoroughly today. I imagine they should like some time on their own."

She put down her bunting and needle and thread and gave Uncle St. John a look as she lifted her chin towards the door.

"Oh, er, yes," said Uncle St. John. "Would you join me for a stroll down to the lower field, my darling?" He offered his arm to his wife.

"Yes," said Aunt Evelyn eyeing Sophie, "I just need a small word with one of the maids first."

They left George and Sophie alone in the drawing room with the door standing decorously ajar. Alone, but not inappropriately so. George was still holding Sophie's hand. When he registered that they were finally by themselves, he dropped to his knees beside her chair.

"Well, don't do that!" said Sophie taken aback. "It's rather much, don't you think?"

"I don't think," said George with a slow smile. "Shall I touch my head to the floor by your feet?"

"Don't be ridiculous!" laughed Sophie. She stood and pulled him up with her.

"So . . . my corker," smiled George. "We have the remainder of the afternoon. What would you like to do?"

"A game?" asked Sophie.

George's eyebrows lifted.

"Not that sort of game," said Sophie, glancing to the open door. "I was thinking chess or cards or—"

"Spillikins?" asked George.

"I haven't played that since I was a child," said Sophie.

"You used to play on your own," said George looking at her carefully.

169

A Baron's Son is Undone

Sophie looked up at him sharply. *How did he know that?*

"Duncan told me," said George.

Sophie pressed her lips together. She didn't like the idea of Duncan sharing her past with George. Mainly because it was somewhat sad, and she did not want to be pitied.

"Your uncle has a lovely chess set," said Sophie turning and walking to a small table at the side of the room where a chessboard was set up—two tiny armies holding their breath, waiting for orders to march.

"Mmm," said George as he watched her step slowly over to the table.

Sophie sensed him behind her before she could turn. She hesitated, closed her eyes. Then his arm was around her waist, pulling her until her back was flush with his chest.

"Are you going to make me play chess instead of kiss you?" asked George in a low murmur at her ear.

Sophie had to muster every shred of willpower at her disposal to respond.

"Yes, that's right," she whispered.

He pressed his face to her hair and inhaled deeply before finally releasing her.

As Sophie sat down at the chess table, she realised that she would have to tell George about her temporary condition or else he would come to her room later that night expecting another round of intimate activities. Uncertain how to broach the subject—it had been difficult enough with Aunt Evelyn—she instead insisted he start the game as white.

Pawn to king bishop four. She matched him with her opposing pawn. A knight came out, another pawn. They struggled quietly for control of the centre of the board.

"My sister Grace will be only too pleased to play any game

you like," said George.

"Truly?" asked Sophie. She had never had someone small to entertain before, but she imagined she might be quite good at it.

"But you must not let her win. She is altogether too confident in her abilities as it is."

"I would never pretend to lose!" said Sophie.

"You say that now, but when you see her little face all scrunched up in disappointment, you will be sorely tempted."

Sophie laughed.

"Have *you* ever let her win at a game?" she asked.

George paused before sliding one of his bishops out to guard his knight.

"When she was small," said George. "I could never have anticipated how insufferable a four-year-old could be after winning a game of snakes and ladders." He grinned up at Sophie. "Never again."

"And what about your sister Patience? She is closer to you in age, is she not? Have you ever let her win a game?"

"Absolutely not!" said George as he took one of Sophie's pawns. "It would never even cross my mind to do so."

"Why?" asked Sophie laughing.

"Because she is my arch nemesis," said George with a straight face, though Sophie could see the twinkle in his eye and the twitch at the corner of his mouth. "Always has been." He placed her captive pawn on the table behind one of his rooks. "Patience is very argumentative," he added. "Stubborn, reckless, incredibly talented with a paintbrush."

Sophie wondered what it would be like to have a sister like that. She saw beyond George's words to the truth. He loved Patience. She must have been his playmate, his competitor,

A Baron's Son is Undone

and eventually, to some degree, his responsibility. He clearly held her in high regard.

"I'm sorry, but she'll be your sister now too," he said with a wry smile.

"I hope I won't disappoint," said Sophie. "I've had no practice as a sister."

She slid her queen along the board.

"Check," she said.

When she looked up, George was gazing at her.

"You could never disappoint, Sophie."

"Oh, I don't know," she said. "I have a feeling you'll be disappointed tonight." *Just tell him. It's not that hard.*

"What does that mean?"

Sophie had never discussed the subject with a man, so it took her a moment to get the words out.

"My courses have come. They are quite heavy." She cringed as she heard herself say the words. "You will want to sleep in your own bedchamber for the next five days or so as it can be a bit of a mess."

She looked to his face to judge his reaction. She knew he would be disappointed, but she had not expected him to be . . . angry. *Why was he angry?*

There was steel in his eyes where before there had been smoke, and Sophie felt exposed and examined in a way she had not previously. George shifted his gaze to the chessboard. He didn't make a move to block her check but instead began slowly lining up all the white pawns down the left side of the board, gently knocking other pieces out of the way as he did so. He seemed deep in thought.

"Well?" said Sophie finally. "Are you going to say something?"

All of You

George looked up at her.

"No," he said.

A footman arrived with a tray of tea things and set it down on a table. Since George's behaviour was unnerving her, Sophie took the opportunity to get up and do something else. She poured two cups of tea.

"Will you not come and sit with me?" she asked George from across the room.

He stood and came over, sat across from her, and accepted his cup of tea. He sipped it gingerly as he stared at her over the rim. They drank their tea in silence, and when George finally drained his cup, he placed it and its saucer on the table with a clink. He leaned back on the settee.

"Why should I care?" he asked.

"Excuse me?"

"Why should I care if there is a mess?"

"Oh!" Sophie was taken by surprise. "I only assumed . . . I thought any man would not . . ." She sighed, not knowing how to continue.

"It would be *intimate*," said George, leaning forward and resting his elbows on his knees. "To know you like that."

"It's unpleasant," said Sophie. "Such a bother." She couldn't meet his eyes. Instead, she rearranged the tea things on the tray.

"It's part of you," said George. "I wouldn't be disappointed with the situation if you gave me permission to sleep in your bed the next few nights. Unless, of course, I am imposing on your privacy."

A Baron's Son is Undone

George held his breath. *Did wives usually sequester themselves in a separate bedchamber during their courses?* He didn't know, and he didn't care. All he knew was that when Sophie suggested he sleep without her, he felt it like a solid punch to the gut.

He wanted her in the most selfish way possible. All of her. He wanted her body and her thoughts, her dreams and her every heartache. He wanted her smiles and her tears, her jests and her censure. He wanted every variation of her there was to have. He would collect it all up and clutch it to his breast like a greedy magpie. It hurt him to think that she would not understand this, that there were some aspects of her experience she would keep to herself.

"It can be messy," she said. "Especially at night."

"I want your mess," said George. He leaned forward and took her hand.

Tell her.

"I want all of you, Sophie. Not just the pleasant bits, the pieces you put out for show. You may not have noticed this yet, but I'm a greedy man."

Her face slowly cracked into a hesitant smile which caused his heart to unfurl like a summer rose.

George took it upon himself to make Sophie's decision worth her while. She seemed to think he would want a physical intimacy that she could not properly give him, and sweet mercy, he did, but he wanted more as well. Over the next few days, he offered her something new each night. He massaged her feet as she laughed and squirmed and bit her plump bottom lip. Pressing his thumb into the pad of each toe, he couldn't help himself—he had to bring them to his mouth and kiss each and every one.

"George!"

All of You

"Don't distract me," he said as seriously as he could, "I'm working."

Her laughter made him feel as if Heaven might not have much to offer in comparison.

The next night, he read to her. Aunt Evelyn liked to keep abreast of the latest novels, and Jane Austen's *Pride and Prejudice* had only just been published the year before. Bare-chested, George propped himself up against some pillows at the headboard, and Sophie snuggled into his side.

"It is a truth universally acknowledged, that a single man in possession of a good fortune, must be in want of a wife," read George.

"Is that what is written, or are you simply making conversation?" asked Sophie chuckling into his side.

"Those are Miss Austen's words," said George peering down at her happy face, her dark tangle of tresses sweeping over the pillow.

"But you are a single man in possession of a good fortune, how is it you have not secured a wife until now?" asked Sophie. Her happy face had dissolved into earnestness.

"Because," said George honestly, "I did not want a wife who only saw me as my fortune, my future title, my name."

"Most men assume that is the currency with which they will attract a wife," said Sophie.

George continued to read: "However little known the feelings or views of such a man may be on his first entering a neighbourhood, this truth is so well fixed in the minds of the surrounding families, that he is considered as the rightful property of some one or other of their daughters."

"Is that what it is like?" she asked.

"Yes," said George. "It is understandable, for all parents

A Baron's Son is Undone

want their daughters to marry well, but it makes it no less exhausting for the gentleman in question. It is impossible to determine whether a lady's proffered affections are true or simply a costume designed to secure her future."

"Do you think mine are true?" asked Sophie looking up at him, her dark amber eyes shining in the lamplight.

"Yes," said George simply.

"Why?"

Because you have seen me as myself. Off the leash. Bloodied in the dirt. And you did not flinch.

He said, "Because fortune hunters tend not to draw pistols on their chosen marks."

Sophie laughed as she shimmied her way up to meet his face. Her mouth was so soft and sweet as she pressed it to his, he felt he might die of the pleasure.

"Sorry," she said pulling away, "I didn't mean to distract from the novel."

Sophie slid herself back down to snuggle in at his side, and he continued to read about Mr. and Mrs. Bennett, their five unwed daughters, and a man named Mr. Bingley in possession of four or five thousand pounds a year. Sophie stroked one hand along his leg, then tossed it across his lap as she curled into him. The golden lamplight, Sophie's laughter and murmured commentary on the story as he read, the warmth of the two of them snuggled under the blue coverlet— George had never known such happiness. He was half-way through chapter three when he realised Sophie had fallen asleep. Placing the book to the side table, he put out the light, and slipped down to lay his head by hers. He gave thanks in the dark as Sophie's soft breath stroked his cheek in a slow and steady rhythm.

All of You

When he awoke the next morning to Sophie's apologies about bloodstains in the bed, he fetched some supplies for her from a drawer and helped her change. Women were quite clever, he decided—belts and cloths and small insertable linens wrapped tightly around smooth short twigs with a length of string for easy removal. That he would know none of this! That Sophie might have kept this all hidden from him like some kind of dirty secret! *It made him feel like a man to have this knowledge. No, it made him feel like a husband—protective, sympathetic, attentive.*

All the while, Duncan had been recuperating his strength and was venturing further from his room near the servants' quarters. George had forgotten what it was like to have the man watching his every move.

"Been talking to the maids," he said one day when he had caught George alone in the back garden.

George stood up from his crouched position. He had gathered a fist full of pink and white columbine and yellow-eyed daisies.

"Maids plural? Or maid singular?" asked George. "I hear there is one in particular who has taken a shine to you. Sophie tells me her name is Angel. How is that even possible?"

Duncan stared at George with open aggression.

"The maids say you have not been sleeping in your room," he said without blinking.

It was George's turn now to return Duncan's combative gaze.

"What do you want me to say?" asked George icily. "I will be marrying Sophie in just over a week."

"You can't just . . ." started Duncan. "She's not . . . She was hurt," he said finally.

A Baron's Son is Undone

"You think I don't know my own bride?! You think I would force myself on her?!"

George was incensed, though at the back of his mind he knew he shouldn't be. They weren't married. He should not be visiting her in her bedchamber.

"Duncan."

George put his free hand to the man's shoulder, and Duncan looked to that hand as if it were a piece of bird shit dropped on him from above. George quickly removed it.

"Duncan," he said again. "She is . . . She is my very breath. She is everything. I have not done and never would do anything to harm her."

"Be that as it may," replied Duncan angrily. "If something happens to you between now and the wedding—you choke and die on a piece of chicken or something—and she ends up with child, it will be the end for her. Hell, *I'll* have to marry her. And she certainly wouldn't want that."

The scar-faced man was red in the face, breathing heavily. Furious.

"She won't be with child," said George with some finality.

Duncan stared at him. George stared back hoping the man would take his meaning, that he wouldn't have to spell it all out for him. *Bloody hell, this was an awkward conversation.*

"And, regardless, I have made preparations for all contingencies," added George.

"You what?" asked Duncan.

"If anything happens to me," said George. "I have made arrangements. You think I take this lightly? That I take my responsibility for Sophie lightly? It's not a game to me, Duncan. I have written to my sister, the Viscountess Winter. If anything happens to me before the wedding, she will make sure that Sophie wants for nothing."

"How do you know your sister would actually do this for you when it came down to it?"

"I know," said George. "There is not a sliver of doubt."

Duncan fondled his knife thoughtfully.

"Stay out of Sophie's room," he said. "You're a good man, Mr. Pemberton, but you must understand that I cannot stand by while you flout the rules. She's under my charge until you are wed."

George looked down at the collection of flowers in his hand. Sophie was not going to like this.

Thirteen

A Man Like Me

"Duncan will not allow it?!" asked Sophie incredulously.

She had become so accustomed to doing as she pleased that the reinsertion of her guard dog's nose into her life was a bit of a shock.

"He's right," said George leaning against the fireplace mantle of the drawing room. "We can wait."

"But . . . but what about the Bennetts?" asked Sophie. "Must I wait an entire week to hear of them again?"

"You could read to yourself," said George with a smile. "Or I could read to you here in the drawing room."

"I don't think so," said Sophie wrapping her arms around herself, trying to contain her disappointment.

"If nothing else," said George advancing on her, "I'm liking how much you dislike our separation."

"Horrible man," threw out Sophie with a shake of her head.

A Man Like Me

She was having a hard time holding back a smile.

George reached for both her hands and kissed each in turn.

"We can survive the week," he said, "and keep Duncan happy. He's done so much for you. For us. And absence, as they say, makes the heart grow fonder."

Sophie furrowed her brow. She knew she could not possibly grow any fonder of this beautiful man.

"If we must," she said.

The next week passed the way time always passes when one is waiting—in excruciatingly slow and mind-numbingly dull increments. Sophie tried her best to distract herself: engaging with Aunt Evelyn to discuss her plans for redecorating the dining room, sewing a plethora of pink-and-yellow bunting, and occasionally slipping out for walks with George.

As the days rolled slowly away, one after another, Sophie realised that she didn't simply *want* George in her bed. She *needed* him there, and it physically hurt her to sleep without him. She felt it as a dull persistent ache in her chest. She craved the intimate time they spent stroking and kissing and laughing and sharing. It certainly wasn't the same in the garden or the drawing room with Aunt Evelyn and Uncle St. John, not to mention a host of servants threatening to interrupt at any moment.

Duncan would make an appearance now and then and give George a respectful nod before disappearing to do who-knew-what. This irritated Sophie more than she wanted to admit. The men making decisions for her. About her. It made her feel prickly and argumentative. She was feeling especially fractious one morning at breakfast after Duncan had peered in to request a word with George once he was finished.

It was a Sunday—the last Sunday the bans would be read.

A Baron's Son is Undone

Aunt Evelyn and Uncle St. John were not at breakfast since they had slept in as they did every Sunday. (Uncle St. John said that the Good Lord would want them to take the opportunity to rest. That was the most important part of Sunday, apparently. Church was optional.)

"When we are wed," asked Sophie, eyeing the back of Duncan as he left the morning room, "will you take decisions on my behalf and tell me what to do?"

"Yes," said George reaching for the butter dish, his face unreadable.

"Yes?!"

"You will be my wife" said George matter-of-factly. "And you will do as you're told."

Sophie was momentarily silenced. She knew she was being petulant because she was annoyed with the sleeping arrangements, but she had not expected him to answer in this way.

George gave her a sideways glance as he buttered his toast.

"Or else," he added.

"You would punish me?"

"Not punish," said George taking a bite of his toast and chewing. He swallowed and fixed her with a serious look. "'Torment' would be a better word."

They stared at each other.

"With my tongue," he added, sliding his sensual mouth into a smile. "So you had better behave, Mrs. Pemberton. I will not countenance a disobedient wife."

Sophie released a puff of breath as heat bloomed between her legs. George leaned forward and poured some tea into her cup from a silver teapot. The woody scent of him wafted over her, and she could feel every pore in her body expanding to breathe him in.

"I will do my best," he said sincerely. "But if I'm being perfectly honest with you, I would have to say it is not my habit to take a census before every decision. If you want your voice heard, I'm afraid you may have to raise it." He placed the teapot back on the table and locked eyes with her.

Sophie didn't know what to say. She had been scolded in a roundabout fashion, but she was not displeased with the way it had been done. And he had not sought to mollify her with false words. All the more reason she desperately wanted this man in her bed. She took a sip of her tea.

"I should like to be part of whatever discussion you will be having with Duncan after breakfast," she said as she took a large bite of muffin slathered in clotted cream.

George paused with his toast half-way to his face.

"Of course," he said looking at her mouth.

Sophie didn't like the way he was smiling at her. Well, actually, she did like it, but she didn't like that she liked it—oh my, she was feeling very frustrated indeed! George did not help matters when he reached his hand to her face and wiped a dollop of cream from the corner of her mouth with his thumb.

"I'm just cleaning you up," he said as he slowly slid his thumb from the corner of her mouth to press it gently between her lips.

What could she do? She sucked the cream from his thumb.

"What's *she* doing here?" asked Duncan when they found him in the kitchen milling about with the maids and the cook.

A Baron's Son is Undone

"I'm part of this conversation," said Sophie trying to stand up a little taller.

Duncan looked to George who shrugged as if the matter had nothing at all to do with him.

"Mrs. Pemberton won't be left out," he said with some amusement.

Duncan led them both through the kitchen door and into the back garden where they could talk away from the prying ears of servants. Sophie thought Duncan looked exceptionally dangerous against the backdrop of the tangled garden. Pink roses climbed a trellis up over his head as purple foxgloves bowed down towards his shins. A fat bee hummed lazily as it flew wobbling past his ear. He waved his hand to shoo it.

"Your father will have sent a man like me," he said to Sophie before glancing at George. "Which means that he will have investigated matters thoroughly."

"But Maddy would have told him we were headed for Scotland," said Sophie.

"If he didn't find a trail leading north, he would have remained here until he could pick up the scent. That's what I would have done. He may not know where we are right now, but if he has found the church in which the bans are being read, he will be waiting for the wedding."

"To kidnap me," said Sophie. She was starting to feel anxious.

"Not sure if it's kidnapping when you belong to his employer," said Duncan quickly. "Arguably, we're the ones doing the kidnapping. Regardless, this man needs to be flushed out and headed off."

"And how do you propose doing that?" asked George as he slid a hand up Sophie's back and gave it a gentle rub.

A Man Like Me

Sophie's body softened against his touch. She felt the warmth of reassurance pass from him to her, through cloth and muscle and bone.

"Simple enough," said Duncan. "A decoy bride. Force the man to show himself, then take him out."

"And by 'take him out', you mean . . . ?" asked George.

"Not kill him!" said Duncan quickly. "Just, you know, maim him or knock him senseless or sit on him until the wedding is over."

"He may not even be there," said George running a hand through his hair.

"I would be," said Duncan. "It's worth planning for just in case."

Sophie looked at Duncan, her faithful guardian. His stern features, the scar dragging his mouth down at one end, the severe shine of his scalp. Freshly shaven. *Who would have done that for him?*

"Who will be the decoy bride?" asked Sophie.

Duncan glanced at George and then quickly looked to Sophie.

"Angel. The maid. She has dark hair like yours, and she is about your height." His voice came out in more of a rasp than usual.

"I couldn't ask her to risk herself like that," said Sophie.

"No risk," replied Duncan, eyeing George. "We are strategising a win."

"Another adventure," said George with a nervous smile. "Let's hope it's all a lot of bother for nothing and that the duke's man is halfway to Gretna Green by now."

Duncan grunted.

A Baron's Son is Undone

George retreated to his bedchamber once Aunt Evelyn was awake and occupying Sophie with yet more bunting. His skin was buzzing with anxious energy, and he needed to calm himself. He stood in the centre of the room and turned slowly, scanning his surroundings and thinking. He moved to the writing desk and adjusted the position of his diary where it lay so that all edges were aligned with the edges of the desk. He slightly shifted the chair that was slid under the desk. The maids had left three cream-coloured towels folded in a pile by the wash basin, but their corners were not aligned properly, so George took three steps in their direction, reached out a hand to straighten them, then thought better of it, and instead knocked the entire pile of towels over into a heap.

Why did he do this? Why did everything need to be lined up? How was this in any way calming? How would it protect him? Protect Sophie?

He sat down on the bed and thought of Sophie. Her head on the pillow, smiling up at him as he read. Her mouth on his, insistent and warm. The feel of her soft skin against him, her fingers trailing up his back. The look in her eyes when she sucked that cream from his thumb. George smiled to himself. Now *this* was calming. He took a breath. Duncan was merely being cautious. Tomorrow would be fine.

"But I was going to lend Sophie my wedding dress!" complained Aunt Evelyn as she sat with a pile of pink-and-yellow bunting in her lap, a needle in her hand. Sophie must have somehow escaped the never-ending bunting task, for she was not in the room.

"Well, now you can lend it to Angel," said George.

"But what will Sophie wear?"

"It hardly matters," said George.

"I think she should wear a pale blue," interrupted Uncle St. John from where he sat in his scroll-armed chair. "It would suit her complexion."

Aunt Evelyn looked to her husband and smiled.

"You're quite right, St. John, and I have just the dress!"

"I know," said Uncle St. John lifting his eyebrows. He turned to George. "We will be coming, of course. You will need witnesses."

"If the duke's man is there, it may be . . . That is, there is a possibility of violence," said George. "I would rather know you are safe and sound at home. Duncan and Angel can act as witnesses."

"For shame!" said Aunt Evelyn shifting the bunting from her lap and standing. "You would not have any family members at your own wedding? Who would give away the bride? Duncan?"

"It would make sense. He did sort of give her to me," said George with a half smile.

"This is the kind of nonsense my brother—your father—would condone, but not I!" said Aunt Evelyn shaking her head. "What would your mother say?"

George thought about what his mother would say. None of it would be good. Patience must have told her by now. He hoped his sister would be able to couch the blow. He also hoped she would be able to talk their mother down off the ceiling. He would have to prepare Sophie for the fact that their reception at home might not be unanimously cordial.

"So in conclusion," said Uncle St. John loudly as he rose

A Baron's Son is Undone

from his chair, "we will *all* be attending the wedding, and that's that! I have a rather threatening walking stick I shall bring along to ward off intruders, interlopers, kidnappers and the like."

His wife smiled sweetly at him.

"And I shall fill my reticule with something heavy," she said.

"Leave the violence to the men, my dear," said Uncle St. John sternly.

Aunt Evelyn cocked her head to one side and then the other.

"Of course. But I shall fill my reticule with whatever I so choose."

She then swept out of the room while calling loudly for Angel who could not possibly hear her because she was in the kitchen.

Uncle St. John looked to George.

"You know *we* don't mind, my boy, but it is quite the scandal, this wedding." He chuckled. "I would never have thought you'd be the one to go full rogue. Patience, maybe. But not you."

George felt a rising discomfort as Uncle St. John quietly studied his face.

"You must love her," said his uncle. "You are not yourself."

Love?!

"I am exactly myself," said George with some irritation.

"Oh ho!" said Uncle St. John. "I have clearly hit a nerve. I do apologise, my boy. Know that your aunt and I, we are always on your side."

"I appreciate that," said George looking to the door.

He felt nauseated, and he was desperate to make an escape before Uncle St. John sought to delve any deeper into the situation. Excusing himself, he walked shakily to the door,

A Man Like Me

down the hall, and out onto the gravel drive in front of the cottage. He paced the drive twice, both hands pulling up at the hair on his head.

Love! He bloody well *loved* Sophie! He could see that now. He loved her so much he felt ill with it. His single-minded devotion to her made complete sense now—it was like a fever that had rendered him blissfully delirious. If he had been smoking opium all day, he would not be able to tell the difference. He was ill, and on top of that, he'd been drugged. This certainly didn't bode well in terms of tidiness and efficiency. But that wasn't what was bothering him. What was bothering him was that Uncle St. John had said it first!

George was up at the crack of dawn the following day. The wedding day. He imagined he was the first person up, but making his way downstairs, he passed by Aunt Evelyn's chamber, and he could hear Sophie's voice from within.

"It's a smidge revealing, don't you think?" she said.

George paused outside the door.

"Nonsense," replied Aunt Evelyn. "It's only because you're used to being buttoned up to your chin."

"The colour is lovely," said Sophie. "Like a pale sky. George took me to a shop once, and the walls were this colour. It was the most magical place."

"Turn around," said Aunt Evelyn.

George knocked at the door. A maid opened it, and he found himself standing and staring at two visions of Sophie dressed in a piece of sky—one was her, and the other was her reflection in a full-length mirror framed in brass. She looked

A Baron's Son is Undone

his way.

"Your Aunt Evelyn says that it is not too revealing," she said tugging at the bodice. "Do you like it?"

George opened his mouth, but he was having trouble forming words. The elegant curve of Sophie's neck, the swell of her breasts, her silken arms were on full display. And she was looking at him with such concern, as if he might not like it.

"Aunt Evelyn, may I have a word alone with my bride?" he asked without taking his eyes from Sophie.

He could hear his aunt sputtering something about Sophie's hair needing to be done, something about leaving the door open, and then she was shuffling past him taking the maid with her.

"If you don't like it," said Sophie, "I can easily wear one of my own. To be honest, I was a bit concerned by your aunt's offer of a dress as she seems to be fond of flounces and frills. But this one is quite plain as you can see." She was looking down and smoothing the skirt.

"Sophie." George stepped into the room.

"Mm." She looked up.

"Sophie."

She smiled. "I'm glad you remember my name."

"Sophie," he said once more taking her hand and pressing it to his chest. "I haven't told you . . . That is . . . you should know . . ."

"George, is everything all right?"

What was wrong with him? Why couldn't he tell her?

For the first time in his life, George understood what it was to be a coward. It was a refusal to test yourself in order to avoid the shame of being found wanting. And Good

A Man Like Me

Lord, there was so much about him that she might find wanting—from his inane and compulsive habits to the single-mindedness that often blinded him to the perspectives of others. *The way he had thought to propose to her! By talking over her head to Duncan! How had he managed to recover from that?*

No. There was enough about him that she liked . . . which was miracle enough. He would not press her into a corner with any declarations of love. This is what he told himself, but shuttered away in a secret compartment of his heart was the knowledge that if Sophie could not honestly return his love, it would destroy him. The devastation would be absolute.

He said, "Sophie, you should know that I will do my best to make you happy."

"Oh," said Sophie. "For a moment there, I thought you were going to say that you didn't like the dress." She laughed somewhat self-consciously.

"I like it," said George stepping back without releasing her hand and slipping his gaze down the length of her and back up to her waiting eyes. He more than liked it.

"Sophie . . . in that dress . . . in any dress . . . you are my sky and my sea, and I am lost in the expanse of perfect blue. You undo me."

That was as close to the truth as he could manage. It would have to do.

Sophie smiled the way she had when he had given her the heart pendant. Genuine surprise and delight lit her face, and George was momentarily ashamed for withholding anything from her.

She stepped in close as her smile fell away to be replaced by a quiet seriousness he found all the more endearing.

"I need you in my bed," said Sophie quietly into his chest.

A Baron's Son is Undone

"It's been a torturous week."

He stroked his knuckles over her bare breast above the neckline of her bodice and took hold of the heart pendant she was wearing even now, lifting it between finger and thumb. He had handed over his heart weeks ago. George let the pendant fall and moved his hand to bury it in her mass of dark hair as he took hold of the back of her head. She clutched roughly at his jacket and pulled him into her.

"George," she whispered. It was a plea.

He gave a shake of his head. The sound of his name on her lips laid waste to everything sensible inside him. He wrestled momentarily with himself as he bent his face next to hers, inhaled the perfume that was her skin. A thrill travelled through him as he felt her breath shudder against his cheek.

"George."

He felt her mouth like an explosion of sensation against his as she crushed herself against him. The way she tasted him with her tongue, the desperate manner in which she gripped at his lapels—she was thick with desire . . . for him! Heavens above, he thought his legs might actually give out!

George rallied himself. It wouldn't do to swoon. He was a man after all.

"Sophie," he said on a gasp. "I'm coming apart rather quickly."

She kissed his neck and stroked one hand up through his hair before settling herself demurely in front of him, a soft smile ghosting her lips.

"All we have to do now," she said, "is get married."

Sophie pressed herself into him once more, and George swelled with pride that this inconceivably brilliant woman could desire him for himself.

A Man Like Me

The carriage was full to bursting with Angel, Sophie, and Aunt Evelyn squeezed on the seat opposite Duncan, George, and Uncle St. John. They were wedged in so tightly, George thought they might need to use St. John's walking stick to pry them loose. Hoisted up into the carriage with Aunt Evelyn was a reticule of purple velvet which appeared to be so heavy it might have been filled with rocks. She had her arms wrapped around it as it rested on her lap.

Duncan had sorted the carriage and driver, but George had his misgivings about the driver who had arrived ill-kempt and seated at a slant with a half-bottle of gin wedged at his feet. When he saw George eyeing his stash, he had said with a lift of his hat and the impudence of someone who had relieved himself of all compunction, "Don't mind my breakfast."

"What the hell, Duncan?" whispered George angrily. "The driver is foxed."

"Not much to do on such short notice," said Duncan apologetically. "It'll be fine."

Inside the carriage, George looked to Sophie who was regarding him with a somewhat apprehensive expression while holding Angel's hand in her lap. The maid had been a surprise all decked out in white and wearing a pretty bonnet decorated with white roses from the garden. She carried a posy of pink roses and white daisies. The perfect decoy bride.

Duncan and George had been waiting by the carriage when she stepped out of the cottage, and George heard Duncan's breath catch when he saw her.

"Lord," he'd said under his breath so quietly George wasn't entirely certain he had heard correctly.

"That's no way to greet my bride this morning," said George stepping forward to take Angel's hand and lend her up into the carriage.

At the top step, she tangled one foot in her gown, and George was forced to catch her before she fell backwards.

"Sorry," she said. "I'm not usually this clumsy."

Duncan shot him an evil look as he took his seat in the carriage. George knew that look. It meant 'hands off'. Well, he didn't want 'hands on', so the look was hardly necessary, though he did grin to himself at the thought that this woman had somehow managed to acquire an unsolicited guard dog.

She looked nothing like Sophie and must have been at least a decade older, but she was the right height with dark hair, and the bonnet would hide her exceptionally pretty face. She was gazing to her own lap, but occasionally she would glance up and catch Duncan's dark eyes with her own pale green. Every time she did so, Duncan would shift uncomfortably in his seat.

"Don't get distracted this morning," said George leaning into Duncan's side.

"For fu—!" Duncan caught himself just in time.

"Now, now," said George with what he assumed was an infuriating grin, "there are ladies present."

Duncan ground down on his teeth and looked out the window. George saw Sophie hide a smile. She was also wearing a bonnet that hid her face from most angles. If the duke's man happened to be there (which was a big 'if'), Sophie's identity would not be apparent.

They arrived at the church before eight o'clock in the morning. There was no one about on the quiet little street except a harried maid carrying a rather large parcel by its string. Duncan dismounted and helped Angel down from the carriage. George followed leaving Sophie, Aunt Evelyn, and

Uncle St. John bringing up the rear. The driver had not even opened the door for them. He had slid down in his seat on the box and tipped his hat over his face as if he were about to take a nap. The bottle of gin was on his lap, now significantly more than half empty.

No point remonstrating with Duncan again, thought George. They were here. They best get on with it.

Just as they were arranging themselves to enter the church, a man stepped out from the corner of the stone building and approached Angel at a brisk purposeful pace.

"Lady Byrd!" He hailed her as he approached. "Your father sent me."

Duncan and George were on him in a heartbeat. Duncan wrestled his arms behind him and tied his wrists with the cravat George had pulled from his own neck. George patted him down for weapons as Duncan stuffed his mouth with a handkerchief.

"Not today!" said Duncan.

"No weapons," said George feeling uneasy. Something wasn't right.

He took another look at the man who was bug-eyed and unshaven. His hat had fallen from his head, and his hair was wild and greasy.

"Duncan," said George in a panic, "This isn't the duke's man. He's a decoy!"

Duncan swore imaginatively, and they both turned to face Aunt Evelyn and Uncle St. John who were watching with mouths agape. Behind them, a tall pale man held Sophie in silence, his hand wrapped around her mouth. In the other hand, he held a pistol. Duncan moved as swift as thought, shoving the bound man to the ground and placing himself to

A Baron's Son is Undone

shield Angel with his body.

George became very still. His mind went quiet. His one thought was that he had only read to the middle of chapter three in *Pride and Prejudice*. What about the Bennetts? It couldn't end here. It simply couldn't. He felt Duncan's hand on his forearm, squeezing like a vice, a warning to do nothing.

"I'll thank you all to take three paces back," said the tall man in a slippery voice.

"You wouldn't shoot her," said Duncan without moving, his grip on George tightening.

Aunt Evelyn and Uncle St. John exclaimed in horror as they turned to see Sophie's mouth muffled against the man's large hand. They didn't shift their positions either. Everyone was immobilised with shock.

"No, but I would shoot any one of you," said the man. "I won't aim to kill, but I'm sure Lady Byrd wouldn't want any of you hurt. She will come with me. Her father is beside himself with worry."

The pale man released his grip on Sophie, his gun aimed at the wedding entourage.

"Be a good girl now, and climb back into that carriage. Any nonsense and I'll shoot one of your friends here." With his free hand, he pulled a second pistol from his coat. "Or maybe two," he added.

"George," said Sophie catching his eye. "Leave it. I don't want anyone injured."

"But this is a wedding!" said Aunt Evelyn practically in tears. "You have no right, Sir!"

Uncle St. John put his arm around his wife, and she shrugged it off angrily and shoved him away from her.

"Don't condescend to me, St. John! I have been sewing

bunting for two weeks, and you won't tell me it was all for nothing—do something!"

"What would you have me do, my darling? The man is holding two pistols."

Aunt Evelyn flushed red with anger and spun around to shoot an accusing look at Duncan and George. She began scolding them in the most inarticulate way. George could make out the occasional "for shame" as he watched Sophie move slowly to the carriage. While Aunt Evelyn was drowning him and Duncan in a tirade of reprobation, Uncle St. John saw fit to make idle conversation with their attacker who was taking one step and then another backwards towards the carriage.

"Are those flintlock pistols?" asked Uncle St. John casually. "Two triggers, eh? I was thinking of purchasing one myself."

And then, in the middle of her demented diatribe, Aunt Evelyn spun fiercely back around, her purple reticule flying out by its handle, but the duke's man was beyond her reach. Making no contact, Aunt Evelyn continued to spin, carried along with the momentum of her weighty handbag as she barely missed striking her husband across the side of the head. Duncan had to catch her before she fell in the street.

Through all of this, George had the strangest vision of himself pulling out his pocket watch to check the time and finding that the second hand was ticking at least ten times too slowly. He looked around. This was one of those moments in life where everything teetered as if it were balanced on the edge of a blade. No day was safe. He had been right about that. But what struck him was that this tragedy was playing out like a comedy. If anyone were watching, they might laugh as his heart turned to lead, as the light in his life blinked out

A Baron's Son is Undone

of existence, and they wouldn't be entirely wrong. It *was* kind of funny. There were layers to this sort of comedic feat, and the first and last joke in this little farce would be the drunken driver.

While everyone had been distracted by Aunt Evelyn's antics and Uncle St. John's incongruous conversation-making, George had seen out of the corner of his eye the driver climb down from his seat at the front of the carriage. *What was he about?* He was surprisingly nimble for a man who had consumed more than a half bottle of gin. As he passed Sophie where she stood by the carriage steps watching the scene, he placed a finger to his lips with his left hand. His right hand which was dangling at his side swung forward lifting a rather large knife as he walked calmly up behind the pale man. As the duke's man took another step backwards, the driver pressed the cold point of the knife to the back of his neck.

"Pistols on the ground if you please," said the driver in a voice as deep as a ravine and as cold as the Thames in winter. "I am not so morally hindered as you," he continued. "If you press me, I aim to kill."

"Christ," said Duncan under his breath.

George watched the pale man's eyes make the appropriate computations. Shoot, you lose. Turn, you lose. Put the pistols down, you lose . . . but perhaps keep your throat intact. He made the reasonable choice and crouched to place the pistols on the ground. Keeping his knife to the man's neck, the driver kicked the pistols over to Duncan who gathered them up.

"I'd like to take a look at the mechanism on one of those," said Uncle St. John with a nervous laugh.

"St. John!" scolded Aunt Evelyn in a whisper.

"Well, what are you waiting for? Tie him up!" yelled the

A Man Like Me

driver.

George and Duncan bound the pale man hand and foot with the remaining cravats belonging to the party. Trussed up like a pig, the duke's man was then shoved into the carriage along with his accomplice. The driver doffed his hat to the wedding party, took his place on the box, and with a flick of his wrist, the horses were pulling the carriage away from the church and down the street.

Sophie ran to George, throwing herself into his arms. He felt the sweet weight of her body, alive and whole, pressing against him. He dropped his lips down onto her brow. Relief flooded his body as he struggled to maintain the integrity of his legs which were threatening to give way beneath him.

"So," said Duncan. "I suppose the parson will be waiting."

"Just a moment," said George wrapping his arms more tightly around Sophie, speaking over her head. "Who was that?"

"Phineas Grave—an old acquaintance of mine I ran into a month or so back.," said Duncan a little sheepishly. "I was merely intending to stay one step ahead of the duke's man. Apologies for his manner. He's a mite overzealous when he has a job to do."

"No moral hindrances, apparently," said Uncle St. John. "What's he doing in Cornwall? No, don't tell me. It's smuggling, isn't it?"

"Something like that," said Duncan evasively. He shook his head. "I'm sure he wouldn't have . . ."

Angel put a hand to Duncan's arm, and he looked to her as if for absolution.

"It's all right," she said. Then she handed her posy of roses and daisies to Sophie who untangled herself from George.

A Baron's Son is Undone

They entered through the large wooden doors into the dim interior. The morning light slanted through colourful stained glass to expose a myriad of dust motes dancing golden in the space between the dark wooden pews.

"Fairy dust," said Aunt Evelyn from behind George.

"Yes," said Uncle St. John. "I think this bodes well, my dear."

Fourteen

What Have We Here?

When they arrived back at the cottage after the wedding, Aunt Evelyn was in high spirits as she led the party through the house and out into the back garden.

"You should have seen yourself, George. I daresay, you were trembling when you placed that ring on Sophie's finger."

Sophie looked to George who was squeezing her hand possessively as they stepped out from the back door and onto the grass.

"Oh!" she said looking around the garden.

Pink-and-yellow bunting had been strung haphazardly from tree to tree and bush to bush. The tiny pastel flags fluttered as a gentle breeze appeared to lift each one in turn. Beneath the bunting were chairs and table set for breakfast among the high grass and flowers. Sunlight laced its way down through the leaves of the silver birch standing sentry

A Baron's Son is Undone

over the table. It landed in dappled patches across the white tablecloth which was strewn with yellow buttercups and pink rose petals. Sophie looked to Aunt Evelyn who was now *her* Aunt Evelyn, her family.

"How magical!"

Aunt Evelyn's face was as bright as the sun. "Yes, well," she said. "A wedding such as yours is always magical. We must celebrate accordingly." The lady of the house turned quickly to catch Angel who was making her way back towards the kitchen. "Stay with us, Angel! I would be honoured if you breakfasted with us today. You are, after all, one of the brides."

Angel startled at this. She glanced to Duncan who stepped up to the table and pulled out a chair for her. George and Uncle St. John followed suit, and soon they were all raising their tea cups to the happy couple. Sophie looked to George and found herself warmed under his molten gaze.

He was silent through most of the breakfast as everyone else chatted and laughed and sighed with relief that everything had worked out so miraculously well. George ate, and in between bites, he stared at Sophie. He even sipped his tea while observing her over the rim. At one point, watching her fumble nervously with a piece of toast, he reached out and gently took it from her, buttered it himself, and then replaced it on her plate. All in silence.

Finally, when the breakfast was coming to a close and napkins were being placed beside plates, George shifted his chair back and stood.

"We should be off," he said.

"What? So soon?!" shrieked Aunt Evelyn. Uncle St. John put a hand to her arm.

"The rest of the family has yet to meet Sophie," said George.

What Have We Here?

"And I should speak with her father as well."

Sophie felt her chest constrict at the mere mention of her father.

"Duncan," said George. "It has been a great pleasure. I will be forever grateful for all that you have done for Sophie, and you will always be welcome in our home."

Duncan looked down at his empty plate, and Sophie knew enough not to attempt to lift his gaze. He was clearly overcome and did not wish to make a spectacle of himself.

"Angel," said George, smiling now. The pretty maid looked astonished to be addressed at all. "Take care of Duncan for us."

At this, her porcelain complexion flushed a hot shade of pink.

"Is . . . Are you . . . Duncan, are you not coming with us?" stammered Sophie.

Her guard dog finally lifted his eyes from his plate. They were shining and rimmed in red.

"Best lay low for now," he said with a crooked smile. "The duke will want my hide for a rug, I should think."

Duncan had filled the dark and yawning chasm in her heart with his gruff affection and his willingness to offer her a glimpse of the world outside her father's walls. There were no words to offer him an appropriate thanks.

"When the fuss dies down, you *must* visit us, Duncan," said Sophie. "I will always have a treat waiting for you." She quirked one side of her mouth in a sad half smile.

Duncan appeared to appreciate the sentiment. He wiped the palm of one hand across his eye.

"That's enough," he said.

Standing from his chair, he strode quickly to the cottage.

A Baron's Son is Undone

Sophie lifted a hand to the table to stay the remaining breakfast-goers before running after Duncan. She caught up with him in the hallway past the kitchen.

"Duncan!" she called.

He turned, and she ran to him and threw her arms around his neck. She found she was sobbing uncontrollably.

"For God's sake," said Duncan, his voice cracking. "Pemberton isn't that bad, is he?"

Sophie laughed a little through the tears, and he patted her gently on the back.

"I'm going to miss you," she said untangling herself and accepting a handkerchief from him. She dabbed at her eyes.

"It'll pass," said Duncan wisely.

"No it won't," said Sophie. "You've been everything to me."

"Certainly not everything," said Duncan clearly struggling to keep his voice steady. "That's his job." He gestured behind her with a lift of his chin.

George was standing there with a concerned look painted over his features. He strode forward in long measured steps, reached a hand out to grasp Duncan's, and pulled him into an embrace.

"Jesus," said Duncan over his shoulder. "Anyone would think we're Americans."

"Thank you," said George when he released him. "I promise to take good care of her."

"You'd better," said Duncan in his usual menacing tone.

Sophie wiped more tears from her eyes as she both sobbed and laughed at the same time.

What Have We Here?

George had hired a private coach to take the two of them all the way to his family's country estate near London. It would have been an uncomfortable trip if attempted in one day, so they overnighted at an inn along the way. It was an especially well-appointed inn, frequented no doubt by wealthy travellers along the route to Cornwall, and George had secured their finest room for the night.

The sudden realisation that it was their wedding night was a jolt to Sophie's nerves. George had promised he would not . . . and she had believed him, but now that the moment was finally here, a sense of dread started creeping its bony fingers up from her ankles, tugging insistently at the hem of her dress, forcing her to take notice of it.

In their room, the fire had been lit against the chill of September as it approached. Sophie stood near the door as George shrugged off his jacket and hung it neatly over the back of a wooden chair. He undid his cravat and pulled the length of it free of his neck so that his shirt fell open. He looked across to her.

"You said you wanted me in your bed," he said with a smile.

Yes, she *had* said that, hadn't she?

He reached out his hand, and she crossed the room to him. He unbuttoned her pelisse, and slipped it down from her shoulders, taking it over to the closet to hang properly before returning to her. He gave her a quick, hot kiss before turning her around. Slowly and methodically, he pulled each of the pins from her hair, until her plait fell loose. He then unravelled it gently from the bottom up, until his fingers were combing through her hair. The soft ticklish tugs to her scalp, his nearness—it all felt quite nice.

Maybe it wouldn't be so bad if he . . . She couldn't help

A Baron's Son is Undone

feeling as if she were being a little unreasonable. He was, after all, her husband, and she was sure that she loved him. So why could she not rid herself of the fear of what was to come? Her own mind warred with itself: she felt so openly wanton in his presence, and even so, the idea of properly consummating the marriage was like coming up against a granite wall—impassable and unmovable. Loving him as she did, she was not entirely certain anymore if this wall existed to protect herself from physical harm or to protect him from some terrible fate. Sophie imagined she was not entirely right in the head, but knowing this and fixing this were two entirely different things.

When George was finished with her hair, he made short work of her dress and underclothes, until she was finally standing before him in nothing but her chemise.

"Arms up," he said.

She lifted her arms, and in one swift movement, he had it off. She was entirely bare, and as he swept an appreciative gaze over her body, she could feel her nipples tighten into hard little pebbles. He shook his head in the subtlest of movements.

"Stand near the fire," he said as he turned away to rummage in a valise.

He stepped up to her by the fireplace with her white nightdress in one hand.

"As much as it's been a pleasure undressing you, I think it will be considerably less awkward if you put on the nightdress yourself."

He handed it to her, then turned and pulled his shirt up over his head. He removed his trousers and hung them over his jacket on the back of the chair so that he was now dressed in nothing but his drawers. Sophie shrugged herself into the nightdress as George stepped to the bed and pulled back the coverlet.

"Climb under then," he said. "Before you catch a chill."

Sophie did as she was told, shimmying over to make room for George. He slipped in beside her, but he did not lie down. Instead, he lifted his pillow and pulled out something from underneath it.

"What have we here?" he said.

It took Sophie's mind a moment to recognise the book in his hand as Aunt Evelyn's copy of *Pride and Prejudice*. Her heart gave a leap, and her face rebelled against the fear that had held it so very still. She smiled.

"You didn't steal it, did you?" she asked.

George pretended affront. "What do you take me for, Mrs. Pemberton? I'm no common thief! A ruffian maybe, but not a thief."

"You stole *me*," she responded.

George laughed as he seated himself up at the headboard, a pillow propped up behind him.

"When I told Aunt Evelyn how much you had been enjoying Miss Austen, she made a wedding gift of it."

"How kind," said Sophie snuggling in against his side, perfectly relaxed.

In one fell swoop, George had managed to cut off the bony-fingered hands of fear that plagued her.

"Where were we?" he asked.

"You'll have to start Chapter Three again," said Sophie. "I drifted off the last time and missed most of it."

George dutifully began reading Chapter Three in earnest. There was an assembly which Mrs. Bennet attended with her many daughters, and Mr. Bingley (of four or even five

A Baron's Son is Undone

thousand a year) had been there and presented himself as a most agreeable fellow with some interest in the eldest Bennet sister Jane. His friend Mr. Darcy, however, proved most distasteful—proud and rude and thinking entirely too much of himself. It seemed that his income of ten thousand a year would not be enough to sweeten Mrs. Bennet in his favour.

"Mr. Darcy seems a horrible man," said Sophie when George had concluded the chapter.

"A real shitter," said George.

Sophie laughed.

"Do you think, perhaps, he is simply guarding himself and his heart with his poor behaviour?"

"Sometimes," said George, "an ass is just an ass and nothing more."

Sophie gave him a playful shove.

"But this is a story," she said. "A romance."

George placed the book to the side table and slipped down into the bed beside her.

"Then it's likely Mr. Darcy will see the error of his ways. He *is* probably guarding himself in some way. Aren't we all?"

He stroked a strand of hair from Sophie's face and looked into her eyes meaningfully.

"George," she said quietly. The word was laden with feeling.

"It's all right," he said. "No apologies and no pretending. I don't want our wedding night to be like that."

"I *do* like it when you touch me," she said. "I more than like it. Please don't be upset."

"Do I look upset?" asked George.

"No," Sophie conceded.

"Tell me if there is anything I can give you, Sophie," said George gliding a finger along the side of her neck. "I'm feeling rather generous tonight." He smiled in that way that he did which had the effect of obliterating all reasonable thought from her mind. Her pulse came rushing into her ears, and her lips parted as if to release some of the heat that had quickly flared inside her. George certainly knew how to take control of the moment in unexpected ways.

"You could . . ." she started.

"Yes?"

"You could . . ."

"I'm afraid," said George, "that the rules of this game require you to make the request explicitly." He smiled mischievously. "What would you like me to do, Mrs. Pemberton?"

Sophie could feel herself grow warm beneath the blanket as her heart began tossing itself about like an excited little bird. She threw the blanket from them and sat up to look down upon her husband lying there with one arm bent casually above his head. She stroked her fingers through the golden hair of his chest.

"I'm glad to see you're thinking about it," said George with some amusement.

He was offering her the most thoughtful gift—the opportunity to explore without any hint of fear that he might push things too far. But try as she might, Sophie didn't know how to form the words, how to say what she wanted. In her mind, it all sounded so . . . so . . . indecent. She hesitated, mustering her courage, then reached for his face as she threw one leg over his torso to straddle him.

"Kiss me," she said. "Kiss me roughly."

A Baron's Son is Undone

Holy hell—George had not expected that!

Sophie's long dark hair fell like a curtain to contain their faces as she leaned in and crushed her mouth to his. Her kiss was a fierce thing, completely unhinged, practically rabid. He had never been kissed in this way before, and he struggled to match her wild abandon. But when she threaded her hands through his hair, gripping and tugging it in her little fists, George felt something give way inside him, like a small stone knocked loose to tumble down the side of a mountain. On its way down, it knocked other rocks loose, and those in turn loosened others, until it was something akin to an avalanche. George felt the weight of it come crashing down as he reached around Sophie with his arms and still kissing her, swung her around so that she was underneath him with her nightdress bunched up at her waist. Her feet slid down his calves and she pressed her nails into his back as he plundered her mouth with his tongue. For a time, they seemed locked in a battle, each of them desperate to take as much as they could from the other, to consume and be consumed. Eventually, George pulled his face from hers and pulled in a ragged breath of air.

"Sophie, what are you doing to me?"

Her face was flushed, and her plump mouth was red from their amorous altercation. She gripped his biceps.

"Kiss me everywhere," she said breathing heavily, the rise and fall of her chest lifting and sinking the golden heart pendant that lay resting there. "Just like that. Use your teeth."

Teeth?

George gave a single shake of his head, but he was certainly not saying no. He reached down and pulled her nightdress up until her breasts were exposed to him. He sank his face into her soft flesh, kissing, licking, gently biting. Sophie arched up into him, groaning and squirming, her hands in his hair holding him tight.

George lifted himself from her.

"Arms up," he said, and her nightdress was pulled from over her head. He tossed it to the floor.

There was the glimmer of a moment in which he realised he had never before tossed an item of clothing to the floor in his life. He shook his head once more as he gazed down into her shining eyes.

And then he was kissing and biting his way down her torso. Rough enough to obey her request, but not so harsh as to leave a mark. Breasts, belly, thighs. She made such appreciative noises as he bit into her silken thighs, he thought he might spend himself in his drawers. He paused between her legs before sweeping his tongue up along the wet petals of her sex. One quick hard lick.

Sophie gasped, and George sensed all her muscles frozen rigid, waiting. He paused. While he had half a mind to give in to his desire to feast on her right now, the other half of his mind was a stickler for the rules of the game. She hadn't exactly been clear with her instructions.

"George." Sophie sat up slowly, her hair streaming down over her shoulders to brush against the swell of her breasts. She seemed almost dazed.

"I await your command, my lady."

"Take off your drawers," she said.

Oh.

He knelt up to unbutton the fall of his drawers, and his cock sprang free. He stood from the bed, and Sophie shifted herself so that she was seated on the side of the bed facing him. She pulled down his drawers. As she bent forward to do so, his cock brushed her cheek. She pressed the side of her face to it, and George had to close his eyes.

"Sophie," he said. "You don't have to . . ."

She cupped his balls in one small hand.

"Do you *like* tasting me between my legs?" she asked pointedly. "Or is it something you do on sufferance?"

"There's nowhere I'd rather be," he said reaching down to take both sides of her head in his hands as she gazed up into his face. "I take especial pleasure in unravelling your composure."

This made Sophie smile.

"I'd like to taste you," she said somewhat shyly as her hand slid from his balls to his shaft. She paused as she considered the tip of his cock. "It's one of the intimate thoughts I've had about you . . . on a number of occasions." She wouldn't look him in the eye as her face flushed rosy in the lamplight. "Would you mind?" she asked in all seriousness.

Mercy.

"I will try my best not to mind," said George stifling a laugh. "Do as you will."

His flippant remarks hid his heart well. That she would want to explore him in this way . . . he did not feel worthy. But oh, there was her pink tongue reaching out to swirl about the head of his cock. As she took him in her mouth, he swore quite soundly, and it was all he could do not to thrust himself into her face. He remained patiently still as she explored him with her lips and tongue and hand, the occasional groan issuing from his mouth. *What was she even doing with her tongue?* If he wasn't careful, he would spend himself in her mouth, and he doubted very much that she would enjoy that. As the tension quickly mounted inside him, Sophie slid a hand around to grip his buttocks and pull him in closer. The simple gesture had him trembling with the effort to restrain his release. Just as he was about to say something, Sophie pulled her face away and smiled shyly up at him.

"You're right," she said. "Unravelling your composure is a special pleasure."

Her hand was still on him, and she squeezed and tugged at him in a brief persistent rhythm as she spoke.

"Sophie. My God, Sophie!"

George felt his tightly coiled control unravel with some alarm as he spilled himself over her fist and onto her chest. Just when he thought he was done, the crude sight of his seed dripping down between her breasts triggered a secondary release that nearly had him lose his footing. Once he was entirely spent, he walked on trembling legs to the washbasin, wet and wrung out a cloth, and then returned to wipe Sophie clean.

He noticed she was entirely flushed, her pulse visible in her throat as she tossed her head back to make room for the washcloth. When he was done, he threw the washcloth aside and pulled her to standing. He gave her a hard kiss, just the way she liked it, and then he wrapped one arm behind her as he reached with his other hand slowly between her legs. He paused with his hand a hair's breadth from her warm sex as he searched her eyes.

"Yes," she said breathlessly, stepping her legs apart to allow him better access.

He had barely made contact with his fingers when she shocked him by taking in a short hard gasp as she clutched tightly to his shoulder.

Sweet Heaven, she was coming already!

He caught her cry in his mouth as he pressed his lips to

hers once more, and she ground down against his hand as wave after wave of pleasure coursed through her. He had to actually catch her up in his arms when it was over to prevent her crumpling to the floor. Cradling her gently, he lay her back down in the bed and climbed in beside her, pulling the covers up over both of them.

"Sophie," he said. "Come here." He pulled her to him and held her tight.

What does anyone even say after that?

"Thank you," she whispered.

"Sophie—"

"—No one else would do what you have done for me," she said burrowing her face into his chest.

Jesus.

"I can't believe you thought to bring the Bennets along." She smiled and planted a soft kiss against his sternum.

George stroked her hair, then ran his hand down her smooth satiny back.

"Sophie, you are my purpose now, and I'm honoured to have your trust. You need never thank me . . . for anything."

She made a sound against him—something murmured, something sweet. Before long, she had drifted off in his embrace, her lips slightly parted, one hand splayed over his chest as if to hold him in place. His heart swelled with an intense and overwhelming urge to encompass the moment, absorb it, and hold it forever inside him.

George knew this carefree honeymoon would be short-lived. They would arrive home tomorrow afternoon, and there would be Mother to deal with. He only hoped Patience would be there as well.

Fifteen

Family Matters

Sophie woke the next morning to more kisses, gentle this time, soft and dreamy with the night's sleep still clinging to them. She stroked her hands over George's warm body, his face, threaded them through his hair.

"Sophie," he kept saying softly between kisses. "Sophie." It was as if he wanted to say more but could not find the words.

They eventually managed to dress and eat and do all those things that seemed quite superfluous when they could be naked in a warm and tousled bed. In the coach, they sat side-by-side as Sophie clutched George's hand. The journey was long, and Sophie eventually dropped her head to his shoulder.

"Shift up," he said, sliding himself to rest his back near the window and lifting one leg up along the seat. "Now sit here."

She rested her back to his chest and lifted her legs to the seat as he pulled her close with one strong arm.

"Rest," he said.

A Baron's Son is Undone

"George, do you think your family will like me?" she asked. "I expect they're not all as immune to gossip as your aunt and uncle."

"Rest," he said again, kissing the back of her head.

She closed her eyes. When next she awoke, George pulled her closer to his chest. He answered her question as if no time had passed.

"When we arrive," he said, "you must not mind a single word my mother says or anything she does."

"She won't like me," said Sophie sitting up and turning to look at him.

"She won't like the *situation*," said George. "She will be hurt that this decision was made without her. And she does so like to read the gossip sheets . . ."

"And your father?" asked Sophie nervously.

"He'll be thrilled," said George with a smile. "How sensible," he will say, "to strike while the iron was hot and to save us all a huge wedding expense in the process—not that I would have minded the expense, but you know."

George had put on a voice that must have been in mimicry of his father's. He laughed.

"What about Patience?" asked Sophie.

"I hope she will be there," said George. "She will always be on our side, and she's not afraid to give Mother a good scolding."

Sophie lifted her eyebrows at that.

"And Grace?"

"She is an incurable romantic, and we are the happy ending of a love story. That, and we will have quite the adventure story to tell her. She loves a good story. Not to mention the magical gifts from Porth La."

Family Matters

"Hmm," said Sophie as she tucked all this information away neatly in her mind.

"We won't be living with them forever," said George. "Only a few weeks until I can have the manor house set up appropriately. I have a small estate not far from theirs, but I rarely frequent it, so it will want a good cleaning, and the staff will need waking up."

When the coach finally pulled up along the gravel drive of the Pembertons' enormous country home, Sophie looked out of the window to see a full-figured young lady in a violet dress running down the steps towards them. A footman followed her out at a much slower pace.

"George!" Sophie could hear the lady's voice from inside the carriage.

Not waiting for the driver, George opened the door himself and stepped down. Sophie hovered by the open door as she watched the young lady who must be Patience give her brother a quick hug. George seemed somewhat startled by the embrace. He stiffened visibly. When his sister released him, she gave him a meaningful look and a slight shake of her pretty blonde head. George then turned to hand Sophie down from the coach.

"Sophie!" said Patience with the brightest smile imaginable. "I'm so pleased to finally meet you."

Another hug! Sophie was enveloped in a soft embrace that felt entirely genuine. She allowed herself to relax a little. She even smiled.

"So George has a wife," said Patience in a teasing sort of voice when she stood back to regard Sophie.

Now that she was trapped under Patience's gaze, Sophie realised that most people simply look, they glance, they skim.

A Baron's Son is Undone

Patience was attempting to *see*. Her eyes darted to Sophie's lips, her neck, her nervously clasped hands.

"George?" said Patience suddenly turning to him.

"No!" he said.

"Please, George. Please."

"She's been through enough for the time being. You can ask her sometime later," said George.

"Ask me what?" asked Sophie.

"She wants to paint your portrait," said George in a tone that suggested long suffering. "But I won't allow you to answer that. You will be polite and say yes, and then you will spend the next several days sitting like a statue up in her studio." He turned to Patience. "Another time," he said. Then added, as if to taunt his sister with the image, "And when you do, you must ask her to wear the red dress."

Patience took in an excited breath and looked to Sophie.

"All right," said Patience. "Later. But it must be done!"

She took Sophie's arm, and the three of them traipsed back to the house. It was not lost on Sophie that neither of his parents had come to greet them at the door. And George himself had not smiled once since greeting his sister.

"Father is not feeling well," said Patience as if reading her thoughts.

George looked sharply to his sister.

"I didn't want to burden you with this from the outset, but you should know that the physician has been to see him. He's up and about, but he's weak."

"A fever?" asked George.

Patience stopped just over the threshold and turned to her brother on the white marble floor of the foyer.

"No," she said. "Nothing contagious. You must speak to

Family Matters

Father about this George. Mother will not entertain that anything is the matter."

Patience guided Sophie up the main staircase, along a hall, and into an extraordinarily yellow drawing room accented in white. George followed close behind. A pretty older lady—Lady Pemberton no doubt—was seated on a butter-yellow settee sewing a sampler. She was wearing a dress of dusty rose that complimented the yellow of the room, and Sophie was reminded of the rose petals and buttercups strewn across their wedding breakfast table.

Lady Pemberton looked up as they entered and then back down at her sampler and continued to sew as if no one had entered the room.

"Mother!" said Patience affronted.

Lady Pemberton looked up once more directing all her attention to Patience.

"I see they have arrived," she said icily. "Do show George the rooms we have prepared for them."

George stepped forward to stand with Sophie, and she felt his warm hand slide over hers.

"Mother," said George. "This is Sophie. My wife."

For the first time since they had entered the room, Lady Pemberton looked directly at Sophie and then at George. Sophie fancied she startled slightly at the look on her son's face.

"She is important to me," said George.

"Oh, well. If she's important to you, then all is forgiven," said Lady Pemberton with some petulance.

She put down her sampler and stood. George squeezed Sophie's hand before the tirade began.

"No warning! No letter except to your sister! I had to hear

second-hand that my only son is to marry a woman from the gossip pages! You always thought of your family first, George. You were my only sensible child!"

Sophie was frozen in place. Her heart felt dull and thick, as if it had become so stiff that it was now a great effort to pump the blood through her body.

"Mother," whispered Patience, clearly taken aback.

"I'm so sorry, Sophie," said George, his voice cracking with emotion. Then to his mother, he spoke in the calmest, most even tone imaginable. "You will not refer to my wife again in that way," he said. "You are overwrought, so I am excusing you this once. But not again. And yes, because she is dear to me, I do believe all should be forgiven. Can you not empathise with the situation in which we found ourselves? There were not many options available to us."

Lady Pemberton stared at her son for a few seconds, her lips pressed tightly together, and then promptly burst into a veritable shower of tears. Patience was at her side with a handkerchief and helped her to sit back down on the settee. Lady Pemberton's sobs eventually came farther apart, bubbling up in hiccups that shook her delicate frame. They eventually slowed to a standstill, and she patted her eyes.

"There is nothing wrong with your father," she said, startling Sophie with the non sequitur. "The physician doesn't know his business, and I shall not be calling for him again."

Sophie looked to George who was now as grim-faced as ever.

"I'm hosting a ball," continued Lady Pemberton, almost to herself. She fiddled with her sampler, then looked to Sophie. "I have not made a good first impression, have I?" She tried for a smile. "Your husband, as sensible as he is, is quite right. All

Family Matters

is forgiven. Truly." She sniffed. "I only hope you can forgive my behaviour this afternoon."

"Of course," said Sophie. "I imagine this has all come as a shock."

"Yes," said Lady Pemberton. "That's what it is—a shock." She patted the settee beside her. "Come and sit with me, Sophie. Let me take a look at you."

George released her hand, and she took a seat with Lady Pemberton who fixed her with an assessing gaze.

"Where was your mother from?" asked Lady Pemberton curiously.

"Mother!" said Patience.

"No, it's all right," said Sophie. "She was from Portugal."

"I suppose that could explain it," said Lady Pemberton examining Sophie's face.

"Mother!" said George and Patience together.

"I will not be scolded in my own home," said Lady Pemberton sniffing once more and dabbing at one eye. "I'm merely trying to become acquainted with the newest member of our family." To Sophie, she said, "Our cook makes the most delightful Portuguese tarts."

"Really?" said Sophie. "I've never tasted one before."

"Haven't you?" said Lady Pemberton. "And your father, the Duke of Somerset . . .?"

Sophie waited. It didn't seem to be a proper question that one could answer.

Lady Pemberton continued, "Your father is not overly fond of my husband, so I suppose we have not lost any love there with this little scandal of a wedding."

She smiled—this time genuinely. Then she laughed, a tinkling girlish laugh that made Sophie herself smile.

221

A Baron's Son is Undone

"The ball will be the perfect opportunity to introduce you to the ton as man and wife. Patience, you must have Richard come so that he can show his support for the happy couple. Tongues will want to wag, but the viscount's involvement will have the effect of numbing a good deal of frivolous speech." She turned to Sophie. "He's a war hero, you know."

"Yes, I know of him," said Sophie. "I read the papers regularly."

Lady Pemberton raised her eyebrows and looked at George.

"Not a bluestocking! George, how could you?" She laughed at her own little joke as she placed a hand to Sophie's wrist and gave it a comforting squeeze.

"What's all this?" The question came from the doorway.

Sophie turned to see a lean, older gentleman with a shock of salt-and-pepper hair step slowly but confidently into the room. He didn't look particularly unwell to her, but then again, she didn't know how he looked when he was well. Sophie stood from her seat.

"Father." George greeted Lord Pemberton with a serious face and an out-stretched hand. "Might I introduce my wife Sophie?"

"Ah! Sophie!" he said gripping her one hand warmly in both of his. "Welcome to the family. We are happy to have you with us. Quite sensible of you both to strike while the iron was hot and to save us all the expense of a wedding. Not that I would have minded, but you know."

Sophie looked to George with a smile on her face as his father spoke the words almost exactly as George had anticipated them in the carriage. But though he caught her eye, her husband's expression remained stony. Sophie felt her smile slide away as a curious confusion began to buzz in her mind. George was not himself.

Patience elbowed George who gave her a glancing glare before returning his attention to Lord Pemberton.

"Father," said George, "might I have a word with you in private?"

"Of course, of course," said Lord Pemberton placing an arm around his son's shoulders and leading him from the room. "Much has transpired since you've been away."

"Tea?" asked Lady Pemberton pertly.

"That would be nice," said Sophie. She looked to Patience nervously, hoping against hope that she would not leave her alone with Lady Pemberton, but Patience was already smiling at her as she took a seat opposite.

"You must tell as all about Cornwall," she said a little too brightly. "And Uncle St. John and Aunt Evelyn."

At the mention of Aunt Evelyn, Lady Pemberton made a small muffled noise that sounded like disapproval.

"Did she make you pray for the slugs?" asked Patience grinning.

Sophie felt herself relaxing as Patience regaled them with her own tales of Aunt Evelyn's special idiosyncrasies. George's sister laughed easily and heartily, and of course, this was contagious. Even Lady Pemberton was tittering away by the time the tea arrived.

Sophie warmed quickly to George's sister who was clearly trying her best to make her feel welcome. If Lord Pemberton was, as Patience had said, unwell, this must have been a considerable effort for her, and Sophie only wished she could relieve Patience of the requirement to be jovial.

After tea, Patience showed Sophie to the rooms that had been prepared for her and George. As they walked arm-

A Baron's Son is Undone

in-arm down yet another long hallway, Sophie took the opportunity to put Patience at ease.

"There's really no need to entertain me as such," said Sophie. "I mean, it is very kind of you to make me feel welcome . . . but if your father . . . that is, if there are more pressing matters, please don't hesitate to ignore me entirely. And if there is anything I can do to help, please let me know."

Patience stopped mid-stride and turned to face Sophie.

"I'm starting to see why George married you," she said. "You have a sympathetic heart." Patience took her hand and gave her a weak smile. "My father is dying," she said. "Three months, maybe six months . . . The physician is not the most accurate fortune teller, but he is confident of the general prediction."

"I'm so sorry," said Sophie. *Where was George? She needed to see him right now.*

"We mustn't waste too much of this precious time crying," said Patience. She was trying to maintain a smile, but she had to wipe a tear from her eye. "He is, after all, still with us. As you have heard, Mother is hosting a ball."

"Because your father likes to dance?" asked Sophie.

"No, he almost never dances," said Patience laughing as she wiped another tear from her eye. "Mother is hosting a ball because she is pretending that there is nothing at all the matter."

"Oh," said Sophie.

When Patience left her to freshen up in the suite of rooms she was to share with George, Sophie sat down on the large four-poster bed beneath its white canopy. She felt suddenly very alone. Kicking off her shoes, she leaned herself down onto her side to rest her head on the pillow. It had been a long day, and her fatigue acted as a weight, dragging her slowly down into sleep.

George had left Sophie with his mother and Patience in the yellow drawing room and walked with his father's arm resting heavily on his shoulder down to the study.

"I suppose you've heard the news," said his father stepping to the side cabinet beside his desk and pouring two glasses of whisky. "It turns out I will be dying sooner rather than later. The specifics are not terribly specific, mind you. A persistent growth in my abdomen. I am more tired than usual—it is an affliction of the blood, I am told. 'Eat some liver,' the physician says. It won't save me, but I may feel less tired for the time being."

Lord Pemberton lifted his whisky glass as if in cheers. George hesitantly raised his, and his father clinked the two glasses in a macabre celebratory gesture.

"Congratulations!" said his father. "You will soon be the new baron. My mind rests easy knowing you will take care of the family, your mother and Grace especially. My mind rests easier still knowing you have someone you can trust and confide in. It is an especially buoyant condition—love. I only hope you will not float away on us." He laughed.

George felt his belly seize as if in the grip of a vice. Everything—his whole life—had been leading up to this moment. He felt suddenly nauseous.

"But Father, I'm not . . . I can't . . ."

"Nonsense," said his father, clearly not understanding at all. "You are and you can. You are an exceptionally clever young

A Baron's Son is Undone

man with a sense of justice, plenty of empathy, a marvellous work ethic. You are my heir, and I have no qualms about trusting my parliamentary legacy to you. Carry it forward. Do good."

"Are you not sad, Father?" asked George.

"Now and then," said Lord Pemberton. "Now and then. But it's not particularly sensible to dwell, now is it?"

"Mother is hosting a ball," said George, trying to provoke something from his father, some acknowledgement of the sheer ridiculousness of the endeavour.

"She loves me," said Lord Pemberton. "She does not know what else to do. And it will be a wonderful party. There is much to celebrate."

"Celebrate?" asked George. He looked at the golden liquid glinting through the crystal glass in his hand. There was no way he would be able to drink it.

"My life," said his father smiling. He took a sip of whisky, swallowed, and then lifted the glass to gaze at it appreciatively. "It has been . . . perfect. An utter joy. From the unlikely event of my marriage to your mother, to your birth, and then Patience. Little Grace—*she* was a welcome surprise! You are, each one of you, the very best that I could have hoped for."

George tried to swallow but found there was some obstruction in his throat. Ever since he had been a child, he had looked up to his father. He had especially appreciated Lord Pemberton's straightforward manner. Unlike every other adult in George's life, his father had never talked down to him no matter his age. If he asked a question, his father would always reply with the truth. And if he was worried or concerned, his father would allay his fears with rational argument and common sense. Growing up with a father like

Family Matters

that was like living beneath an enormous and sturdy tree whose branches held up the weight of the sky overhead. Who would hold up the sky when this pillar of support eventually crumbled to dust? It seemed inconceivable that George could take his father's place, that he would be able to provide that kind of solid assurance and protection to his family with his mere presence. He knew for a fact he did not even deserve to be considered as Lord Pemberton's heir. He was, after all, no son at all.

When finally, he left his father to attend to some matters in his study, George walked quickly down one hall, turned down another, and stepped down a flight of stairs stumbling near the bottom so that he had to catch himself on the bannister. The white marble foyer lay before him at the bottom of the stairs. He struggled to take a breath to settle himself. And then in several hurried steps, he was across the foyer and out the front door, practically running down the front steps and out onto the drive. He turned left and stepping onto the grass, he heaved the contents of his stomach onto the green carpet beneath him. It went on and on—a gagging, retching affair until he was dragging up yellow bile. Then nothing—dry heaves that left him kneeling in the grass with bruised ribs and a raw throat.

When Sophie awoke in the bed, George was lying beside her on top of the bedspread fully clothed, his face as pale as ash.

"George."

She reached for him and he for her. He kissed her brow softly, his face solemn.

A Baron's Son is Undone

"I'm sorry about your father," she said. "Patience told me."

He was silent for a long time.

"You can talk to me," she said.

"There's nothing to talk about," said George.

Sophie furrowed her brow, then reached up to stroke her fingers over his forehead. His jaw was visibly clenched as he took her hand from his brow and placed it down at her side. He wasn't looking at her but rather staring off to the wall behind her.

It was grief, she told herself even though she knew he had been behaving strangely since the moment they had arrived.

"What can I do for you?" she asked.

His eyes finally focussed on hers, and his countenance softened.

"Sophie," he said. "My wife." He pulled her to him and wrapped his arms around her. "Don't hate me," he said.

"What?"

"I'm trying," he said cryptically, "but it's no easier than it was before I left." He paused, and she felt his next breath shudder through his chest. "If Father . . . I can't . . . I'm not . . ."

Sophie pulled his face down to hers to find his grey irises looking like two soft pebbles glimpsed beneath the shifting sea—his eyes were brimming with tears.

"What's this all about?" she asked.

George blinked and several tears spilled down his face. He shook his head.

"Do you need to punch someone?" asked Sophie. "Would that make it all better?"

George actually smiled then—his first smile since they had arrived at his family home.

"Maybe," he said. "For now, I just need to hold you."

Sixteen

Accounts to Review

Sophie sat in the yellow drawing room feigning interest in a book. It wasn't *Pride and Prejudice*—no, that book was still packed away, unread since her wedding night which was now several days past. The book in her hand was . . . well, she didn't know what the title was. It didn't matter since she was only holding it to disguise the fact that she was bored and alone.

Lady Pemberton had kept herself busy for days with preparations for the ball, and Lord Pemberton spent part of each morning with Patience in the library. She diverted him with clever logical riddles and questions of mathematics from a book given to her by her good friend—a Mrs. Serafina Thornton. Not that Patience knew the answers. She would ask each question, and Lord Pemberton would grin and lift a pencil as he pulled a piece of paper towards himself across a side table. When he had finally worked it out, Patience would

A Baron's Son is Undone

say, "Let's see what Serafina says," and she would consult the answers at the back of her book. It was all "a lot of good sense" according to Lord Pemberton, and when Sophie occasionally passed by the library, she would often hear him laughing delightedly as Patience read out a solution that he himself could not solve. They would often invite her to join them, but Sophie knew it was their special time together, time that was in increasingly short supply, so she would politely decline, pleading some other plan for the morning.

Those plans, however, never included George since he would disappear each morning after breakfast to "review the accounts", and Sophie did not know how to question this or whether she should. Lord Pemberton would take a post-luncheon rest after which he would sequester himself and George in his study for the remainder of the afternoon. George would inevitably emerge from the study looking weathered and worn—stoically so. He never smiled with his family, Sophie noticed. He seemed to keep himself apart. They would laugh and chat and gossip, and he would observe them as he leaned back in his chair with a grave expression clouding his features.

It was afternoon now, and that meant Patience and her generous heart would seek Sophie out to keep her company. While Sophie appreciated the thought and the effort, she knew Patience had much on her mind and was probably in need of some solitude after the morning spent with her father. So that was why Sophie was pretending to read—to give Patience a break.

And here she was now, right on schedule, peeking into the drawing room. Sophie pretended to be so engrossed in her book that she didn't notice Patience's presence.

Accounts to Review

"Is it that good?" asked Patience, walking up to her. Her wide hips swayed confidently as she made her way across the room, green skirts swishing against her legs.

"Excuse me?" said Sophie looking up.

Patience swiped the book from her hands in a most unceremonious and sisterly gesture that made Sophie feel for just that one moment as if she actually belonged.

"What have we here?" asked Patience.

The playful words tugged at Sophie's heart. George had spoken exactly those words when he had pulled *Pride and Prejudice* from under his pillow on their wedding night.

Patience read the title aloud: *"L'art de conserver pendant plusieurs années toutes les substances animales ou végétales* by Nicolas Appert." She looked at Sophie. "Are you planning on preserving fruit this autumn?" she asked.

"Perhaps," said Sophie without batting an eye. "It's all very compelling."

Patience lifted a finger to silence her, then opened the book up to the first page.

"Yes, I can see how this might have diverted you," she said flipping the pages. "This Nicolas Appert has included diagrams and everything."

Sophie reached out her hand for the book, but Patience lifted it up into the air.

"I don't think so, Sophie! I'll not have you sitting here all on your lonesome reading about preservation methods and machines with crank handles."

"But I *like* preservation methods and machines with crank handles," said Sophie, a small smile playing around the corners of her mouth as she stood and reached for her book.

Patience lifted the book just out of reach and took a quick

A Baron's Son is Undone

step to the left.

"Give it back!" Sophie lunged for her, and Patience shrieked as she darted behind a chair.

Cheeks flushed and eyes shining, Patience led Sophie on a merry chase about the room until they collapsed onto the yellow settee giggling. Sophie took the book gingerly from Patience.

"I might want to preserve lemons," she said through her giggles.

"George would never allow you to work in the kitchen," said Patience in a scolding tone. "You're to be the baroness one day soon."

The smile dropped from Sophie's face just as the clatter of carriage wheels over the gravel drive sifted up through the window and into the drawing room. Patience stood quickly.

"That'll be Richard. Thank the Lord for small miracles!"

She took Sophie's hand and pulled her at a run down the stairs and out to greet the carriage at the front of the house. The viscount saw himself out of the carriage, bending his large frame to duck through the open door. Lord Winter was huge, not only in height, but in muscled bulk. Sophie took in his dark hair, his beard, and his stern features. Yes, this was definitely the war hero she had read about so often in the papers. He turned to hand a little girl down from the carriage—Grace. She was Lord Winter's opposite in every way—small with golden ringlets and bright eyes shining with excitement. She was clutching a small brown pug under one arm, but the dog did not seem to be in agreement with the arrangement, and she was wriggling and yipping in annoyance.

"Don't be so contrary, Potato!" said Grace to the dog. "I'm

Accounts to Review

only carrying you out." She proceeded to place the dog down on the ground, and she immediately ran over to sniff at Sophie's shoes.

"Mind your slippers," said Patience. "She'll chew them right off your feet."

"That's no way to speak about Potato!" said Grace. "She can hear what you're saying."

The dog looked over to Grace as she spoke, then scampered across the drive towards the front door of the house as Patience ran forward and threw herself into the viscount's outstretched arms. He cradled the back of her head with one large hand as he looked over her to Sophie standing in the drive. She lifted a hesitant hand in greeting.

Grace began chattering away as if everyone had been introduced.

"I could skewer a Frenchman in a matter of seconds!" she announced. "Richard says he's never seen such a young fencer attack with such ferocity!"

Patience laughed at her sister and glanced adoringly up into her husband's face. After an awkward moment, Patience finally thought to introduce Sophie to Lord Winter and would have introduced her to Grace, but the little girl was not to be slowed down with matters of protocol and social etiquette.

"Sophie!" she said, smiling as if they had known each other for years. "I'll show you how to fence if you like."

Sophie's eyes went wide as did her smile.

"That would be excellent. But I must warn you, your brother tells me I'm not to let you win."

"He *would* say that, wouldn't he?" said Grace to Patience. "Where is he anyway?"

"With Father," said Patience unwrapping her arms from

around her enormous husband.

The way her voice landed on the word 'Father' had Grace glancing from face to face.

"What's going on?" she asked.

"Come on," said Patience taking her hand. "Let's get you cleaned up, and then tea."

Grace looked backwards to Sophie as Patience pulled her towards the house.

"*You'll* tell me what's going on, won't you, Sophie?" she said.

"I believe George has a surprise for you," said Sophie in an effort to change the subject. Someone was going to have to tell her about her father, but it certainly wasn't Sophie's place to do so. She glanced over and up at the viscount who was striding beside her.

"Patience will tell her," he said, "if Lord Pemberton doesn't do it himself."

Sophie heaved a sigh. The strain of the last few days was beginning to take its toll.

"I'm sorry your honeymoon has not been more joyful," said Richard. "George deserves a bit of happiness."

"Do you know him well?" asked Sophie. She was curious to get someone else's perspective on her husband.

"I wouldn't say *well*," said Lord Winter simply. He took a few more strides in silence.

"He did attack me once," said the viscount. "He has a mean right hook—I know that much about him. That, and he will do absolutely anything for his family. As far as husbands go, you could have done much worse." He gave her a slight sideways smile as they walked.

At the front door, Lord Winter stopped to regard Sophie.

"Patience showed me his letter," he said solemnly. "I've never seen the like. And to think it was George who wrote it . . ." He shook his head in disbelief. "You are his family now, and he will move Heaven and earth for you if required. You can be assured of that."

Sophie absorbed all of this as her mind attempted to arrange and rearrange all the pieces of the puzzle that was George.

Grace, it turned out, would be the most helpful informant of all. Her mind was quick, her speech unfiltered, and the subject of George appeared to be a favourite of hers. Sophie engaged the little girl in a game of checkers so as to allow the rest of the family an opportunity to discuss matters among themselves.

"So," said Grace as she jumped her black marker over two of Sophie's red. "You married George."

"Yes," said Sophie sliding a red marker across the board.

"Not a good move!" said Grace, claiming another piece. She looked up with a mischievous gleam in her eye. "What was it that recommended him to you?" she asked.

"Excuse me?" said Sophie.

"George. What was it about him that made you think, 'Aye-aye, I'd like him for a husband'?"

Sophie laughed.

"I liked his smile," said Sophie in an attempt to tread lightly. "And he is quite funny sometimes."

"George doesn't smile," said Grace, stacking up the red pieces she had already claimed into a little tower. "I used to think he had a reason not to smile, but maybe it's just something he can't do. Like how some people can't wiggle their ears." She paused to demonstrate to Sophie that this was not a particular handicap of hers. "And he's certainly not funny, so it must be something else." She looked questioningly

A Baron's Son is Undone

at Sophie.

"He's surprising," said Sophie.

"No, he's not!" countered Grace. "He is completely predictable. There's the schedule and the lining things up and the rules—don't do this, don't do that. If there's any fun to be had, George will squash it like a plump little bug." She eyed Sophie with a grin. "Bug juice everywhere! And that's another thing," said Grace. "He needs everything to be clean and tidy, or he becomes very irritable. I don't envy you."

Sophie smiled back, but her nerves were starting to sing an odd note of disquiet, like a tuning fork humming into the silence.

"I *like* his schedule," said Sophie somewhat defensively. "And he *is* funny."

"Oooh," said Grace picking up on Sophie's tone of voice. "I suppose love will make fools of us all." She looked down at the board. "Your move."

That evening in bed as George lay stiffly beside her (for that was how he had slept for the last few nights), Sophie stared up at the white canopy above them. They no longer read together at night or laughed or talked. It was all George could do to climb into bed at the end of each day and kiss her brow before falling into a light and fitful sleep. Everything was such a tangled mess.

At first, Sophie had assumed George's withdrawn and tense demeanour had been due to grief for his father's plight. But according to Grace, he was always this way with his family—unsmiling and severe. And then there were the tears that he had shed the other night. He had almost told her something that night, something important. But instead, he had kept it to himself. Confusing all of this was something Sophie could not

Accounts to Review

bring herself to overlook—the fact that she was withholding something from him as well, something any husband had a right to expect. George had told her it was all right, but he was a man, and she had a feeling that the well of male patience did not run so deep. Eventually, he would be frustrated with her if he wasn't already. Frustration would soon transform itself into resentment, and she couldn't bear the thought. George had done so much for her, she couldn't help but feel that she owed him something—proper consummation of the marriage would be the bare minimum.

Sophie reached for his hand and gave it a squeeze. The movement had the effect of stirring him slightly from sleep. He rolled towards her and reached an arm across her to pull her body towards him. She closed her eyes as she shimmied into his embrace.

"Sophie," she heard him say in his sleep. He mumbled something unintelligible. Then, "I'm so sorry, Sophie."

She lifted his hand and kissed it before wiping away her own quiet tears with a corner of the coverlet.

George could not believe his ears. He looked down at his ham and toast and eggs, then back at his mother across the breakfast table. Every single member of the family had their mouths agape. Only Grace was not present, having eaten much earlier.

"Excuse me?" he said.

"I've invited His Grace the Duke of Somerset to the ball," she repeated with a prim little smile painted on her face.

"Why would you do that?" asked George evenly, careful to

A Baron's Son is Undone

control the tone of his voice.

"It's your coming out ball as it were—you will be introduced for the first time as a couple." She looked to Sophie. "I thought it would be obvious that the families should be seen to stand together."

"But they don't stand together," said George through gritted teeth.

He glanced worriedly over at Sophie who was fiddling nervously with the napkin in her lap.

"Of course they do!" replied Lady Pemberton. "The duke will see sense. I've sent him a letter."

"Not just an invitation," said George to clarify. "You wrote him a letter as well? Without my permission?!"

"I'm your mother, George. I don't need your permission," said Lady Pemberton pertly. "Tell him, Edward." She turned to her husband who reached for her hand across the breakfast table.

"George will be the baron soon, my love. You must become accustomed to taking his concerns into account," said Lord Pemberton to his wife.

"Don't talk rubbish, Edward!" said Lady Pemberton pulling her hand away angrily. "The duke will attend the ball—" She stood from the breakfast table. "—If he knows what's good for him!"

And with a swirl of her bronze-coloured skirts, she departed the room leaving the faint scent of lilies in her wake.

George looked to Sophie whose gaze was fixed down on her lap. Eventually, she reached with a shaky hand for her teacup, then seemed to think better of it and instead placed her napkin to the table.

"If you will all excuse me," she said. "I'm in need of some

Accounts to Review

air."

George watched as she stood and made her way slowly from the room. She had not looked to him once all morning. He squeezed his eyes against the pain that suddenly seized at his temples.

"You need to rein Mother in," he said to his father.

"I'm afraid that will be your job soon," said Lord Pemberton. "Best to get practising."

George reached both hands up into his hair in a gesture of exasperation. Then he whipped his napkin from his lap and strode from the room. He was just in time to see Sophie's lilac dress turn the corner. He followed her out into the garden where a blaze of morning light slanted through the trees and bushes sending slender shadows falling across the green lawn. Sophie took off across the grass at a run heading towards a copse of trees in the distance. George pulled out his pocket watch and checked the time. This was *not* part of his schedule for the day.

"Sophie!" he called, but she didn't turn back.

He slipped his watch back into his pocket and sprinted after her, catching up just as she reached the trees. Reaching out, he grabbed her sleeve and spun her towards him.

"I'm sorry about Mother," he said, his chest rising and falling rapidly with the exertion of his run.

"Wonderful," said Sophie irritably shaking his hand from her arm. "That's everything sorted then."

He was a little surprised at her tone. She had been so quiet for the last few days as he himself faced each day with grim acceptance. Each morning, he familiarised himself with all the various estates and accounts, and then in the afternoons, he listened attentively to his father's instructions and made detailed notes. His family would be counting on him. He could leave nothing up in the air.

"Sophie," said George.

"Who are you?" she asked stepping back. "What has happened to you?"

Her bald questions startled him, like a grouse bursting suddenly from the underbrush.

"Father is dying," said George briskly. "You can understand that. I'm sorry if I've been distant. I'm very preoccupied."

He knew his speech was clipped and his tone severe, but he could not find the means to soften his response. Sophie took another step backwards and away from him. She shook her head.

"No, that's not it," she said. "I can understand grief, but this is not simply grief: you're different here."

He didn't respond. He couldn't. Her words struck a little too close to home, and George found himself pulling out his pocket watch as some sort of shield.

"Do you have somewhere you need to be?" asked Sophie. "Oh, that's right—you must *review the accounts*."

Her voice was dripping with sarcasm.

"Life isn't a holiday, Sophie. We're no longer in Cornwall, and I have responsibilities to attend."

She heaved a breath as if she were struggling to take in air.

George couldn't understand why he was speaking to her like this. He had run after her to console her about what Mother had done. This conversation should be about Mother's poor behaviour, not his.

"I thought," said Sophie, her bottom lip quivering, "that you could be intimate with me."

"I can!" said George closing the distance between them. "I

have been."

She shook her head.

"I sleep beside you, but I'm alone." She wiped an angry tear from one eye. "And I know that's partially my fault, but George, I need you to talk to me."

"About what?!" George was nearly—not quite, but nearly—yelling now.

"About what the hell is going on with you!" Sophie raised her voice to match his.

"I don't know what you want me to say," said George.

"The truth," said Sophie more quietly. She stepped up to him and placed her hand over his heart. "Please don't pretend with me. I don't think I will be able to bear it for much longer."

He felt the heat of her palm seep into his chest like warm honey. *Sweet Heaven, he needed this. He needed her touch.* His hands were fisted at his sides with the strain of holding himself together, and he had to consciously unfurl them. Lifting his right hand, he realised with some dismay that it was trembling as he slowly placed it over Sophie's on his chest.

Sophie took in a deep breath and let it loose. Her shoulders relaxed.

George wanted to tell her his secret. She was his wife, and he loved her. She should know everything. But wanting to do something and doing something were two entirely different things. He looked down into her pleading face, those dark amber eyes shining with intelligence, her lips gently pursed with concern. His free hand strayed to her cheek and she leaned into it, closing her eyes.

He said, "I do not know how to reverse what Mother has done, but you will not be pressed to attend the ball if your father is present. I, however, must at least take the opportunity to talk with him. But now, I must go inside and review the accounts."

Seventeen

Target Practice

Grace had been told about her father. This was obvious from the fact that the little girl had been silent for nearly two days. Sophie had lost her mother at a similarly young age, and she knew how devastating the loss would be. To contemplate that loss ahead of time was more than any child should have to endure. On the third day, however, Grace awoke and entered the breakfast room with a spring in her step.

"Good morning!" she said to the family who was already seated around the table. She took her seat and hitched her chair in towards the table noisily. "Father, can I show you what Richard has been teaching me? After breakfast? I promise not to injure you, though I could do it in a heartbeat if you were an enemy soldier."

"Of course, my darling," said Lord Pemberton beaming. He turned to his eldest daughter. "You don't mind, do you,

A Baron's Son is Undone

Patience? We *have* done quite a lot of maths over the last several days." He chuckled.

"Not at all," said Patience leaning in towards her husband's side. "Do you need an audience, Grace?"

"No!" said Grace quickly. "Just me and Papa."

Lady Pemberton looked to Lord Winter. "You've given her all sorts of ideas, Richard. I'm not entirely certain they suit a young lady."

"Mother," said Patience taking her husband's hand on the table, "A lady should be able to defend herself. Richard has given Grace a wonderful gift."

"Yes. I just worry about her confidence," said Lady Pemberton with a sly smile and a sparkle in her eye. "She has a great deal too much already."

Everyone at the table laughed except George.

Sophie looked over at her husband. He would have accounts to review after breakfast. *How many accounts could there be?* It had been days and days of this with no end in sight. And at night, he continued to sleep stiffly beside her with no attempt to go beyond a peck on the forehead. She couldn't help but feel as if she were losing him before they had even had a chance to fully explore one another. The thought saddened her, but as often happened with Sophie's sadness, it descended upon her as if lit from behind, a thin bright halo at the edges. Perhaps she could do something small to tease the light from the darkness. Sophie took the opening in the conversation she had been fortuitously granted.

"Patience is right: a lady should be able to defend herself," said Sophie. "I for one should like to learn to shoot a pistol."

She carefully kept her eyes averted from her infuriatingly efficient and productive husband.

Target Practice

"Oh! I should like that as well!" said Patience practically bouncing in her seat as she turned towards Lord Winter. "Richard, will you teach us? We could have a lesson this morning."

Sophie noticed that Lord Winter had a way of regarding his wife—as if he couldn't quite believe that she existed. He was looking at her like that now as a smile slowly spread over his face, warm and wondering and indulgent all at once.

"That's a 'yes'!" said Patience excitedly, and she leaned forward and gave him a quick kiss on the mouth before sitting back in her chair and surveying the family with her violet-blue eyes.

Lord Winter was still looking at her, but his countenance had shifted to something considerably more heated. Lady Pemberton cleared her throat, and it was then that Sophie noticed George was silently and repeatedly adjusting the placement of his cutlery beside his plate.

He was thinking.

Sophie's heart felt as if it had paused between beats as she held her breath, willing him to speak.

"*I* was going to teach you to shoot," he said quietly as he lined up his fork alongside his folded napkin.

Yes.

She turned to him.

"But you have accounts to review," she said.

She was seated beside him, but George didn't look over at her. He kept readjusting his fork.

"Yes," he said, thoughtfully drawing the word out. "But I think I will join you anyway."

"Well, if your hearts are all set on a morning of violence, I'll have to inform the servants to stay clear of the back lawn,"

A Baron's Son is Undone

said Lady Pemberton. "Please be careful!"

Patience grinned as she hefted the ivory-inlaid pistol in her hand.

"Oh yes," she said. "This feels good."

The sunlight glinted off her golden hair and the silver metal of the gun. Sophie thought it would make a pretty picture.

"Watch yourself!" said George. "Keep it aimed elsewhere."

Lord Winter gently took his wife's shoulders in his hands and turned her towards one of two archery targets that had been set up down the lawn.

"George is simply worried that I will show him up," said Patience casually swinging the pistol to take aim at the brightly coloured target. She closed one eye. Richard stepped behind her and took her free hand to place it on the gun as well.

"Those are *your* archery targets," said George in response. "Funny—I don't see any holes in them."

Patience gave Sophie a sideways glance.

"Are you hearing this, Sophie? He's not terribly kind to his sister."

Sophie covered her mouth to hide a smile, but the corners of George's mouth remained firmly under control. His eyes were steel and his countenance firm and unyielding.

"I didn't take to archery," continued Patience in all good humour. "My arm guard was always twisting away, and the bow string kept stinging me."

As George demonstrated to Sophie how to load her pistol, Richard gave Patience her own lesson. He stood behind her, his dark head bent low beside her bright one, and his voice

Target Practice

was so low and so soft, he might have been murmuring sweet nothings to her in bed instead of instructing her on a makeshift gun range.

"Are you listening?" George asked Sophie in a clipped tone.

"What? Yes," said Sophie, tearing her attention back to her husband.

As George repeated his demonstration one more time for good measure, the sudden earth-shattering sound of Patience firing her pistol made Sophie's heart leap in her chest. When she looked over, Patience had either stepped or fallen back against Richard's enormous chest.

"Hah!" she cried "George, look! I hit the target."

"In the white," said George barely glancing up. "Call me when you hit an actual colour."

"Well done," said Richard wrapping his arms around her from behind and taking the gun from her hand.

"You're up, Sophie," said Patience with a grin.

George handed her the pistol, and the weight of it in her hand made her think of that day on the beach so many weeks ago. She could almost hear the rush of the ocean as she looked out over the lawn.

Sophie stepped into place in front of the second target and took aim with both hands. She could sense George's presence just behind her even though he wasn't making any actual contact.

"I'm seeing double," she said.

"Bring your focus in," said George, his mouth near her ear. "Let the target blur."

"Oh."

"Take a breath, and as you let it go, squeeze the trigger."

Sophie did as he said, but as the gun discharged its bullet

A Baron's Son is Undone

with a shocking report, she was thrown off balance by the recoil. Before she could even stumble, George had his body flush against hers, his arms around her. Sophie found herself laughing with the sudden joy of it all. Shooting guns, it turned out, was quite a rush.

"Yellow!" said George, and she could hear the smile in his voice. "Are you seeing this, Patience? My wife is a bloody excellent shot!"

He gave her entire body an enthusiastic squeeze from behind, and Sophie turned to him in his arms grinning like a giddy little girl.

"I'm not sure this is entirely healthy, George. You mustn't pit me against your sister." Sophie was laughing as she said it. "I hope your affection isn't conditional on my shooting skills."

Her husband's eyes were soft and glossy and full of mirth as he looked down into hers. Sophie felt a momentary pang to see him as himself if only briefly. And then he let loose one hiccup of laughter followed by another and another. It was like liquid sunlight pouring over her. Sweet Heaven, after the tension of the last several days, to hear him laugh was a kind of release that sent sparks of tingly hope shimmering through her veins.

"I'm serious," said Sophie trying to school her own amusement. "You are entirely too competitive."

George cocked his head as if he might kiss her, and Sophie was reminded that they were in company. She looked over to Patience and Richard who were standing side-by-side with their mouths slightly open.

"Winter," said George taking the gun from Sophie and ignoring the astonished expressions. "Best of five?"

"As long as you don't try to shoot me in the head when I

Target Practice

win," said Lord Winter amiably.

"You know I can't make ridiculous promises like that," said George as he set to reloading the pistol.

"All right," said Patience as if she had been consulted. "But I want another turn when you're both done. I'm sure Sophie does as well."

"Watch and learn," said George to his sister as he took aim.

The men took turns firing shots at the targets, and Sophie was pleased for the opportunity to simply watch her husband—his blonde hair flashing under the sun, his confident stance, the way he swung the gun up into position. At one point, he shrugged off his jacket and tossed it to the ground. His waistcoat followed so that eventually he was dressed in only his white linen shirtsleeves. Each time he hit close to the centre of the target, he would turn smiling to Sophie. Unfortunately, *all* of Lord Winter's shots seemed to be pulled as if by some magnetic force to the exact centre of his bull's eye. But it didn't seem to matter to George. He looked pleased as punch each time he stepped up to take aim, even remarking on the extraordinary shots made by his brother-in-law. By the end, he was laughing as they debated whether Lord Winter's last shot had even hit the target. Patience was of the opinion that the lead ball had actually flown through a hole that had already been pierced by a previous shot.

"When will you come to terms with the awful truth?" asked George of his sister. "The fact of the matter is that regardless what the papers say, your husband is not a terribly good marksman."

His eyes were twinkling with mischief as he spoke.

"All I can do is try my best," said Lord Winter, joining in the game.

A Baron's Son is Undone

Patience rolled her eyes and reached her hand out towards her husband.

"She wants your gun, Winter," said George. "Thanks for the game," he added.

The rest of the morning was spent teaching Patience and Sophie their technique, until finally, Patience and Lord Winter excused themselves and returned to the house. Sophie joined George where he was sitting on the grass leaning back on his hands and gazing out over the lawn.

When Sophie had stumbled backwards into George's arms laughing after firing the pistol for the first time, a small lamp had been lit inside him, and he had suddenly seen clearly for the fist time in days that which had been shrouded by his own self-serving habits: Sophie herself was the lamp, his beacon in a dark world.

As she sat down beside him on the grass, it felt to him almost criminal, his withholding the secret part of himself from her. There should be nothing between them.

He placed his hand over hers where it rested on the earth.

"That was fun," she said.

"Mmm."

"I like watching you and your sister spar." She grinned at him.

"Sophie," said George, taking her hand in his and lifting it to his lips. He pressed a grateful kiss to her delicate knuckles. "I need to tell you . . ."

He looked into her beautiful waiting eyes and found he couldn't continue. The secret was somehow a part of him now, woven through the fabric of his soul like darning thread through a damaged stocking. It was what held him together, in one functional piece. To speak it aloud felt to him as if he would be pulling out the thread to reveal something so damaged and useless it might as well be thrown on the rubbish heap.

"You can tell me anything, George. I will guard every confidence with my life."

George felt a chill as a breeze stroked over his face. He realised that his brow was clammy with anxious sweat, and his heartbeat was a gallop inside his chest. *He wasn't the baron's son, and if he wasn't the baron's son, who was he?* As if reading his mind, Sophie spoke.

"You're my husband," she said lifting his hand to her lips. "For longer than death do us part, I promise you."

It was precisely what he needed to hear. He was only a partial brother, no son at all to the man he considered his father, but he was entirely, with every frayed edge of his battered soul, Sophie's husband. He wrapped an arm around her and pulled her to him, clinging to her as he might a piece of driftwood on a wide and otherwise empty sea. He pulled her down to the grass and cradled her head against his chest.

"Heaven help me," he said, his voice cracking. "Sophie, I can't do this without you."

"You don't have to. I'm here," she said wrapping her free arm around him and placing a comforting hand to the middle of his back.

He lay there with her for quite some time with the warm sun beating down on them and the prickle of grass against his cheek where it rested on the ground. The smell of earth and crushed chamomile and Sophie helped to calm his nerves.

A Baron's Son is Undone

His heartbeat slowed to match hers, his sweat evaporated, and eventually he loosened his fierce embrace, and Sophie rolled onto her back to look up at the sky. George gazed at her profile from where he lay, watched her breast rise and fall. She was so incredibly clever, his wife. He had a feeling she had instigated this entire morning of target practice just for him. To give him a chance to play. To forget himself in the moment. To live.

He smiled.

"I'm going to have to kiss you," he said.

She turned her head to him on the grass, then rolled her body back into him. George tipped her over onto her back once more, but this time his body was over hers, and he propped himself up with his forearms.

"Go on then," she whispered.

He pressed his lips to hers, and sweet mercy, they had been warmed by the sun. Her mouth was as ripe as a summer peach. He sipped at her gently at first. Just a taste. Her arms came around him as she responded in kind—soft, tender kisses, that made his throat feel thick with emotion. She pressed herself up against his body, and he felt desire kindle low in his belly and lower still. He regretfully reminded himself that they were in full view of the house. On the lawn. This could only go so far. Slowly, he pulled away and sat up. She sat up with him.

George twisted one arm to take a look at his white linen sleeve—grass stains!

"Look what you made me do," he said with mock seriousness, showing her one sleeve and then the other.

She pressed her lips together, but he could see the smile she was trying to hide. And then as a laugh burst forth from her

Target Practice

lips, she actually lunged for him, knocking him to the ground! Sophie knelt up above him, straddling his torso, one hand to his chest to hold him down.

"If you don't mind your tone, Mr. Pemberton, you'll have more than grass stains to worry about."

"Oh, will I?" asked George, tumbling her down and underneath him once more.

She let out a happy little shriek as he did so. He kissed her then. Not gentle this time. It was rough and needy and joyful all at once. And then he dragged his mouth along her jaw to her neck where he set her vibrating with that special sound she loved so much. It pleased him to the very depths of his soul to hear her laughter, to feel her wriggle delightedly beneath him.

When George finally lifted his head from hers, something caught his eye. There were four startled faces staring from the drawing room window! His entire family had been watching their little display.

"Bloody hell," he muttered, standing up and dusting himself off.

"What is it?" asked Sophie, allowing herself to be pulled to her feet.

"We have an audience," said George gesturing to the window with his chin.

When Sophie looked over, there were only two faces left in the window—Patience and Grace. His parents had at least known to pretend they had not been watching. Grace lifted a hand to wave, and Sophie waved back.

"Don't acknowledge them," said George gathering up his jacket and waistcoat from the grass while studiously ignoring the window.

A Baron's Son is Undone

Sophie laughed, and when George met her eye, he couldn't help the smile that broke through his annoyance.

By the time he and Sophie had cleaned themselves up, everyone except Lord Winter was already gathered in the dining room for luncheon. They were whispering among themselves as George and Sophie entered, but their whispers died to silence when they noticed the latest arrivals. George pulled out a chair for Sophie and took his own seat. Everyone was staring at them.

Grace finally broke through the quiet of the room: "Why do you only smile for her?"

"Grace!" scolded Lady Pemberton.

"I suppose it has to do with all the kissing," said Grace thoughtfully.

"I won't warn you again," said Lady Pemberton as the baron let out a low chuckle.

"Sophie is his soul mate," said Patience pulling a basket of bread towards her and reaching for the butter dish. "That is so much more than a wife."

Patience was entirely right. He wouldn't tell her so, of course.

"Where's Winter?" he asked.

"In the stable," said Patience. "One of the horses is poorly, and he is discussing next steps with the groom."

George passed a plate of fruit over to Sophie, and she helped herself. She was still flushed from their encounter on the grass, and her eyes were sparkling as she popped a blackberry into her mouth. She had redone her hair and changed her dress before lunch, but now all he wanted to do was muss her up again.

Lord Pemberton cleared his throat.

Target Practice

"I think we've covered a lot of ground over the last several days," he said to George. "Perhaps we could do something else this afternoon. As a family."

"A three-legged race!" declared Grace.

"Well," said the baron. "That wasn't top of my list, but I suppose . . ."

"No races with any number of legs," interrupted Lady Pemberton. "We shall all go for a nice walk." She looked to her husband. "Would you be up for that, Edward?"

It was her first public concession that perhaps her husband was not entirely well.

"Yes, my dear. I'll rest after we eat, and then yes, a walk will do just fine. Very sensible of you."

Lady Pemberton beamed at her husband.

"And then after the boring walk, whoever wants to do so can join in the three-legged race," added Grace.

Lady Pemberton made a muffled sound of disapproving agreement, and Patience gave her sister a wink from across the table. George forked some cold meat onto his plate and offered the same to Sophie who ignored the meat platter and instead stole a slice of roast beef from his plate. When he locked eyes with her, she gave him a challenging look full of good cheer, and he realised that he had not seen her this happy in days. He knew, of course, that this had been entirely his fault. In his stress and his grief, he had completely shut her out, isolating himself inside the role that he always played among his family.

As Sophie laughed at something Patience had said from her place across the table, George made a decision that set his heart hammering once more.

Eighteen

The Sensible One

Sophie lay in bed as George fussed about the room. It was late, and he had not even taken off his jacket. Instead, he adjusted the position of a chair under the writing desk and then proceeded to rearrange several of the implements upon the desk. Sophie pretended to be resting as she watched him out of the corner of her eye. He walked up to the enormous brown-and-cream patterned carpet that stretched itself across the centre of the room and kicked at one of its corners.

"It won't lie flat," he muttered.

Then he strode to the wardrobe and opened the dark wooden doors.

"The maid is always hanging these shirts bunched together at one end of the rail," he said as he slid the hangers and shirts into a more pleasing position.

"I'll have her pilloried in the morning," said Sophie from the

The Sensible One

bed.

George looked over at her as if he was just now realising she was in the room with him.

"I suppose you think you're being funny," he said without smiling.

"Yes," said Sophie, defying him with a grin. "Leave the shirts, George. Come to bed."

He didn't make a move towards her, but instead sat down in an armchair in the corner of the room and resting his elbows on his knees, placed his face in his hands.

"George?"

He didn't look up, but she could see him heave a breath. Sophie carefully pulled back the covers and swung her bare feet to the floor.

"Give me a few minutes," said George rubbing his hands up over his face and into his hair.

Sophie stayed exactly where she was, her eyes never leaving her husband. They might have sat there like that at opposite corners of the room for ten minutes or more before George finally stood up.

"Come with me," he said, reaching out his hand. "And bring that blanket. It's cold in the house after dark."

Sophie tugged the blanket from the bed and bunched it under her arm as she joined George at the door to their bedchamber.

"Here," he said taking the blanket gently from her and wrapping it around her shoulders.

He didn't make eye contact as he did so, and Sophie watched his solemn face go about his task with all the gravity of a sacred ritual. When he had her all bundled up, he lifted a candle and led her out into the darkness. Down one hall and then another.

A Baron's Son is Undone

Stairs. Another hall. Until finally, he led her into the darkened library. He put down his candle on a table and stepped to a window where he pulled back the enormous velvet drapes onto a view of the lawn over which hung a white crescent moon.

"I was sitting right here," he said pointing to a place on the wide window sill just behind the fall of the dark curtain.

Sophie pulled the blanket tighter and waited. *He was going to tell her.*

"I was ten, and we—Patience, Serafina, and I—were playing The Invisible Game, so that is why I was hiding."

He proceeded to tell her all that he had overheard that day between his mother and his aunt while he kept his eyes fixed to the window sill. When he was finished, he looked sharply up at her.

"I still look nothing like Father. When I was small, the occasional guest or acquaintance would comment that I had his eyes or his nose, but with each passing year, the difference in our features became more prominent." He paused and looked out the window. "I'm not Father's legitimate heir, but I must pretend to be for the sake of the family. Up until now, it seemed an abstract thing—all I could do was play the part I had been given. But now . . . with Father unwell . . . and they will all be looking to me when he goes . . . I'm not . . . Sophie, I feel as if I can't . . . and if they found out—Patience and Father . . ."

He reached up to the curtain to draw it closed once more, and Sophie realised his hands were trembling. She dropped the blanket, and the cold of the room swept itself around her as she stepped up behind him. He turned towards her.

"There should be nothing between us," he said. "I should

The Sensible One

have told you sooner. I'm not who you thought I was."

Sophie drew her arms around his waist and nestled her cheek against his chest. She felt his body shudder with a silent sob as his arms came around hers. After a minute or so, when she felt his body soften against her, she spoke.

"George, you are exactly who I thought you were. I never wanted to marry the baron's son. I wanted to marry you." She felt his arms tighten around her. "You're not going to like what I'm going to say next," she said looked up into his glistening eyes. "I think you should speak with your mother."

George stared at her for a period of time that slowly stretched itself out into the darkest corners of the room. Finally, he spoke.

"You're right," he said quietly. "I don't like it."

Back in their bedchamber, Sophie helped George to undress. When she had him down to his drawers, she pulled her night dress up over her head and climbed into the bed. From where her head rested on the pillow, she watched as George stepped out of his drawers. She reached for him as he climbed under the covers, and they slept together that night skin-to-skin, their warm limbs entangled, breathing together as one.

In the morning, Lady Pemberton called Sophie into her private parlour. Patches of sunflower yellow accented the blues and creams of the room, paying a sort of homage to the more audacious decorating choices of the main drawing room.

"Please take a seat," said Lady Pemberton when Sophie had stepped into the room.

A Baron's Son is Undone

Her mother-in-law was regarding her with a curious look overlaid with a smile.

"What can I do for you, Lady Pemberton?"

"Ah, that is the question, now isn't it?" she said, her smile growing wider. "However, I fear you have already done it, my dear."

Sophie didn't understand.

"You have brought my son to life," she continued.

Lady Pemberton's smile dropped, and she placed a hand to her mouth as if overcome with emotion.

"I didn't—" started Sophie.

"Don't tell me what you have or haven't done, my dear. I saw it with my own eyes. He smiled yesterday. For Heaven's sake, he actually laughed! I haven't seen him laugh since he was a boy. Always so serious and with that determined look on his face. I feared that whomever he chose for a wife would be shackled to a fairly grim existence . . . though he *is* handsome, so there would be some degree of compensation, I suppose." She caught Sophie's gaze in hers. "You *do* think he's handsome, don't you?"

Sophie could feel her face heat.

"Well, I . . . yes, my lady. Facts are facts."

Lady Pemberton laughed.

"See! That is it right there. That is why you are suited. *Facts are facts*. It's exactly the sort of thing George or my husband might say." She tittered once more.

"Sophie, my darling, I must apologise once more for the terrible way in which I greeted you. I was not myself. No, that's not true. I was completely myself, and I behaved abysmally."

"It was entirely understandable, Lady Pemberton."

The Sensible One

"Please, you must call me Mother."

Sophie's heart stumbled against her chest. She thought she must have heard wrongly.

"Unless . . . that is . . . if you would prefer not to," added Lady Pemberton.

"No," said Sophie quickly. "No, I would be honoured."

"Good girl! Now. To business. I'll not be one of those mother-in-laws who begrudges handing over her title. No. You shall be the baroness soon."

"There's no need to speak of it now," said Sophie feeling the sad weight of Lord Pemberton's illness settle over the room.

"My husband likes it when I'm sensible," said Lady Pemberton. "So I'm trying to be sensible. Do indulge me." She shifted in her seat and rearranged the pleats of her dress. "There is much to learn, and I should like to teach you, beginning with the organisation of this ball we are to host. From what I know of your past, you have not had any experience managing a household or hosting events."

"No," said Sophie simply.

No one had ever entertained the idea that she had something to offer. She had simply been a possession kept in a cupboard waiting for the day she would be traded for money or esteem or perhaps even a political favour.

"Do not be deceived, my girl," said Lady Pemberton. "A ball may seem like a trivial affair, but as the baron's wife, it is an opportunity to make connections, to sway hearts and minds. We may not sit in the House of Lords, but we can still have some effect on what happens there.

"Come then. Let me explain a few things." Lady Pemberton stood and walked over to a desk strewn with papers. "Parties don't materialise on their own. Although a good housekeeper

A Baron's Son is Undone

is worth her weight in oolong tea." Lady Pemberton gave her a mischievous grin. "By weight, it's worth more than gold, you see."

Sophie found herself laughing.

"I'll remember that," she said as Lady Pemberton pulled up a chair for her, and they both took a seat in front of the desk.

As pleased as Sophie was with the way Lady Pemberton had taken her under her wing, she felt ever-so-briefly a flutter of tension over the fact that she would be helping to organise the ball her father might be attending. How would she be able to excuse herself from attending the ball now that Lady Pemberton had so graciously included her as a proper member of the family, now that she was co-organising the event? Sophie suspected that her new mother-in-law was, not conniving exactly, but certainly a clever woman who was adept at moulding circumstances to her will. Which was not to say that the lady's sentiments were not heartfelt—Sophie knew them to be genuine. She also knew that she was now trapped within Lady Pemberton's machiavellian plot.

It was late afternoon, and George had been dismissed some time ago from his father's study. He thought to seek out Sophie. He had seen her at lunch chatting animatedly with his mother at the other end of the table—something about flower arrangements and cheeses. Sophie had caught his eye at one point and flared hers wide as if to acknowledge the shift in his mother's general demeanour towards her. After lunch, Patience had whisked Sophie off for a tour of her old studio she still kept at the house.

The Sensible One

"And if you're not interested in art," said Patience as they left the room, "we can always go hunting for some lemons to preserve." George could hear Sophie and Patience laughing as they disappeared down the hall.

Now, as George stood in the entrance of the house, his black shoes reflected in the well-polished marble floor, he felt the overwhelming need to have Sophie near. To hold her, to talk to her. He hadn't spoken properly with his wife since last night, but he knew what she would say to him if he found her: *talk to your mother.*

The words repeated themselves in his head like a taunt. George didn't think so. Talking to his mother was a step too far, an irreversible act, like dropping a crystal vase from the roof of the house. Nevertheless, within the next few minutes, he found his feet had taken him to the drawing room where Lady Pemberton was seated at a writing desk in the corner going over some correspondence.

"Mother."

She looked up, and if George was not mistaken, she winced at the sight of him. Her face quickly transformed itself into a smile.

"George! I was just about to come looking for you."

Why?

He waited, standing in stillness by the door.

"Close the door," she said.

He did so and then stepped into the middle of the carpet which was covered in tiny yellow canaries lifting vines in their sharp little beaks.

"What's this about?" asked George.

"His Grace, the Duke of Somerset—" began his mother.

"Dear God, he is coming to the ball!" George shoved a hand

A Baron's Son is Undone

up over his head. "What have you done, Mother? Do you have any idea how he has treated Sophie?!"

"Contrary to what you may think, George, I am not slow-witted," said his mother. "But this is about your future and hers. The duke must be seen to stand with us." She paused to adjust her skirts as she stood from her chair. "And yes, he is, in fact, coming."

"Well then Sophie will not be attending," said George.

"Don't be so dramatic," responded Lady Pemberton with a dismissive wave of her hand. "The duke will be on his best behaviour."

"Mother?"

Lady Pemberton licked her lips and looked sideways across the room.

"I may have threatened him," she said.

"With what?"

"This and that, George—you don't need to know. It's all a bit *low* if you take my meaning. I couldn't rightly speak it aloud."

Holy hell. George thought he might pull his hair out by the roots. He was beginning to feel more than exasperated. There was an anger surging inside him, working its way up past his throat.

"You're very creative with your solutions, Mother," he said. And his mouth continued as if it were in no way attached to his brain: "Was *I* also once a problem that required a creative solution?"

Lady Pemberton blinked twice and then froze. Her face drained of all colour.

"What?" she whispered.

"Was marrying Father an ingenious solution to a difficult

problem?" asked George.

"Your fa-father," stammered Lady Pemberton, clearly thrown off her guard. "How . . . ?"

"I once heard you talking with Aunt Sara—that time when she came visiting unannounced."

"That was twenty years ago," said his mother.

"Yes."

"George . . ."

She stepped up to him, reaching for him, but he stepped away.

"It is unforgivable, Mother," he said. "To have deceived Father in that way."

She looked as if she had been struck, and he immediately regretted the words he had spoken.

"I would never deceive your father," she said quietly.

"Father knows?!"

"Of course. It was his idea. He is, after all, the sensible one."

She reached her hand to a chair, and George realised her legs were giving way. He rushed over to give her his arm and lowered her into the seat.

"Oh, George, I was such a foolish young girl. And so trusting. It is a hard thing to learn that your heart can be led so easily astray. Your father found me crying in the garden at a house party. He had overheard me speaking of my . . . condition with my sister. I knew he fancied me, but I never thought he was glamorous enough to entertain as a suitor. And yet, he offered for me. On the spot. He offered to save me from certain ruin."

"A marriage of convenience," said George.

"Yes, but not for long," said Lady Pemberton looking up into his eyes. "Your father, he is the beating heart of my world."

A Baron's Son is Undone

Her tears started to fall then.

"I'm so sorry you had to find out like that. And you were so young . . . You should have come to us."

"Would you have ever told me?"

"There didn't seem to be a need." She dabbed at her eyes with a handkerchief. "You are our son."

Father knows, thought George. *He has always known.* Every moment in George's life had to be rewritten with this in mind. He didn't understand. He had not even entertained the possibility.

The door to the drawing room clicked open, and Lord Pemberton stood on the threshold surveying the scene.

"Who made my wife cry?" he asked.

"It's nothing, Edward."

"George?" said his father.

"He knows," said Lady Pemberton. "He's known since he was ten."

"Ah." Lord Pemberton placed a hand to his jaw. "Put it out of your mind, son. It's of no consequence."

"What? But I'm not . . . and when you go . . . Father, I'm not your son. I'm not the legal heir!"

Lord Pemberton regarded him then with what George could only describe as anger. George quailed quietly inside himself. His father never appeared angry. He was always so even-keeled, so matter-of-fact and calm. Lord Pemberton stepped forward and took both George's shoulders firmly in his hands.

"Look at me, George! Have I ever lied to you?"

George shook his head. *Never. Not once.*

"That's right," said Lord Pemberton. "Now listen carefully. You are my son, and I love you. You are the pride of my life, and you are my consolation in death. If Patience or Grace had

The Sensible One

been born boys, you would still be my heir because you would still be my eldest son, not simply in name, but in concrete absolute fact—a fact that resides in my heart and in my soul forever."

George could feel his eyes well with all the emotion he had taken so much care to keep hidden for the last twenty years.

"But I don't deserve—"

"—don't deserve what?" asked his father. "The barony?"

George nodded as he regarded his father through tear-clouded eyes.

"And you think your cousin Giles does? Because he's next in line you know. That man doesn't know his arse from a small hole in the ground. Look, now you have me swearing. You think Giles *deserves* to inherit? I'll tell you something in case you haven't noticed, my boy, but the members of the House of Lords no more deserve their seats than children deserve to be working in the various factories that are springing up all over England. It's not a question of deserving. It is a question of what is best, and it just so happens that what is best for the country and for this family align.

"I know you will take your seat in Parliament, and I know you will do your utmost, if not to make things better because that is a tall order, then to at least temper the worst of what our government might seek to do. I also know you will take care of this family, including my lovely wife here, but you must promise not to reduce her to tears ever again. I'll not have it."

George took two long juddering breaths.

"Now then," said his father. "Is there anything else you need me to set straight?"

When George did not respond, his father pulled him into

A Baron's Son is Undone

a strong embrace. Lord Pemberton was not in the habit of handing out hugs, and George was quickly overcome with a mixed feeling of poignancy and bone-melting relief. His tears began to fall silently.

"What will I do without you?" he asked over his father's shoulder.

"Your best," responded his father. "It will be more than good enough. I promise."

The simple words spread like a balm over his battered soul. After a time, George realised he was leaning into his father who was probably feeling quite tired. He pulled away and forced himself to look at his mother.

She waved a hand and shook her head at him to preempt any apology. Then dabbing her eye with a handkerchief, she said, "You do see why I love him, don't you?"

"Come, my love," said Lord Pemberton to his wife. "Let us leave George to his thoughts."

When they had gone from the room, George leaned his weight down into a chair. His body and soul felt ravaged, yet strangely light, as if he had recently emerged from some lengthy battle. Belatedly, he realised that the battle had been waged with no one but himself. If that was not a fool's errand, he didn't know what was.

Sophie.

The last several days could not have been easy for her. And yet, somehow she had managed to find a way through to him. The shooting lessons to lift his spirits, the quiet manner in which she had listened to his secret and reassured him that it was him she wanted and not the baron's son. The way she had stripped down to her skin in order to hold him against her that night with nothing between them. And the advice to

The Sensible One

speak with his mother—he had not wanted to hear it, but she had been right.

George was jostled from his thoughts by girlish laughter coming from the hallway, and then Sophie and Patience burst into the room. Sophie was carrying a piece of paper in her hand and grinning widely.

"George, you must settle a dispute for us," she said.

"Don't be ridiculous," said Patience. "George has no conception of art."

Sophie thrust the paper at him, and he looked down to see a rudimentary (and that was putting it generously) drawing of what appeared to be a bird struggling to take shape.

"Patience says this is a wonderful attempt at a swallow," said Sophie, suppressing a laugh. "What would you say?"

Patience snatched the page from Sophie's hand.

"Did *you* draw that?" asked George looking at Sophie. He could feel a small smile tugging at his mouth.

"Yes," said Sophie. "According to your sister, I'm a natural." Her eyes grew wide in that amused yet challenging way she had of looking at him.

Sweet Heaven, she was beautiful.

"But I want to know what *you* think," she said. "No pretending," she added.

"I think . . ." said George, stalling for time as his face broke into a broad smile. "I think . . . it is a bird."

Sophie turned laughing and gave Patience a playful shove.

"See!" she said. "It's awful! You must admit it now."

"I'll admit to nothing!" said Patience holding the drawing aloft as she made for the door. "George wouldn't know good art if it bit him on the—" She turned quickly at the door. "—You-know-what!" And with that she took herself from the

A Baron's Son is Undone

room, leaving Sophie and George grinning after her.

"Your sister has been very kind to me," said Sophie.

"That's just how she is," said George.

"*You've* been very kind to me," said Sophie.

"No, I haven't," said George.

Nineteen

A Disobedient Wife

"How is it," asked George, his eyes gone all smoky as he examined her face, "that you can find joy, that you can *play*, even when you find yourself in the saddest of circumstances?"

Sophie shook her head. She didn't understand.

"When I met you, apart from Duncan, you were all alone, with your reputation in ruins and the threat of your own father's next plan for you hanging over your head like the executioner's axe. And yet, you went out to find company, played at dice and cards, even took a lonesome picnic to the beach, packing a pistol no less! . . . And you gave me a chance despite the absolute ass I made of myself."

"I don't know," said Sophie slowly. "When I look back, there is always some sadness looming like a dark mass. But when I think about it like that, I usually notice that the edges of that sadness are lit from behind. The light is there. It's just a

A Baron's Son is Undone

matter of teasing it out bit by bit. The sadness doesn't actually go away, but it has more and more trouble hiding the light if that makes any sense."

She felt almost embarrassed saying these things. They sounded quite foolish. But George was looking at her now with more than smoke in his gaze, so she continued.

"And you're not an ass," she added.

He stepped closer to her so that she had to tip her face up to look at him. His eyes were slightly bloodshot, and it looked as if he had been crying. She placed a hand to the side of his face and rubbed a thumb across his cheek. It was damp.

"Don't lie to me, Sophie," he said sternly.

"Fine," said Sophie. "You are the veriest ass who ever lived! Does that make you happy?"

"It's a start," he said wrapping an arm around her waist and jerking her against him.

The motion had the effect of producing an involuntary pant from Sophie's lips.

"I've been neglecting you," he said, his warm breath against her ear. "You promised me that you would tell me if I ever made you unhappy."

"I tried," whispered Sophie.

"Not hard enough," said George. "I would say you've been somewhat disobedient on that count . . . and I've already told you how I will deal with a disobedient wife."

Sophie didn't think she had been disobedient in the slightest, but she wasn't going to argue. Her breath hitched in her chest, and heat flooded the space between her legs.

Holding her tightly against him, George walked her backwards until her back was up against the door of the drawing room. Reaching down, he turned the lock, and Sophie heard the dull thunk of the mechanism falling into place.

He wasn't going to . . . Surely, not here in the yellow drawing room!

"Now," he said, "untie your bodice."

She hesitated, and George fixed her with an admonishing look.

"The door is locked," he said as if to reassure her.

Slowly, her hands came to the ribbon at the front of her dress. When she had it loosened, George tugged down her bodice exposing her breasts to his eyes which were now clouded over in a sensual haze. Sophie could feel her nipples gathering themselves into tight little peaks from the stroke of his gaze alone. He kissed her then, full on the mouth. Hot and needful but with an edge of tenderness that Sophie imagined was apologetic more than anything else.

He was trying to say he was sorry.

Her bare breasts were crushed against the rough fabric of his waistcoat, and Sophie couldn't help but revel in the contrast of her naked skin with his fully clad body. He dragged his warm velvety tongue down her neck, and lifting both breasts in his hands, he gave them a tender squeeze before taking one nipple and then the other in his mouth.

"Ah!" Sophie was pressed up against the door, squirming as he licked and sucked at her.

He lifted his head and gave it a solemn shake.

"Quiet, you naughty girl!" he said before giving her a quick and hungry kiss on the mouth. He pulled away and looked at her with mischief in his eyes. "We don't want to attract any attention now, do we?"

Sophie shook her head. George kept his eyes fixed on hers as he reached down to pull up her skirt, bunching it in his

A Baron's Son is Undone

hands until she was exposed to him.

"Hold this," he said, handing her the bunched-up fabric.

"George," whispered Sophie.

He froze. "Do you want me to stop?" he asked seriously, his face flushed and his breath ragged.

God, no! She shook her head.

"Don't stop," she said.

He leaned in to inhale the skin by her ear. Then he took her free hand and slipped her first two fingers into his mouth. The wet heat of his mouth sucking at her fingers sent a wave of molten pleasure sweeping down the length of her arm and spearing her between the legs so that she bucked roughly up against him.

"Oh!"

He pulled her fingers from his mouth and looked her in the eyes as he placed her hand between her thighs.

"Touch yourself," he whispered. "Quietly," he added.

Another searing kiss pressed against her lips, his tongue probing and tasting her as she responded in kind. She was feeling quite desperate at this point and was only faintly aware of the impropriety of it all as she pressed her fingers against herself, stroking and rubbing as George took one nipple between his fingers while he continued to delve into her mouth. Sophie found her breath coming faster. Her mind shut down as a wave of pleasure rippled through her, surging and cresting, but George pulled himself and her hand away before it could come crashing down.

She was left panting and breathless and feeling extraordinarily wanton with her breasts exposed and her skirt pulled up to her waist in front of this gorgeous man who was still entirely clothed and seemingly in complete control of himself.

A Disobedient Wife

"I should like to worship you properly," he said in a hoarse voice as he dropped himself to his knees before her.

Mercy.

She looked down as his golden head tilted up to her, and her grip loosened on her skirt.

"Up!" he said firmly as he lifted her dress. He sat back on his haunches, and his grey trousers pulled tight across the muscles of his thighs. "Hold my shoulder with your other hand."

Sophie did as she was told, and George slipped his hand around her stockinged calf. Gently he lifted it over his opposite shoulder as she balanced with one hand to him and one hand holding her dress. Once her leg was firmly hooked over him, she shifted her hand from his shoulder to rest lightly on the top of his head and leaned back against the door.

"Fuck, you smell good," said George as he pressed his face to the curls between her legs and inhaled.

What was it about his indecent words?

Sophie could feel herself swell and throb with an almost painful need as George slid one hand up her standing leg, past her stocking to stroke itself lightly, almost ticklishly up the bare skin of her thigh. He reached around to cup the flesh of her bottom and draw her firmly towards his face. Sophie tilted her head back, knocking it against the door as his fingers slid from her bottom to part the petals between her legs. Gently, he pressed a finger inside her as his tongue reached out to touch her in that special place. For a time he stroked her with his tongue gently, then harder, rougher, until it was all she could do to remain standing. Her entire body strained and quivered against the insane pleasure coursing through her. George turned his face to kiss and lick at her thighs, biting,

A Baron's Son is Undone

tormenting, and then shocked her senseless as he returned to take her bud of pleasure in his mouth and suck! George had his hand to her bottom again, holding her securely in place as his lips and tongue mercilessly pulled at her peak of pleasure to send a firestorm pulsing through her.

Sophie banged her head back against the door and attempted to muffle a scream as she pressed herself down against his face. It was no good. The scream forced its way up through her throat, a harsh keening sound that broke loose to be followed by several heavy panting breaths. Her vision blurred, her body began to crumple, and she was vaguely aware of George holding her back against the door with one hand as he lifted her leg from his shoulder with the other. His fingers glided up between her legs, a single tender sweep as he stood. By the time Sophie's full set of faculties had returned, she was seated across his lap on the settee as he cradled her against his waistcoat.

"George," she said pressing a kiss to his jaw wonderingly, "what have you done to me?"

He gave her a tender look.

"You knew the consequence for disobedience," he said. "You can hardly complain that it was a surprise."

The corners of his mouth twitched, and then he smiled. Lazily he reached a hand across to cup one of her still bare breasts.

"I think you should wear your dresses like this more often," he said.

Sophie laughed and pressed herself against his chest.

"It's unlikely I would spend so much time reviewing the accounts if I knew you were dressed this way as you read a book or sewed a sampler in the drawing room."

"Indeed!" said Sophie. "It would be that easy to garner your attention, would it? I should have thought of it sooner."

George dropped his smile. He gingerly pulled up her bodice to cover her, deftly managing the laces to tie her back into the dress.

"You were right," he said. "About talking to Mother."

He told her all that had happened with his parents.

"I've been such a fool," he said stroking her arm. "I had everything all along, and I couldn't even see it."

Sophie watched his face transform from thoughtful to painfully earnest.

"I'm sorry," he said. "For everything. For living inside my own head in a world of my own creation and leaving you to fend for yourself in a new place with new people and no one to lean on. And for being too afraid to tell you that you are the light in my darkness, the jewel in my life. Sophie, I love you. Now. Tomorrow. Forever. I love you so much, I am ill with it."

Sophie's fingers curled around his lapel as she felt a sharp pricking behind her eyes.

He loved her.

"And if you are ill with it, what would be the cure?" she asked quietly, trying her best to keep her voice steady and the tide of tears from rising.

"No cure," said George smiling wistfully. "But the symptoms can be treated with small doses of your affection taken at regular intervals."

She gripped his lapel tighter.

"And what about me?" asked Sophie. "What am I to do about my ailment?" Her voice cracked on the last word.

George went still. Sophie thought he might even be holding

A Baron's Son is Undone

his breath.

"Pardon?" he whispered.

"I'm lovesick as well," she said. "What would you recommend treatment-wise?"

"So-Sophie," he stuttered.

She realised with some surprise that he was genuinely taken aback, and she felt the need to press on, to make herself absolutely clear.

"I love you, George. Being with you is . . . I don't know how to explain it. Just the thought of you looking at me or touching me is quite thrilling . . . but at the same time, you make me feel entirely safe. I didn't think I'd ever feel that way with anyone. I love the way you devote yourself to your family, and sweet Heaven, I love seeing you stripped to the waist and sweaty from a fight. I love your schedule, and I love to mess it up. But mostly I love your heart, George—it's pure and true and gentle. You are the best of men, and I am honoured to be your wife."

All these words were true, and yet Sophie felt an odd sinking sensation as she said them. She knew she was . . . not digging her own grave exactly but rather backing herself into a corner with this admission of love. He would expect . . . As her husband and knowing that she loved him, he had every right to expect . . .

"I'm sorry I haven't . . ." she said. "That is, you should know . . . I want . . . I want to give you more."

She looked up into his face meaningfully.

Good Lord.

A Disobedient Wife

George reached a trembling hand up to cup her cheek, and she pressed the side of her face into it. The aching sweetness of the subtle gesture coupled with the slippery tears that began to spill from her dark amber eyes threatened to overwhelm him. He felt full to the brim, both a tight and expansive feeling at once. George opened his mouth to speak, but he choked on a sob. Thinking better of speaking, he clutched her to him. It was all he could do, seated with his wife on the yellow settee above the carpet with its canaries and their golden vines, in the room made of sunshine that his mother had fashioned.

He knew now why his mother had created it. This brilliant golden room. It was how she felt about her life, about the love contained within it. And now, it was how he felt about his life. The sadness of his father's predicament still weighed on him. It would be wretched. He anticipated some of the worst days of his life were yet to come, but Sophie would help him to tease out the light from behind the darkness as it descended. It would be bearable. He would survive, and he would carry his family along with him.

A knock sounded at the drawing-room door. George lifted Sophie from his lap and strode over to unlock it.

"Who locks a drawing room?!" said Grace before the door was even open. "What are you doing in here?"

She peered past her brother to Sophie standing by the settee as Potato raced into the room and leapt up onto a chair.

"Down!" yelled George.

Potato stared up at him defiantly with her squished-in nose and her pink tongue protruding in a way that suggested she did not take him particularly seriously.

"But that's her favourite chair!" said Grace. "Mother says she can sit on that one if she doesn't sit on the others."

A Baron's Son is Undone

George looked to Sophie whose face was still most becomingly flushed from their encounter. She pressed her sweet pink lips together and shrugged.

"I don't mean to be rude," said Grace, "but there's been some talk of a surprise or a gift of some sort, and so far, none has been presented to me." She placed her hand on her hip as Potato barked her agreement from the chair. "See! Potato has noticed as well."

George advanced on his sister.

"Oh, really?" he said. "None has been presented to you?" he repeated darkly. He stepped up close to her. "And you don't mean to be rude?"

"I *hate* being rude," said Grace, holding her ground. "But needs must."

Something cracked and broke inside him then—something cold and hard and useless to him now. He laughed.

"You little imp!" he said. And then he surprised his sister by actually picking her up and swinging her around.

"George!" she shrieked. "Put me down!"

He obediently set her down on the carpet.

"Actually," said Grace who was smiling once she had regained her footing, "can you do it again?"

"All right," said George. "But just once. You're a bit hefty, and I'm not entirely certain my back will survive too much more."

Grace looked to Sophie.

"'Hefty,' he says. Always the gentleman, isn't h—?" Grace's sentence ended on a shriek as George lifted her up and spun her around.

His sister was thrilled to pieces with her blown-glass gifts, especially the tiny fragile dog.

A Disobedient Wife

"It's a mini you!" she said lifting it up so Potato could sniff at it somewhat indifferently.

Grace lined up the dog and the swan and the unicorn on the table in front of her, and then she threw herself into her brother's arms.

"Thank you, George!"

"I'm sorry I ruined the last trip to Cornwall for you," said George as he held her small frame against him. She struggled up from his embrace and gave him a startled look. He continued, "I'll take you again sometime . . . with Sophie as well, and you can help me write the daily schedule."

"That would be . . ." said Grace quietly as she looked over to Sophie. "That would be brilliant."

That evening, George found himself enjoying dinner with his family in a way he had not enjoyed it before. He took part in the conversation and even laughed once or twice. It was difficult not to notice both his parents eyeing him with concern at the beginning of the meal, but their faces soon melted with gentle delight as they saw him emerge from the cold shelter he had built up around himself over the years.

"It's going to be a grand party!" said his mother of the ball.

"Are children allowed?" asked Grace.

"No," said Lady Pemberton, setting her mouth firmly to dispel any argument.

Grace groaned.

"Perhaps," interjected Lord Pemberton. "Perhaps, Grace could attend for the first hour or so. I could be her escort."

"Yes!" said Grace. "Papa knows best, I daresay."

"I daresay," said Lady Pemberton as she regarded her husband with a warm smile spreading over her face. "That sounds entirely sensible, my dear."

A Baron's Son is Undone

She then reached across the table to place her hand over Sophie's wrist.

"Sophie and I are putting the finishing touches on the ball. The florists should be arriving in a few days to discuss the arrangements."

Sophie's eyes met his, and George's heart sank an inch. His mother had somehow commandeered Sophie into organising the ball—a party that his mother knew full well would be difficult for Sophie to attend with her father present. Oh, she was a wily one, his mother. It was just like her to do such a thing. George calmly told himself that he would have a word with Sophie—she should not feel obligated to attend.

The day of the ball approached like a tide bearing upon it the unwelcome arrival of Sophie's father the Duke of Somerset. George had imagined she would shrink in on herself with each passing day, a kind of closing up for purposes of self-preservation, like a hedgehog curling into a prickly ball. Instead, she appeared to be blossoming with confidence and joy as she went about organising the party with his mother.

The Pembertons' servants were not ill-informed. They knew quite well that Lord Pemberton was unwell and that Lady Pemberton was paving the way for Sophie to take her place. As the days progressed, Lady Pemberton appeared to fall back more and more, allowing Sophie to take the reins. The maids, in particular, loved their would-be mistress and would often bypass Miss Tindale, the housekeeper, to speak with Sophie directly. After a meeting with Sophie, he would see them traipsing out of the reception room smiling and chatting quietly to one another. Once, he even caught a few snippets of conversation as they passed him unnoticed.

"A duke's daughter should rightfully be floating away on her airs and graces," said one maid.

A few muttered agreements.

"But she seems to actually care," said another.

"Potato is going to be the diamond of the season!" laughed another, and the rest of them giggled as they jostled each other down the hall.

What did that mean? thought George.

On another occasion, he watched from atop the main staircase as Sophie and Miss Tindale discussed logistical operations with a fleet of footmen in the main foyer. Even when Miss Tindale was speaking, he noticed that all the footmen were looking at Sophie. When the housekeeper had finished, Sophie took her hand before addressing the footmen. The woman looked so thoroughly shocked by this that George half-thought he should descend the stairs to catch her before she fainted.

"Miss Tindale's word is law as far as Lady Pemberton and I are concerned," said Sophie. She smiled at the housekeeper, then directed her beautiful beaming face towards the footmen once more. "You have your marching orders . . . so march!"

Sophie laughed as she said it, and George noticed that all the footmen were grinning as they disbanded.

He trotted down the red-carpeted steps to greet his wife as Miss Tindale took her leave after the footmen. Sophie was wearing a new dress—sea-green silk with capped sleeves and a low sweetheart neckline that drew his eye down between her breasts.

"You seem to be getting on quite fine," he said pulling her

supple body into an embrace and sliding his hands down the whispery fabric to softly cup her buttocks.

"The staff have been tolerant of me," she said, tilting her face up to his.

"Mm . . . 'Tolerant' is not the word I would use," he said. "Everyone seems to be having fun now that you're here."

"Don't be ridiculous," said Sophie. "The staff are working very hard to have everything ready for the party."

"With smiles on their faces for some reason," added George.

He was suddenly overcome, and all he could do was press his lips to hers. His gentle kiss soon turned rather heated as Sophie's hands slid up his back beneath his jacket. She pressed herself to him, and he responded by delving deeper into her hot mouth as he stumbled forwards, catching them both against a wall.

"My, my!" said a familiar voice.

George turned towards the front door with Sophie still in his arms. Patience and Lord Winter had just stepped inside. They were dressed for riding, and while Winter had carefully arranged his face into a polite mask, Patience would do no such thing. She was grinning from ear to ear, eyes darting from Sophie to George and back again.

"Your bedchamber is up the stairs and along the hall," she said pointing with her riding crop. "For pity's sake, if you must debauch each other, please do it there!"

Patience had made some attempt to make her words sound like a reprimand, but both she and Sophie burst into laughter as she landed on the final word of her last sentence.

George found that holding Sophie in his arms as she laughed was like holding a hothouse rose in the middle of winter, the sheer improbability of the situation lending it an air of magic and wonder. It struck him then that his sister and Sophie were actually friends, and the thought warmed him in a way he could not have anticipated.

He released Sophie from the embrace, and as she watched Patience and Lord Winter make their way to the stairs, he saw her smile fall and an odd look cloud her features.

Had his sister's comment disconcerted her?

Sophie's laughter had been genuine, but George knew quite well that a heart can hold many contradictions. He was well aware of the fact that although she had made it clear she would like to give him "more", that "more" had not actually been forthcoming. Of course, he would not press her. He loved her too much to do so. Part of the reason he had married her had been to save her from a situation she might not be able to endure.

George lifted his eyes to watch Patience and her husband disappear around the second-story balustrade.

"Sophie," he said.

She looked at him with an almost startled expression.

"You should know that I am grateful for every tiny moment you choose to share with me."

"Oh," she said.

"Every touch, every kiss is a blessing," he continued. "You never need feel . . . compelled."

She smiled, but it was a melancholic smile, and George was reminded of the fact that Sophie's optimistic and often light-hearted approach to life did not mean that she was not also drowning in her own sadness.

A Baron's Son is Undone

The days passed quickly by, and with only one day left before the ball, George couldn't help feeling increasingly agitated. No matter how many times he maintained that it was not necessary, Sophie stubbornly insisted on being present for the party. She refused to sacrifice his family's social standing for her own comfort.

Rolling over towards her in bed that morning, he attempted to dissuade her one more time, but as usual, she wasn't having it.

"I cannot sit it out, George. I'm organising the whole thing with your mother."

"That was her plan from the beginning—don't you see?" said George.

"She's very clever," said Sophie smiling softly up into his face. "And she's right. The families should be seen to stand together. There's no need to invite extraneous gossip. My past is enough to deal with—we need not provoke suspicion that this was an elopement."

"Then, tell me, Sophie, how would you feel if you found yourself alone with your father?"

A shadow flitted over her features, a flicker and it was gone.

"I'm sure it can be avoided," she said.

"You wouldn't like it," said George.

"No, I wouldn't, but if it came down to it, I'm sure I would survive."

"I don't want you to have to survive anything," said George stroking a strand of hair from her face. "It's all so bloody ridiculous."

She kissed him then, her lips softened by sleep, her mouth warm with their argument. George felt a pang of heartache and concern for his wife shoot down through his body as the

A Disobedient Wife

pleasure of her kiss melted his sensible mind.

"Is this how you plan on getting your way?" he asked. "In our marriage?" he added. "You'll say one thing. I'll say another. Then you'll kiss me and destroy all my resolve."

"Mhm," nodded Sophie.

"Sophie..." he said, but she wasn't listening to him anymore as she pressed her lips to his neck. He realised with a stifled groan that she was going to get her way.

Several hours later, as George strode along a hallway on the second floor of the house, he was still ruminating over the situation. He was so engrossed with matters of his own mind, that he barely registered the sound of someone whistling—a brief bird-like call. He continued making his way along the hall before hearing the same sharp whistle once more. Glancing behind him in the direction of the sound, he found his sister Patience leaning with one foot out of the doorway to her art studio. The morning light from her studio windows spilled out of the doorway and into the hall illuminating her face and hair so that she seemed almost angelic—*'almost' being the operative word*, thought George with a smile to himself.

Patience beckoned him with a tilt of her head towards the studio, and George hesitantly joined her inside the well-lit room. His sister was wearing a white apron that was smeared with a jumble of colours so vibrant it would have sparked envy in a rainbow. There was a smudge of yellow across one temple where she must have rubbed a hand.

"Mother," said Patience to her brother as if he should know what she meant with just the one word.

He was touched and surprised by what she said next: "She may have cornered Sophie into attending this ball, but I'll not have her left alone for a second with that father of hers."

A Baron's Son is Undone

"I'll watch her," said George.

"That's the problem, though, George. *We're* hosting the ball. Father is unlikely to last the night as he will be too tired, and Mother may need us to attend to matters of hospitality. She can't expect Sophie to manage everything on the day. You know how it is: a fleet of carriages and horses to stable, not to mention elderly guests who need special attention, servants with last-minute questions. We may be run off our feet. And Richard is always mobbed with various lords and their attempts to sway his vote in Parliament."

"So what are you suggesting?" asked George.

"I'm not suggesting anything," said Patience. "I'm telling you what I've organised."

George couldn't help feeling irritated by this. She hadn't even consulted him!

"And what is that?"

"I've sent for Thomas."

Captain Thomas Walpole.

"What?! That joker?"

"He likes to laugh," said Patience defensively. "There's nothing wrong with that."

"He also likes to drink and gamble and womanise," said George. "That man doesn't take anything seriously."

Patience gave her brother a scolding glare.

"Richard says he's seen Thomas snap a man's neck in less time than it takes to draw a breath. Thomas may be a joker as you say, but he's also a battle-hardened soldier. If we give him a task to watch Sophie, he will, and God help her father if he presses his luck. She will have an armed guard, George. You won't have to worry. And more importantly, *I* won't have to worry."

A Disobedient Wife

George didn't know what to say. His sister had succeeded in both irritating him and setting his mind to rest over Sophie at the same time. How very like her to do so.

When George didn't say anything, Patience spoke once more.

"You're welcome," she said.

George ran a hand through his hair and allowed a smile to play slowly over his lips.

"Quite the sister," he said.

Patience grinned.

"It's going to be all right," she said. "I won't allow it to *not* be all right."

"We'd best run this by Sophie," said George.

"You like to consult your wife now, do you?" said Patience in a teasing tone.

George narrowed his eyes at her, and Patience laughed.

"Obviously, George! By all means, consult Sophie. But I do think she's going to like my plan."

Twenty

A Vision of Sunshine

Sophie was touched to her core to realise that Patience had so much concern for her well-being. If she was being perfectly honest with herself, now that the ball was upon them, she was feeling somewhat reticent despite her protests to the contrary.

"An armed guard?" she asked George as she placed her glass of sherry on the gleaming wooden surface of the table beside her.

They were alone in the library, stealing a quiet moment to themselves before dinner.

"Well, not literally, but I've been told that Captain Walpole's hands are fairly lethal."

"Indeed!" said Sophie.

"We will greet your father publicly, as a family," said George. "After that, you need not interact with him again. If you choose to do so, it will be with either myself or Thomas on hand. You

A Vision of Sunshine

will not be left alone for a moment."

Sophie heaved a sigh. She did feel relieved to know that she would not be cornered by her father.

"Thank you," she said. "This does, in fact, make me feel better."

"You can always change your mind," said George reaching over and taking a sip from her glass of sherry. "We could take a bottle of champagne up to our bedchamber and have our own party."

Sophie touched her fingers to her lips. It was certainly an appealing alternative . . . but it was an alternative that was becoming increasingly psychologically fraught. Throwing herself into organising the ball with Lady Pemberton had been one way for her to demonstrate that she could be a proper wife despite her shortcomings—she had honestly not realised how much she would enjoy the task. With each passing day, however, she could feel the guilt piling up around her. Despite the fact that George had never once complained about what they did in bed, she knew that he must want more. She had said she would give him more. And she did want to. She loved him for God's sake! So what was the problem? Occasionally, during moments like these, Sophie felt like banging her head against a table until she knocked some sense into herself.

Sophie regarded the well-polished table on which George had replaced her glass of sherry. She could see a perfect reflection of the glass on its surface, and she imagined slamming her head into that reflection. Just the once. Sherry spilling all over the carpet and George gawping at her with the realisation that his wife was perhaps just a little bit mad.

Would he still love her then? Would he continue to love her if she couldn't . . .?

A Baron's Son is Undone

"I'm going to the ball," she said firmly.

The sun was struggling to shine through a bank of low cloud when Captain Walpole arrived early on the day of the ball. He leapt from his carriage and bounded up the steps of the house to greet Patience and George and Sophie before they had a chance to descend down to the drive. Sophie did not know what she had been expecting, but the merry man with the twinkle in his eye and the cheeky smile playing about his lips was definitely not it.

This man didn't look like he would be capable of hurting a fly!

Patience introduced them, and Captain Walpole swept his lean yet muscular frame into a rather dramatic bow.

"At your service, my lady," he said.

Sophie glanced incredulously from Patience to George and then back to Captain Walpole who unfolded his body to stand upright once more. Sophie thought she actually saw him wink at George before settling his eyes back on hers once more. He was perhaps in his mid-thirties with longish chestnut brown hair that fell forwards into his face in the most unassumingly boyish manner.

"So you are the damsel," he said with a handsome grin. "Pemberton's damsel," he added.

George stepped forward to shake his hand.

"Thank you for doing this," he said with a polite smile. "It's very good of you."

Captain Walpole appeared frozen in shock for a moment before his features slowly melted back into place.

"It smiles!" he said with an air of wonder. "Are you seeing

A Vision of Sunshine

this, Patience?" And then, to Sophie with mock accusation: "Is this *your* doing?"

Sophie didn't know how to answer, and she found herself cocking her head to the side and giving a little laugh. She was surprised when Captain Walpole gallantly offered her his arm. She gave George an amused look before placing her hand to the captain's sleeve and allowing him to lead her inside the house as if it were his own.

"Now," said Captain Walpole looking around the foyer, "where is my boy Richard?"

The sheer naughtiness of referring to the massive and important Lord Winter as "my boy" was enough to ruffle Sophie's composure. She wanted to laugh, but obviously that would be terribly rude.

"In the stable," said Patience without batting an eye at the indiscretion. "My hunter threw a shoe."

Captain Walpole leaned down to Sophie as if taking her into his confidence.

"No doubt he'll want a hug and a kiss when he sees me."

Sophie found she was very much enjoying herself with this Captain Walpole. He had somehow managed to set her immediately at ease. Patience led them all to the brilliant yellow drawing room where whisky was poured instead of tea, and before long, Captain Walpole ("Call me Thomas") had them all in stitches over a story involving a wager to see whether one portly gentleman could walk a half-mile in less time than it took another man to eat twenty-four herrings and three ounces of mustard.

The captain had not been entirely wrong about his enthusiastic reception by the formidable Lord Winter. When Patience's husband entered the room, he took several long

A Baron's Son is Undone

strides over to Thomas who was barely on his feet before his hand was clasped and then his body tugged into a powerful embrace.

"He wasn't always like this," said Thomas to Sophie as he took his seat once more. "He used to be quite the stone-hearted monster. No hugs as a rule. Certainly no kisses."

"Don't make me regret inviting you," said Lord Winter in a dark voice, but his eyes were dancing.

Thomas downed the remains of his whisky and set the empty glass down on the table with enthusiastic force.

"Will there be a card room?" he asked no one in particular.

"Oh yes!" said Sophie. "Not everyone cares to dance all night."

"Jolly good!" said Thomas. "Perhaps I shall show you a trick or two. There are always a few feather-brained dandies—no offence, George—in want of lighter pockets."

Sophie looked to George who was holding himself together admirably. She had a strong feeling that Captain Walpole was not entirely her husband's cup of tea.

"As long as you keep your attention on your task," said George seriously.

Captain Walpole looked stricken.

"Have no fear," he said placing his hand to his breast. "That is the last whisky I shall imbibe today. I will be stone-cold sober as I fleece your guests while keeping both eyes on your lovely wife over here—not exactly a chore to do the latter, now is it?" he asked George before sending a wink Sophie's way.

George ground down on his teeth but said nothing as Lord Winter placed a hand to his shoulder and squeezed.

"I will be there as well," he said as if to reassure George.

A Vision of Sunshine

"Right!" said Patience brightly. "That's settled then. You'll have to excuse me and Sophie as we have party matters to attend. Richard, can you show Thomas to his room?"

Lord Winter gave a nod of his head as Patience took Sophie's hand and tugged her to her feet before leading her from the drawing room.

"Best leave them to it," said Patience quietly as they walked down the hall. "You may have noticed that George is not the most ardent admirer of Captain Walpole."

"You don't say?" remarked Sophie with a grin.

"But the good captain is entirely trustworthy, and George knows it, at least *intellectually*," said Patience with a laugh. "Now, *emotionally*—" began Patience.

"—Emotionally, George would like to punch the good captain in his very handsome face," supplied Sophie with a suppressed smile.

Patience threw her head back and laughed.

"I'm sure George would love to knock him into the middle of next week," said Patience. "Did you hear Thomas? What did he say? 'Feather-brained dandies—no offence, George!'" Patience laughed until she was gripping her stomach as if in pain.

Sophie waited patiently and with much amusement as Patience struggled to regain her composure.

"There," said Patience squeezing her cheeks with the palms of her hands, "I think the fit has passed." She gave a small giggle but managed to take control of herself once more. "Now. Where do you think we might find Potato?" she asked.

Sophie's eyes lit up.

A Baron's Son is Undone

"Your mother says it's a surprise," said Lord Pemberton as he joined George on their walk from their respective dressing rooms to the yellow drawing room.

It was evening, and they were both wearing their formal black coattails in anticipation of the ball. Crisp white shirts and cravats folded with geometrical precision.

"Apparently, it was your wife's idea," said his father.

George felt his father's arm come around his shoulder, and he closed his eyes for just a moment in an effort to preserve the memory of that sensation. How many more times might his father hold him like this? And would George even realise when it was the last time? He resolved to treat each moment with his father as if it were the last—the last hug, the last breakfast, the last argument over ledgers and numbers only to find that his father had been right all along. This would be the last ball. That was for certain. His father had not the strength to attend another.

They approached the drawing-room door, and as George reached out to turn the handle, he could hear faint feminine laughter coming from the other side. When he opened the door, it was onto the yellow room accented in white and lit with candlelight. His breath caught in his chest as Sophie turned towards him. She and every other female member of the family was dressed in yellow silk—a golden kind of yellow, like early morning sunlight pouring through a pane of glass. As the ladies moved to acknowledge his and Lord Pemberton's appearance, it was as if pieces of the yellow room had come to life.

"You should have knocked!" scolded Grace who was seated on the yellow settee. "We were going to arrange ourselves into a tableau."

A Vision of Sunshine

Potato barked and scampered across the room to leap onto Grace's lap . . . which was when George realised that Potato was wearing a yellow dress as well!

He looked over to his father who had his palms together as if in prayer with both index fingers pressed against his lips. He looked as if he might cry.

"Agnes," he said, lowering his hands and stretching out his arms.

George's mother stepped forward into his embrace, her silk gown shimmering in the candlelight almost as if it were the candlelight itself.

"Mind my hair," she said as Lord Pemberton held her.

"Of course, my dear. Of course. I always mind your hair." He laughed.

"You do, don't you?" she said looking up into his eyes lovingly.

When Lord Pemberton released his wife, he took the hand of each daughter in turn.

"A vision of sunshine!" he said over and over again. "The light in my life."

Finally, he took both of Sophie's hands in his.

"A third daughter!" he said. "I am truly blessed."

"What about Potato?" asked Grace lifting up the dog who was wriggling excitedly in her grasp. "She's a light in your life too, isn't she?"

"Without a doubt, my dear," said Lord Pemberton placing a hand to the dog's head. "And she is surprisingly fetching in a frock, isn't she?"

"This was your idea?" asked George quietly as he stepped up beside Sophie.

There was a luminosity to his wife that seemed to emanate

A Baron's Son is Undone

from her very skin, her soul shining with such radiance it could barely be contained by her body.

"I thought it would make your mother happy," she said.

"And Potato?" asked George with a crooked smile.

"That was a hilarious suggestion from one of the maids," said Sophie. "Once it was spoken, it had to be done!"

Lord Winter and Captain Walpole arrived just then at the door to the drawing room, one dressed in dapper black, the other in his smart red captain's jacket. George tried to imagine Captain Walpole killing someone—anyone—but the man resembled nothing more than a scamp with a face and a manner that seemed designed to reel in one willing lady after another. Still, Patience trusted the captain . . . and George trusted Patience.

"Are you ready?" he asked Sophie, offering her his arm. "You know you can excuse yourself at any time?"

"Yes," she said. "To both questions." She slipped her hand into the crook of his elbow and squeezed.

When the family was announced and entered the ballroom to greet their guests, George scanned the crowd for Sophie's father. It wasn't hard to find him. He was an exceptionally tall man who moved much like a stork, knees bending gingerly to take slow methodical steps with his long legs. Lady Pemberton placed a hand to George's free arm as he stood with Sophie at the edge of the ballroom.

"Show time," she whispered.

His mother took a moment to catch Sophie's eye, and when she did, Sophie gave her a nod, but George could feel his wife's entire body stiffen through the simple touch of her hand on his sleeve.

"You don't have to," he said quietly.

A Vision of Sunshine

"I'm ready," said Sophie lifting her chin.

They approached the Duke of Somerset as a group of four—Lord and Lady Pemberton leading the way as George and Sophie brought up the rear.

"Your Grace," said Lady Pemberton by way of attracting his attention, for he was speaking with two lords and did not notice their approach.

When he turned, there was a brief spark in his eye as he took Sophie in, but the small flame died quickly and was replaced with a calculated look of indifference.

"Ah," he said. "Our hosts."

Lady Pemberton and Sophie curtsied in the proper manner.

"You are most welcome," said Lady Pemberton.

"Well, you were most persuasive in your invitation," he replied. "How could I not come to see my daughter settled so well among you?"

"She is a credit to you," said Lord Pemberton.

"Is she?" asked the duke. "I should think she takes after her mother in most regards."

George was watching Sophie carefully, but she had arranged her features into the blandest expression imaginable.

"Then she must have been a wonder, your late wife," said Lord Pemberton. "For Sophie is truly a marvel. She has brought so much joy into our home."

The duke lifted his eyebrows and looked over at Sophie.

"I should like a word with my daughter alone," he said.

George was surprised when Sophie actually responded.

"Of course, Father," she said with a forced smile. "But the music is starting up right now, and I have promised the first dance to Captain Walpole over there."

She pointed to the jolly man in red who lifted a hand to

A Baron's Son is Undone

wave from across the room. George was momentarily pleased that Thomas was actually paying attention.

"In the meantime, I hope you will enjoy yourself. It is so good to see you. My lords," she said dropping another curtsy to the men standing with her father.

By the time Sophie turned to leave, Thomas was upon them. How he had managed to press his way so quickly through the crush of the ballroom, George could not comprehend.

"Your Grace!" said Thomas with a bow. "You will excuse me, but I must commandeer your daughter for a dance. With your permission, of course, Mr. Pemberton."

George gave him a nod, and Thomas swept Sophie away on a tide of murmured confidences that George imagined were both clever and uproariously funny. His eyes followed his wife as she stepped into the crowd and then out onto the dance floor with her armed guard. By the time George turned his attention back to the duke, the lords and his parents had taken their leave without his noticing.

"Mr. Pemberton," said the duke in a tone dripping icicles.

"Your Grace," said George.

"If you think for a moment that you will be able to extract a dowry out of me—" started the duke.

"What?!"

The duke continued, "Your mother's threats notwithstanding, I swear I will ruin you."

"I don't want your money, Somerset," said George through gritted teeth.

His hands were fisted at his sides. *Breathe.*

"Then what do you want?" asked the duke.

George looked at the man incredulously.

"I have what I want," he said slowly. "I want Sophie to be

A Vision of Sunshine

safe and happy."

Having said the words, George couldn't help wondering if Sophie was, in fact, happy. He may have to settle for safe for the time being.

"To the devil with you!" said the duke. "Don't play innocent with me! You went to considerable effort to wrest her from me. So. What. Do. You. Want?"

A strange calm settled over George as he realised what kind of man the Duke of Somerset was: he was a man who knew the price of everything and the value of nothing. He was also a man who would not let the matter go until he felt he had come out on top.

"What do *you* want?" asked George.

The duke did not have to think about his answer for a second.

"Compensation," he said. "For assets stolen."

"Fine," said George. "How much does Sophie cost?"

As he said the words, a scorching anger surged within him like molten rock pressing itself slowly up from beneath the surface of the earth. With a great deal of stoic resolve, George held himself in check as the duke actually opened his mouth to put a price on his daughter.

"Done," said George when the duke had named the sum. "I'll have my man of business contact yours. From now on, however, the matter is settled. You will be agreeable when in the presence of my family, and you will never contact Sophie or seek to speak with her alone. Is that clear?"

The duke looked so shocked by George's agreement to his request that George did not think he was actually listening to anything that followed.

"Is that clear, Somerset?!"

A Baron's Son is Undone

"What? Yes. Of course. Why wouldn't I be agreeable? I'm a reasonable man, Pemberton. And I've no need to speak with that ungrateful daughter of mine now that the matter is settled."

George swore violently inside his own head. How had Sophie survived a childhood in the keeping of this man?

"If you'll excuse me," said George. He needed to find a fucking drink.

As George knocked back his second glass of champagne, he caught a glimpse of Sophie's black hair and golden silk gown among the crowd of dancers in the centre of the room. She was with Lord Winter.

"Obviously," said Patience who had sidled up beside him in her matching gown of sunlight, "she can't have *two* dances with Thomas, so Richard has stepped in to keep her out of harm's way."

"Much obliged," said George.

"I'll need you to come with me," said Patience. "Lady Leveson-Gower has been asking after you, and she will not let the matter drop. I have a feeling she knows something about your spontaneous nuptials (don't ask me how) and would like a few juicy details in exchange for her silence."

George gave his sister a hard look. Two drinks was clearly not enough.

"She's fairly harmless—a bit like Mother. Come on!" said Patience taking her brother's arm.

The things one had to do to keep the social wheels greased and turning. For Sophie, thought George, as he allowed his sister to guide him across the room. *For my family.*

After George had spoken with Lady Leveson-Gower, sorted out a disagreement over a carriage between a young gentleman and one of the Pemberton footmen, and then seen a completely inebriated lord to one of the guest rooms, he found himself back in the ballroom. Sophie was nowhere to be seen. Neither was Thomas, thank God. *He had better be with her.* Despite the deal George had made with Sophie's father, he was reluctant to trust the man.

Now, where was his beloved?

Feather-brained dandies in want of lighter pockets, thought George.

He made his way to the card room where Sophie and Thomas were easy to spot—two bright splashes of colour in a sea of black jackets. George stood in the doorway watching his wife as she lit up the room with her laughter. Thomas was sat across the card table from her as they played at whist with two other gentlemen George recognised as inveterate drinkers and gamblers. Thomas was pulling a jumble of cards towards himself as the two gentlemen sat watching with severe faces.

"Last hand!" said Sophie. "It's not looking good for our friends here, is it Thomas?"

"That's because Lady Luck herself is playing," said Thomas with a grin as he shuffled the deck of cards. "I may think of borrowing you from time to time if your husband is amenable. You would go down a treat at Crockford's!"

George had approached the table as Thomas was talking. He placed a firm hand to the man's shoulder as he shuffled.

"You will not be taking my wife to a gaming hell," he said. "I would not be, as you say, amenable."

George watched Sophie press her lips together in amusement as she looked to Thomas for some sort of witty response.

"Have pity on me, Pemberton," said the captain in all good humour. "All I have are my good looks and my charm, but I

A Baron's Son is Undone

live in darkness. And while you may be sadly lacking in both looks and charm, you have Lady Luck here to light up your days."

Thomas sent Sophie a wink, and she pressed a hand to her mouth to hide her smile as she looked up into her husband's face.

What could George do? He laughed.

"And here I thought he was going to clock me round the side of the head," said Thomas dealing out the last hand.

"He still might," said Sophie smiling as she picked up her cards.

George watched as the last hand was played. A rather large purse was won, and when Sophie slid it across the table to Thomas, he pressed it back her way.

"You can have my share," he said standing. "A wedding present. Buy your man here something nice."

Sophie was in high spirits as she left the games room with George to stroll out into the crowded ballroom. He could feel her practically shimmering with joy—a kind of effervescent energy that lifted his own mood up on a sparkling tide.

"You had fun with Captain Walpole, I take it?" he asked.

"Oh yes!" said Sophie. She looked at George. "I think he likes you," she said. "He wouldn't tease you so if he didn't."

"Is that right?"

"You're very likeable," said Sophie.

"Am I?"

"Very *loveable*," she corrected.

"Do you think Captain Walpole *loves* me?" asked George with amusement.

"Not the way he loves Lord Winter," she said with a laugh. "But *I* love you—will that do?"

A Vision of Sunshine

"It will more than do," said George seriously.

Sophie led George across the ballroom and out the door at the far side.

"Where are we going?" he asked.

"Come along," she said with a grin as she led him down a flight of stairs and along a narrow hall to the kitchen which was full to the brim with staff rushing hither and thither.

"Could we steal a bottle of champagne?" said Sophie to one of the kitchen maids.

"Oh, Mrs. Pemberton! Mr. Pemberton!" said the maid, clearly surprised to see them both in the kitchen.

She rushed off to fetch and uncork them a bottle.

"What's all this about?" asked George as Sophie, with bottle in hand, led him up the servants' stairs, past the ballroom and higher still towards their bedchamber.

She turned to him on the staircase.

"You said I could leave the ball at any time. You said we could have our own little party instead." She lifted the champagne bottle to her lips, took a cheeky sip, and smiled.

George could feel his pupils dilate to take her in. His gaze swept down the golden silky length of her and back up to the mischievous expression on her beautiful face.

He caught up with her on the stairs and slipped a hand around her soft waist. She leaned into him, and he took the bottle of champagne from her hands.

"Well, if it's to be a party," he said lifting the bottle to his lips.

By the time, they reached the hallway to their bedchamber, they were walking in stops and starts, pausing to kiss the champagne hungrily from each other's lips, stumbling along as they fumbled at each other's clothing, tugging laces and

A Baron's Son is Undone

ripping buttons.

They were both panting with need as the bedchamber door slammed closed behind them, and George placed the bottle down on a table.

"Off!" said George tugging at Sophie's dress. He had her down to her chemise in a matter of seconds.

She was smiling. Her face was flushed. He had never seen her look more devastatingly beautiful. She pressed herself against him and tilted her head to expose her neck. He kissed her there, dragging his tongue up to her ear. She moaned, and he could feel her tugging at his shirt, trying to pull it out of his trousers. George broke away, his heart hammering with desire as he shrugged out of his jacket, tearing at the remaining buttons of his waistcoat. When he looked up, Sophie was standing naked in front of him looking like a goddess, her body golden in the lamplight. She gripped him by the waist of his trousers and pulled him to the bed. He tumbled on top of her, fumbling frantically with the fall of his trousers.

Good God, he wanted his wife with a kind of mad frenzy that was beginning to frighten him!

He took a few stabilising breaths as she worked his trousers and drawers down from his hips. His cock was so hard it was almost unbearable, and he groaned as he pressed it up along her soft belly. He kissed her again and again, revelling in the sensation of her hot and eager response. He took one nipple in his mouth and then dragged his cheek across the other. Somehow, he managed to kick himself free of his trousers and drawers. Sophie had pulled his cravat from his neck so that his shirt fell open. She then dragged his shirt up, and they both laughed as he struggled free of the sleeves. George took her sweet mouth in his as he rubbed his erection up and down

A Vision of Sunshine

over her belly.

"You can take me, George," she whispered. "I would like to give myself to you."

A haze of lust descended over him as he took in her words. He could barely see straight as he manoeuvred his cock down between her legs. Sweet Heaven, she was so hot and wet. Gathering every ounce of his restraint, he resisted entering her, and instead gently slid the length of him along the slick petals of her sex. Merciful heavens, it was the most exquisite pleasure, touching himself to her in that way.

Then something about the situation changed.

It was a subtle shift, barely noticeable, but he did notice despite the rush of blood in his ears and his blurred vision. Sophie had stiffened ever-so-slightly beneath him. George forced himself to focus his eyes and take in her face, and what he saw gave him pause. She looked absolutely terrified!

Jesus.

With an effort that cost him quite dearly, he shoved himself from her, toppling over onto his back. He lay there beside her waiting for his heart to stop pounding. When it did, he turned to her on his side. She was still staring up at the ceiling and did not look at him.

"I'm sorry," she said and then hiccuped as he watched a tear slide down from the corner of her eye to her ear. She rolled away from him, pulling her knees up as she lay on her side.

"Sophie," he said, placing a hand to her upper arm and tugging her back towards him. "Come here."

She rolled into him, but she wouldn't look him in the eye. Instead, she burrowed her face into his chest as her body trembled against him with the effort to keep her sobbing contained. He held her and stroked her hair in what he hoped

A Baron's Son is Undone

was a comforting gesture.

"It's not necessary," he said.

"Yes, it is," she said into his chest.

"I love you, and I know you love me. Sophie, you don't have to prove it like this."

George continued stroking her hair as her sobs came softer and farther apart.

"I think," said George, "that one day you may be ready, Sophie. But we can't force it. You've been through an ordeal that is still affecting you." He paused. "And if you want to talk about it. Not the details. I mean, if you want to talk about how it's made you feel, I'm here, and I'll listen."

Then he had one more thought.

"And Sophie . . . perhaps it's best not to think of it as *giving yourself to me*. You should wait until it's something you want to take from me instead."

It was all he could do. He hoped it would be enough.

Finally, she lifted her face to look at him. Her eyes were rimmed in pink, her dark hair was a mess, and her face was damp—she was the most gorgeous creature he had ever seen in his life.

"In the meantime," he said lifting her chin with his hand, "I think we have a more-than-satisfactory repertoire, do you not think?"

She smiled half-heartedly through her tears.

"You're not upset?" she asked.

"I would only be upset if I ended up hurting you," he said. "I love you, Sophie. I've told you before, nothing about this relationship is transactional. There's nothing you need to give me."

"And you don't mind if I . . . if I talk about . . . it?"

A Vision of Sunshine

"If you would like to," he said stroking her arm.

George thought he had been intimate with Sophie before, and he had been. But when she quietly and slowly began to speak—began to bare herself to him—he realised that *this* was what it was to have nothing between them. Removing their clothing was only a symbolic gesture.

At first, she spoke only to his chest, her knees up as if to guard herself. Soft murmurs into the lamplight. He held her hand. He listened. He cradled every word as if it were a fragile thing offered up to him. How his heart broke for her. He had known the bare facts before, but not the depth of the betrayal, nor the extent of her distress, nor the guilt and fear she still carried. To crack your heart open in front of someone else as Sophie was doing . . . It was the bravest thing he had ever witnessed.

Gradually, her knees came down, her legs stretched alongside his, and still she spoke into his chest. When she was finished, she looked up into his face searching him for something. He took her face gently in his hands as he felt her breath shudder through her.

"Sophie, your feelings are completely understandable," he said.

"You don't think I'm being . . . that I'm being unreasonable?"

"Jesus, Sophie. From what you've told me, you're hardly being unreasonable. I'd say you've managed unbelievably well."

She wiped a stray tear from her face.

"Father was so angry with me for what happened and later, for not being able to pretend that it hadn't happened. He said I was over-reacting."

George felt a sharp pain along the side of his neck as anger flared within him.

"Your father is wrong," he said simply as he opened his free arm to invite her closer.

She moved herself in towards him, and he pulled the blanket up over them. George had never felt so protective of someone in his entire life. It was an altogether overwhelming feeling—fear and anger and vigilance all tumbled together like a dark storm rolling in over the sea. He wrapped one arm around Sophie as if he might shield her with it, as if he could prevent what had already happened from happening.

In the morning, George woke to Sophie's soft kisses pressed gently over his entire face—his brow, his eyelids, his cheeks and nose and lips. He opened his eyes to her soft smile.

"Good morning," he said sleepily as he pulled her glorious naked body into an embrace.

That was the day that everything began anew. In the days and weeks and months that followed, Sophie seemed somehow more at ease—with him and with herself. Their conversation had by no means solved the physical issue. Rather, it had been more like cracking open a rusty gate that had previously barred their path. The road was now accessible and lay stretched out before them. While George did not know how long it would take to traverse it, he committed himself to holding Sophie's hand as she drew him along. The journey was hers, and he would follow.

Epilogue

Nearly one year later . . .

Sophie sat on the red blanket with her toes in the sand as she gazed out across the expanse of blue. The wind was blowing the clouds in overhead, but it didn't matter.

On the beach in front of her, George and Grace paddled in the surf looking for interesting pebbles and sea glass beneath the surface of the water. In the distance, she could see the wind-flapped dresses of Aunt Evelyn and Lady Pemberton as they walked arm-in-arm towards her along the beach.

"All I'm saying is that the water is deceptive!" yelled Grace to her brother over the sound of the sea. "The pebbles look so brightly coloured when they're wet, but then when they dry out, they're just regular old rocks."

George looked across to his sister.

"So keep them in a glass bowl of water," he said. "That way they'll never lose their shine."

"Ooh!" said Grace. "That's actually not a bad idea!"

"Don't look so surprised," said George handing her a pebble. "I'm full of good ideas."

A Baron's Son is Undone

"You're full of something," said Grace with a cheeky smile.

"You'll do well to learn that is no way to speak to a peer of the realm," said George in a scolding tone.

"Isn't it?" asked Grace. "Father always said that the House of Lords was as a whole, and I quote, 'A large pot of feculence brimming with its own self-importance.'"

At the mention of his late father, George's face fell. But it was only a fraction of a second before he began to laugh.

"Fair enough," he said through his laughter. "Father's wise and sensible words have nailed me to a post. Just as they should."

Lady Pemberton and Aunt Evelyn approached Sophie on her blanket.

"I think that's me for the day," said Lady Pemberton. "All this sea air has me pining for a nap."

"I'll walk you back," said Aunt Evelyn. "Sophie?"

"Thank you, but I think I'll stay right here for the time being," said Sophie digging her toes deeper into the sand.

"Grace!" called Lady Pemberton. "Are you ready to head back?"

Grace came running across the sand, her hands full of pebbles as her brother watched from the water.

"Aunt Evelyn, do you have a glass bowl I could borrow?"

Aunt Evelyn's eyebrows lifted in amusement.

"I have several," she said.

As the older ladies traipsed off with Grace chatting happily between them, George approached Sophie across the sand, the wind ruffling his golden hair. He was wearing that grey jacket again, the one that brought out his eyes.

"Aren't you going to check your pocket watch?" asked Sophie smiling up at her husband with undisguised adoration.

Epilogue

"I've nowhere else to be," he said reaching down for her hand and pulling her to her feet.

They gazed into each other's eyes for several long seconds before Sophie placed a hand to the middle of her husband's chest.

"George," she said. She knew he would know what she meant.

A smile spread across his handsome face.

"Not this again!" he teased.

"Yes, this again," said Sophie with mock seriousness. "It's your duty."

His smile fell.

"Say it," he commanded in a low gravel that made her breath come slightly faster. "Ask me."

Sophie rolled her eyes.

"Ask me," he repeated as he crowded her body with his and reached an arm around her waist.

Sophie shook her head, but she obeyed him as the heavy bloom of arousal sank down between her legs: "Would you please put a baby inside me?" She attempted to smother a giggle. "Or at least," she added, "I would like you to try your best."

"My best?" he asked darkly as he walked her slowly backwards until they were sheltered under a rocky overhang.

Sophie leaned her back up against the stone wall of the cliff.

"I should like you to try a little harder than last time," she said gazing up at him from under her lashes.

"Harder?" he asked in a low voice as he brought his forehead down to meet hers.

"*Much* harder," she responded as she fumbled with the fall of his trousers.

A Baron's Son is Undone

"You wouldn't like to wait until we have a bed at our disposal?" asked George as if stalling for time though she knew he was as desperate for her as she was for him. She could feel the heat of his breath on her, see the rise and fall of his chest.

"No beds," said Sophie. "They're too soft."

"Mmm." Her husband had his mouth to her neck as she slipped the eager length of him free of his trousers and wrapped her hand around his thick shaft.

The sensation of his lips against her skin still sent shivers all the way down to her toes. He shifted to kiss her full on the mouth as she slid her hand down and then up along him.

"I want you inside me," she said as he slipped down her to suck and tease at her nipples through the fabric of her dress. "Ah! George!"

He stood again to his full height, his face as serious as ever. He glanced around and up to make sure they were hidden from view of the cliff path.

"Up with your skirts," he said hoarsely.

When she had bunched up her skirts in one hand and lifted them to expose herself to the salty sea air, he reached a hand down between her legs to stroke her with agonising gentleness over and over again until she was trembling as he kissed her.

"More," she said breathlessly.

He slipped a finger inside her, then a second. For a moment, Sophie thought it might all be over. She felt her composure begin to crack as she panted into the velvet cave of his mouth. But George was as sensitive to her changing state of arousal as he had ever been.

"Not yet," he whispered, as he withdrew his fingers. "I thought you wanted a baby."

Epilogue

Sophie bit her lip as George lifted and hooked one of her legs over his arm. Knowing what he was about to do, she felt almost mad with need as the sweet ache between her legs became almost unbearable. She clung to her husband as he pressed himself slowly up inside her, and she exhaled with a sigh as George growled softly at the back of his throat.

For the last two weeks, she had craved this sensation to the point of distraction. It was a second honeymoon for them, and the fact that George had been so incredibly patient and understanding over the past year had made it all the more wondrous.

George rocked himself up inside her as she clawed her fingers into his shoulder. She could feel the heat surge within her as he pressed insistently and rhythmically into her with one hand to the rock wall to keep her from knocking against it. The sensation of him filling her up was almost too much to bear as he repeatedly passed over a small pressure point inside her, sending flames licking up from the depths.

"Sweet Heaven, Sophie!" he said on a gasp.

"George, I . . ."

"Don't tell me you can't," he purred. "You'd best touch yourself. Now."

Realising his hands were both engaged in holding her up, Sophie reached her own hand down between their bodies to stroke her fingers over her swollen bud. She immediately came apart with a cry as George released himself inside her with a tremulous groan. He kept her leg hooked over his arm, and as their breathing settled, he pressed Sophie gently back against the cliff wall and took her mouth in his for a slow and sensual kiss that seemed as if it might last a blissful eternity.

Eventually, George lowered her leg to the ground, and

A Baron's Son is Undone

Sophie smoothed out her skirts in a business-like fashion. She could feel his warm seed between her legs, and the knowledge of it made her feel a little wild, like a wind-tossed blossom.

Good Lord, she wanted him again! She could never have enough of him. Looking up, she caught his eye, and they both started to laugh.

"It's not funny," said George. "Making a baby is serious business."

"Is that what we're doing?" asked Sophie.

"No," said George seriously as he tucked a stray strand of hair behind her ear. "We're simply enjoying each other. A baby would be lovely, but being with you is more joy than I can manage right now."

"If I didn't or couldn't become with child . . ." started Sophie. She did wonder sometimes. She thought of her own mother and all she had been through.

George took her face in his.

"There are plenty of children in need of parents, Sophie. A true family need not be tied with blood."

Sophie allowed the love in her husband's words to melt over her as a light drizzle began to fall. A rather fat drop of rain smacked her across the cheek. Another hit George on the forehead. Within moments, they were being pelted with a torrent of water. George turned his face skyward and into the rain.

"Game's over," he said.

Sophie tugged him from the cliff wall. They went in search of their shoes, then gathered up the sopping red blanket and ran hand-in-hand laughing across the beach as the sky grew even darker overhead.

Thank You

Thank you for reading *A Baron's Son is Undone.* It's been an emotional journey, and I've tried my best to give Sophie and George the happy ending they deserve. Love is at its most magical when it finds a way to weather the storms of life.

- If you would like to know when my next book is available, you can sign up for my mailing list at oliviaelliottromance.com.
- Reviews help other readers decide if a book would suit them. I appreciate all reviews, both positive and negative, so please think about leaving a star-rating or, if you have the time, a few thoughts about my book.
- *A Baron's Son is Undone* is the third book in *The Pemberton Series*, and I am currently working on the fourth, so stay tuned!

Also by Olivia Elliott

If you haven't read them already, you may also enjoy the first two books in *The Pemberton Series.*

A Dangerous Man to Trust?
Bridgerton meets *Jane Eyre* in this spicy, slow-burn Regency romance written with humour and wit. A strong yet vulnerable hero who feels he's unworthy of love, a feisty governess who has sworn off marriage, and a world of heartache and longing between them.

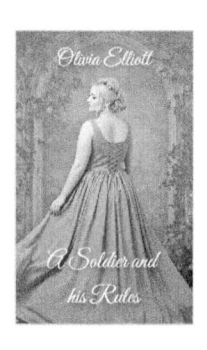

A Soldier and his Rules
He is a stern and brooding soldier who is used to giving orders. She is a passionate artist who rarely does as she's told. His haunted past and secret shame stand like a wall between them in this hot and spicy Regency romance.

Printed in Dunstable, United Kingdom